THE WEATHERMAN'S DAUGHTERS

Books by Richard Hoyt

THE WEATHERMAN'S DAUGHTERS

A John Denson Mystery

Richard Hoyt

A TOM DOHERTY ASSOCIATES BOOK

NEW YORK

This is a work of fiction. All the characters and events portrayed in this book are either products of the author's imagination or are used fictitiously.

THE WEATHERMAN'S DAUGHTERS

Copyright © 2003 by Richard Hoyt

A Forge Book
Published by Tom Doherty Associates, LLC
175 Fifth Avenue
New York, NY 10010

www.tor.com

Forge® is a registered trademark of Tom Doherty Associates, LLC.

ISBN 0-765-34226-X
EAN 978-0765-34226-X

First edition: July 2003
First mass market edition: February 2005

Printed in the United States of America

0 9 8 7 6 5 4 3 2 1

For my wife, Teresita Artes Hoyt

What is the end of human life? It is not, believe me, the chief end of man that he should make a fortune and beget children whose end is likewise to make a fortune, but it is, in a few words, that he should explore himself.

—Ralph Waldo Emerson, *Nature*

THE WEATHERMAN'S
DAUGHTERS

1 • What goes up

The Darth Vader cloud formation, a large black whorl a couple of miles wide and surrounded by a sky as blue as an iceman's eye, drifted ominously to the east off the Pacific Ocean. If I had lived in rural Kansas or Oklahoma, I would have started looking for a hole to crawl into. Instead, I pulled my Volkswagen minibus to the side of the highway and snatched my 35mm Nikon. I clapped a telephoto lens onto it. I popped a fresh cartridge into my Sony video camera.

I piled out of the bus and snapped two still photographs, but I knew that the real action was with video. I glanced at my watch before triggering the Sony. Into the camera's mike, I said, "It is now 3:25 P.M. I am taping this from the highway flanking Elk Creek about fifteen miles east of Astoria, Oregon, and two miles south of the Columbia River."

I kept shooting as a huge, spooky black funnel lowered from the cloud bank and touched down on the river, forming an awesome waterspout. Determined to stand my ground, I kept my finger hard on the trigger, tracking the huge waterspout that moved slowly to the east, up river. I couldn't see the river itself. My view was blocked by the trees.

Then the funnel left the river and turned south, my direction. The front edge of the Darth Vader cloud moved overhead, plunging the landscape into darkness. My mouth dry, my heart beating like Ringo's drums, I leaped inside my bus and gave that forty horsepower beater all it had, driving pedal to the metal, gripping the steering wheel with whitened knuckles.

A lacy sheet of lightning turned the Douglas firs on either side of me into luminous, brooding ghosts. A whopping crack of thunder directly overhead nearly sent me out of my skin. I wanted deliverance. I drove on through the popping, booming and rumbling. Jagged sheets of lightning danced above the tops of the trees from horizon to horizon. Hard gusts of wind rocked my minibus. I felt like it was going to topple.

Was I being pursued by the tornado? Amid the crazed static on my aging radio, I could barely make out a weatherman's breathless description of the waterspout. His voice sounded familiar, but I couldn't make it out. I rarely listened to the radio, preferring to leave the vacuum between my ears undisturbed by the lamentations of youth seeking love and recovering from love gone awry. Now, when I needed it, I discovered that the radio was on the blink, threatening to quit any second. If the eyewitness descriptions coming through the static weren't all hyperbole, this wasn't just any old tornado. It was a huge father.

Then I recognized the voice on the radio. Portland's famous television weatherman, Jerry Toogood, popularly known as T.G., had been pressed into emergency service. T.G. gave his listeners a quick meteorological primer. A mass of moist warm air pushing up from the warm Pacific waters near Hawaii had collided with a high pressure of frigid air coming down out of Alaska. As a storm it was a freak, this not being the heartland where cold continental air masses routinely collided with moist air pushed up from the Caribbean or the Gulf of Mexico.

In his inimitable style, T.G. told us yes, an occasional twister did hit the Pacific Northwest, but rarely anything like the spooky force three, four, and five monster tornadoes that roared through small towns in corn country sending Toyotas, Winnebagos, and urinating Holstein cows aloft. And water-spouts, that is, tornadoes above water, were commonplace in the United Kingdom. The Brits had the temerity to claim that more twisters hit the U.K. in a given year than the U.S., although their tornadoes, more numerous and more often over water, were far smaller then those that formed over amber fields of American grain.

Folks out there in Kansas and Nebraska and other targets of major league twisters, prideful sufferers, would scoff at the idea that a genuine howler could ever hit Oregon or Washington. Everybody knew that it rained all the time in the Pacific Northwest, where babies were said to be born with webbed feet and folks had mildew on the brain. A waterspout on the Columbia River?

T.G. said the hogbody twister, an "anomalous phenomenon," was as strong as a force two tornado, and, if the accounts of the breathless eyewitnesses were to be believed, maybe even a force three or four. "We're getting reports in that the tornado has lifted from the water and has turned south at a point . . ."

My radio fell silent.

Dammit to hell! I played with the cracked-plastic knobs. Nothing. Hoping to knock some sense into its aging transistors, I gave it a healthy whack with the heel of my hand. Nothing. Doing my best to keep my sphincters from leaking, I drove on. My windshield wipers, clicking like brave little metronomes, struggled to clear the rain as a gusting wind rocked my bus with broadside gusts.

My bus emerged from the gloom. I was bathed in wonderful light. Clear blue skies. A warming late afternoon sun. It was tweet bird weather. Picnic weather. The funnel had passed me by. Hot damn! Yippity skip! Life was good! I rolled down the window, savoring the sweet mountain air. I twisted my neck to see what had happened to the Darth Vader storm front. I saw the back edge of the dark whorl as the storm front moved southeast in the direction of Portland. The tornado had apparently lifted and dissipated.

I closed the door, relieved. Dead ahead, I saw a grand double rainbow. I buzzed on, grateful to be alive. I felt suddenly hungry. I had a hankering for a big old cheeseburger with lots of onions, comfort food.

As I entered a stretch of highway flanked by towering Douglas fir, something thumped hard on the roof of the bus.

Then another thump.

A large wriggling fish bounced onto the highway in front of me.

A fish?

I pulled to the side of the road and leaped out. I squatted beside the mystery fish. It was a coho, or silver salmon, one of the two main species of salmon that ran up the Columbia River, the other being the larger Chinook, or king salmon.

A coho had mysteriously plopped directly in front of me on a mountain highway.

How in hell had that happened? I looked about, but couldn't see any possible source for the fish. Where had it come from? I retreated to my bus and continued up Elk Creek.

I felt something else slam against the top of my bus. Again I pulled to the side of the road. I got out and inspected the top of my bus. I saw two bloody dents. A tree branch didn't bleed. I ran my finger through the blood. Scales. Slime. This was fish goo. Coho? Couldn't be. Impossible. Then I spotted a second fish, apparently the source of the second hit on my bus, just off the shoulder of the road.

The coho made a spring run in May or early June and a

fall run in August or early September. We were now square in the middle of what was said to be the largest spring run of coho in fifty years. Was it possible the coho had been sucked up by the waterspout, which released them when it dissipated?

I got back into my bus. I had no sooner cranked up the air cooled engine than the roof and sides of my bus really took a beating.

Bum. Bum. Bum. Bum.

Fish! More of them. Yes!

Whack. Whack. Whack. Whack.

Down they came, sailing out of the clear blue sky. Fish. Coho or silver salmon to be precise. They bounced onto the highway and smacked into my bus. Fish, fish, fish. Hundreds of coho raining down from the sky. Sweet Jesus, I was caught in a salmon storm! Live salmon they were. A still camera and a video camera were tools of my trade, being necessary to obtain legal evidence of thieves, cheats, liars, philandering spouses, corporate polluters and other dwellers in the universal zoo of miscreants. I grabbed my video camera and jumped outside.

BUM-BUM-BUM-BUM!

WHACK-WHACK-WHACK-WHACK!

Faster they came and faster and faster still. A cloudburst. Staying close to the bus, I aimed my camera skyward. What I caught in the viewfinder was nothing short of surreal; thousands of living, shimmering silver salmon plummeted out of the clear blue sky at high speed. It was such an eerily beautiful, bizarre, spooky vision that it literally gave me goosebumps. If ever an amateur photographer had been in the right place at the right time, it was me.

BU-BU-BU-BU-WH-WH-WH-WH!

The salmon must have been sucked up by waterspout. What went up, both fish and water, had to come down. I remembered reading somewhere that in the U.K. waterspouts

sometimes sucked up sprat or frogs and dumped them onto
land. When the spout was the real deal running atop the big-
gest run of coho in fifty years, what got sucked up were
salmon. And once up there . . .

BU-BU-BU-BU-WH-WH-WH-WH!

Only then did I see the Ford Explorer and the young
woman. I had run into the fish storm where a silver Explorer
had slid off the side of the road. A young woman lay on the
edge of the pavement beside the driver's open door.

BU-BU-BU-BU-WH-WH-WH-WH!

Had the woman gotten out to look up at the falling fish,
only to be knocked cold? However much I wanted to continue
shooting the falling fish, I felt my first responsibility was to
help the woman.

BU-BU-BU-BU-WH-WH-WH-WH!

Putting my arms over my head to protect myself and my
camera, which I kept running, I sprinted through the falling
fish toward the woman. A salmon bounced off my back. Another sailed into the back of my knee, buckling my leg and
sending me sprawling.

BU-BU-BU-BU-WH-WH-WH-WH!

I kept my finger on the trigger of the camera. I got up,
camera running, and a salmon whacked into my shoulder,
turning me around. The fish had survived their ordeal still
living and were everywhere, pitching and flopping on the
ground.

BU-BU-BU-BU-WH-WH-WH-WH!

Finally, I made it to the prone figure, dressed in blue jeans
and a nylon windbreaker. She had not been knocked silly by
a falling fish. She had a bullet hole high in her chest and blood
coming out of her mouth, but she was still alive. Her eyes,
wide open, hypnotic, translucent cornflower blue, looked
straight into mine, imploring me.

I dropped quickly to my knees and hands with fish bounc-

ing off my back. I turned my left ear to her mouth and held
it close. When she talked she gurgled the blood that was welling up through her throat. I could only discern fragments of
words.

"Gurgle, gurgle, gurgle ther. Gurgle, gurgle, ister. Gurgle,
gurgle ill gurgle."

Then she was dead.

Her eyes were hypnotic. I sat up, using my elbow and arm
to shield myself from the falling fish. Her blue eyes, though
now lifeless, were still talking to me, imploring me. It was
spooky. With fish pummeling me, I stared, transfixed, into the
blue pools.

BU-BU-BU-BU-WH-WH-WH-WH!

I turned and caught a fish square in the face—it almost
knocked me out. I dropped to my knees, dizzy, but I continued with my chore of capturing the moment on tape. I could
taste blood, which poured out of my nose. I struggled to my
feet, still focusing on the falling fish, only to take the mother
of all coho at an angle on my chest, slamming me flat on my
back. The blow knocked the air from my lungs, and I couldn't
breathe. I struggled to breath, *hoooooop, hoooooop, hoooooop*,
as the fish pummeled me hard. I was slimy with blood and
guts and scales.

BU-BU-BU-BU-WH-WH-WH-WH!

I was closer to the rear of the Ford Explorer than my own
bus. Instinctively, I knew that I should try to crawl under the
Explorer, the nearest refuge, but I couldn't do anything except
struggle to breathe with pain shooting through several ribs
that were likely cracked.

Bum. Bum. Bum. Whack. Whack. Whack.

The hail of fish began to ease and there I lay there twisting,
gasping for air amid hundreds of flopping salmon whose own
systems were struggling to obtain water. The highway was covered with them. Directly in front of me a salmon on his stom-

ach twisted violently, desperately trying to swim, his mouth opening and closing, gills pumping frantically. The struggling fish appeared to look at me straight on as if somehow sharing the agony of our silent desperation. His run up the Columbia River was not finished. Evolution pushed him forward. Did he think I was an odd variety of sturgeon that he had never encountered, also sucked up from the water while I was going about my business? Did we share something on the order of a fish-human, spiritual understanding? Likely not, but it was an unsettling moment.

Bum. Bum. Whack. Whack.

At last I was able to breathe, and I continued taping the waning moments of the fish storm. My nose was still bleeding and my mouth was full of blood. The fish that had slammed into my face had mashed my mouth against my teeth, cutting the inside of my cheeks. I looked up at the bumper of the Explorer. On it was a metal symbol of a fish. But it was no Christian fish. It was one of those skeptical Darwinian fish, its mouth open wide, swallowing a smaller fish.

I started to tape the Explorer and the dead young woman, but quickly took my finger off the camera trigger. If I taped either the body or the Explorer, the police could lay claim to my videotape. The fish that had been in front of me was dead. A few floppers still remained, but it was time to switch cameras. Okay to take still photos of the body and the Explorer. If they wanted copies of those, no problem.

I went back to my bus and wrote down gurgle by gurgle, syllable by syllable what the dying young woman had told me. I popped in a roll of ASA 200 film into my 35mm Nikon and checked the light with a meter so I could manually set the correct f-stop. My hands were trembling. I glanced back at the body on the highway.

What had she been trying to tell me? Who had killed her? Those eyes!

2 · The unfathomable "I"

Stepping carefully between fish so as not to slip on one, I made it back to my microbus, whose chassis, a dented slime of blood, guts and fish scales, was virtually destroyed. I grabbed my cell phone and punched 911. Upon hearing my story of coming upon a murdered body amid a storm of falling salmon, the operator, a young man, paused, "A fish storm, sir? Falling salmon? Riiiiiiiiight."

He wasn't being a jerk. I understood his skepticism. I was Denson in Wonderland. It had been stupid of me to mention the fish. I hung up and asked information for the number of the Oregon State Police. This time I didn't mention the fish, only that I had come across a murdered woman. "In unusual circumstances," I told the desk officer.

"Aren't all murders unusual?"

"You got me there. I'm calling from a cell phone. If you can put me in touch with a patrolman, I can explain it all to him. Please humor me." I couldn't stop thinking about the dead girl's eyes looking up at me. Imploring me. Even when she was dead, the spirit behind her eyes haunted me. Even in death, they implored. Impossible, I knew. Nothing behind those eyes. She was gone.

The desk officer said there were a lot of patrolmen in the area because of the waterspout and gave me a number of a squad car to call.

I hung up and called the number, getting Sgt. Lewis Jakes of the Oregon State Police, who turned out to be only a few miles away. I told him about coming upon a dying woman on the highway flanking Elk Creek, omitting any reference to fish. "Fair warning, sergeant. Brace yourself. What we've got here is something straight out of Guinness. This'll be one for your grandchildren, guaranteed."

"A murdered woman? Hard to believe that would rate Guinness."

"You'll see."

"Stay well clear of the crime scene. Don't touch the body or her vehicle."

"She was still alive for a few seconds after I got here. I thought I might be able to help her. Other than that I've kept my distance," I said.

"She's dead. You're sure of that."

"Positive," I said, still unable to shake the vision of the young woman's eyes, alive in the beginning, had turned to lifeless mirrors.

"I'm on my way," he said.

I could hear the *boop-beep* of his siren in the background.

I hung up the phone to wait. Willie Sees the Night, a.k.a. Willie Prettybird, was out and about on a case. I tried his number on my cell phone. No answer.

For years after we threw in together, Willie had called himself Prettybird. Then one day I saw William Sees the Night on the top of his federal income tax form. I asked him about it. He said he was born Sees the Night. That was the name on

his birth certificate. But over the years he had grown weary
at uptight people blinking at the mention of his surname. Was
that one word or three? Which letters were upper case and
which lower? He had seen some dandy European names,
having known a woman named Underman and men named
Cowherd and Godlove, but never mind. As a joke, poking fun
at the ferocious and colorful names given to Indians by Hollywood scriptwriters, he began calling himself Prettybird.

Willie believed himself to be Coyote, a sorcerer in human
form. Although coyotes hunt mostly at night, they are diurnal
like human beings. Willie saw "the night," meaning he saw it
literally and in other ways as well, looking into the darkness
and allegedly seeing what mere mortals could not.

I asked him why on earth would I want to have Prettybird
as a partner when I could have Sees the Night. Prettybird
sounded like a finch or starling flitting from branch to branch.
That was not Willie. Sees the Night was mysterious and suggestive. I urged him to take back his name.

The truth was I wasn't surprised so much that he had surrendered to morons unable to accept his name, but that a
shape-changing animal spirit would have a birth certificate in
the first place, much less fill out his IRS Form 1040. An animal
spirit giving his due to the Internal Revenue Service? The
thought of Uncle Sam getting his nick from denizens of the
spirit world was jarring. It was as though the IRS pursued
people into dimensions the nature of which the rest of us
could only speculate. If that were true, could any of us, ever,
escape the IRS?

While I waited in the Sea of Dead Fish, unable to forget
the eyes of the dead young woman, I recalled reading about
Plato's discussion with two of his students on the prideful

nature of *thymos* or what we moderns would call soul, spirit, or consciousness—the unfathomable "I." For years, I had operated on the assumption that the dominant motive for most crime was covered by the two Latin words, *cui bono?* Who profits? The German philosopher Herr Friedrich Hegel, whose dialectic had been fancifully appropriated and mangled by Karl Marx, thought the great drive of human history was for *recognition*.

Young African-Americans had coined the word *dissed*, short for disrespected, by which they meant that their *thymos* had been not been acknowledged. Their fury over being forever dissed left them enraged. The protagonist of Ralph Ellison's novel *Invisible Man* was so named because white people looked right through him like he didn't exist. He didn't count for anything. His lack of value had rendered him transparent. Dissed teenagers opened fire on their fellow students. Husbands and wives and lovers eternally wrangled over the question of who dissed whom. The bitch! The bastard! *Thymos* was what it was all about. The comedian Rodney Dangerfield hit a nerve with his trademark lament, *I don't get no respect. Where's the respect?*

In a way, I felt that the drama of a crime contained the heart of history, and just as history was not driven by economics alone, as we learned with the collapse of the Soviet empire, so the motive of criminals was more complicated than the simple question of who profited. *Cui bono*, yes. Dissed *thymos* too.

The dying girl had looked up at me with blue eyes alive with *thymos*. Her spirit talked to me. I had heard moronic television reporters, needing desperately to fill up air time, talk of "closure" when a murderer was brought to justice. Closure? There was nothing to replace *thymos*, not justice or revenge, certainly not closure, whatever the hell that was. It was one of those pretentious nonwords that took up space but meant nothing. If it had been me lying on that road with a bullet hole in my chest, blood welling out of my mouth, I would have wanted whoever found me to obtain some form of elemental payback. Not closure. Revenge. Justice. The murderer had to sacrifice. There had to be a price. The knowledge that committing murder carried a cost was the glue of civilization.

The religionists had various explanations of what happened to the *thymos* with the end of its corporeal host. The Hindus argued that the spirit underwent a series of reincarnations; the Christians held that, for the blessed at least, the soul continued in eternal afterlife. I found all those theories fascinating in the abstract, but for me, John Denson, the interest lay in what I believed was a personal epiphany:

The human condition is the search for the answer to one simple question: what comes next?

We each ask the question a thousand times each day. It gives meaning to our lives. Imprisonment is so barbarous because the question is largely eliminated when all days are almost exactly the same. What comes next is the core of all drama from *Moby-Dick* and *Gone with the Wind* to Bobby Thompson striding to the plate to face Ralph Branca in the bottom of the ninth.

The question loomed larger, ever larger, as Branca threw that fateful pitch.

Baseball fans across the country listened on the radio.

Thompson swung . . .

The crack of white ash meeting ball still reverberated in baseball lore.

Death, the final question of what happens next, has never been satisfactorily answered. Perhaps it is unanswerable. As the ration of our years grows shorter, the tension of that question tightens.

A fish storm. A murdered young woman. What next?

I was jerked from my reverie by the crazed *boop-beep* of a siren.

Glancing down at the dead body, the Oregon state policeman all solemn and spiffy in his dark blue uniform and polished boots waded through the sea of salmon. They were mostly dead, although a few still had it in them to give half-hearted flips of their tails. A tag on his chest said he was Sgt. Lewis Jakes. He stood self-consciously erect. He wasn't very big, but once he donned his uniform, he swelled with pride, pumped like an overinflated balloon by the power of the state of Oregon.

Jakes, who had a camera dangling around his neck, found it impossible to maintain his air of self-importance in view of what he had stumbled into. "Jesus Christ, what is this?" He looked about, mouth open.

"The aftermath of a fish storm," I said as though nothing unusual had happened. My left eye was swollen nearly shut and the left side of my lips was swollen bigger than boiled Bratwurst. "I told you this is something for Guinness. They sailed out of a clear blue sky after the storm moved. Straight from the heavens. I was able to get a lot of it on videotape."

Looking around in disbelief, he said, "A fish storm. Right."

"My guess is that they got sucked up by the waterspout. You put a force two or three waterspout on top of a river glutted with salmon run and this what you get. What goes up, comes down. Einstein apparently explained how gravity works, but I could never understand it."

"My God, you're right. That has to be it. And your name is?"

"John Denson," I said.

He looked amused. "I tell you what, Mr. Denson, you better get a cold fish on that eye and your lip before it gets any worse."

"Isn't that what Bill Clinton supposedly told that Arkansas woman after he bit her lip? I guess that was ice, though, not fish."

He gave me a look.

"You're right. I need to stop the swelling." I grabbed a smaller salmon and held it over my bruised face.

"Your chest is bleeding. I think maybe you better check that out too."

My shirt was soaked with blood. I unbuttoned it.

Jakes stepped back, eyes wide. "Jesus!"

I looked down at myself and saw what he meant. I had a purple bruise running at an angle from the top of my left hip to my right shoulder in a near perfect shape of a fish. It reminded me of a fish leaping over a barrier in the river, determined to reach that golden place where it was conceived.

He liked his lips and blinked. "Spooky."

"You mind using my camera to get a couple of shots of that?"

He shrugged. "Not as long as you let me shoot a couple with my camera."

"No problem. Let's do it."

He photographed the bruise on my chest, taking several shots with each of our cameras, then I followed him to the corpse so he could get on with investigating the murder.

He gave me a notepad and said, "I want you to write down whatever it was the girl said to you word-for-word, as well as you can remember. Think about it. I want it accurate as possible."

While I wrote the young woman's dying words, he took some shots of the corpse and the vehicle. He set up some flares on the highway to detour traffic around the crime scene, then went to his vehicle and called for help.

When he finished, I gave him the pad. "She was still alive when I found her. She talked to me, but blood was coming out of her mouth, and she mostly gurgled. This is what she said. Or at least what I was able to hear."

He glanced at the note and slipped the pad into his pocket. "Hang tight. We'll talk about this in a few minutes."

"I'm not going anywhere."

The dead woman, who was in her mid- to late twenties, had left a handbag on the passenger's seat of the Explorer. Jakes put on some rubber gloves and opened the handbag to find out who she was. He shined his flashlight on her driver's license. Standing behind him, I was curious, but didn't say anything. This was cop business, and I wasn't a cop.

He said, "She is Sharon Toogood."

I blinked. "Toogood! Related to T.G.? I was listening to him tell us about tornadoes and waterspouts a few minutes before the, uh, fish storm." Toogood, the amiable television weatherman, was scion of a local family that had gotten wealthy from the timber industry forty years earlier. His familiar long, grinning mug with *T.G.* under it was ubiquitous on bus and light rail placards and on billboards around town.

"Likely his daughter. Look here."

Jakes showed me a photograph of the dead woman beside T.G.'s familiar visage. He put the photograph back in her handbag. "A fish storm and Jerry Toogood's murdered daughter all in one shift. Some kind of night for me." He removed a business card from her wallet and glanced at me. "You a private investigator?"

I nodded, wondering how he knew that.

He slipped the card into his shirt pocket.

He paused, thinking of what he should do next. Given the murder of the famous weatherman's daughter, every move he made would be reported in media, and he knew it. He was also aware that any mistake he made no matter how small or insignificant would be pointed out by eager critics of everything a cop did no matter what the circumstances. Equally important was his responsibility to get an accurate account of the bizarre fish storm. He was a state cop, an official witness. "I guess I better ask you a few questions while we wait," he said.

"No problem," I said. "You think this is going to land me on Oprah or Larry King?"

He laughed and retrieved a small tape recorder from his squad car and punched it on. He identified himself and gave the time, date and place of the discovery of the body of Sharon Toogood. He asked me for my full name, date and place of birth, and my address. I gave him all that, telling him that I lived in a cabin on Jump-Off Joe Creek on Whorehouse Meadow about fifteen miles southeast of Clatskanie and received my mail at a post office box in Clatskanie, which I gave him.

"Whorehouse Meadow?"

"There used to be a gold mine at the headwaters of Jump-Off Joe. The miners needed a little recreation for their morale, so the company, uh, provided for their various needs."

"I see."

"The federal government renamed it 'Naughty Lady Meadow' on its maps, but folks around here still call it Whorehouse Meadow."

"Whorehouse Meadow, the very idea!" Jakes pretended to be embarrassed.

I said, "The Department of Interior bureaucrats never heard of Blue Balls, Pennsylvania, or French Lick, Indiana.

There's a scattering of summer cabins higher up Elk Creek, and this is fishing season. Other than that nobody home out this far."

Jakes removed the business card from his shirt pocket and handed it to me. It was the one Willie and I used. "I take it this is yours?"

"Yes, it is."

"Willie Sees the Night?" He arched an eyebrow.

"He's a Cowlitz."

"I see. Is Sharon Toogood your client?"

I shook my head. "I've never heard of her. I know who Jerry Toogood is, of course. I may have heard him mention having daughters on his weather program, but I can't remember."

"Who lives up here besides you and your partner?"

"Nobody. There are a few fishing cabins along Elk Creek, but no permanent residents."

"Is it possible that she was coming to see you about something? She had your card in her wallet."

"She might well have been. I've never talked to her. Maybe Willie has. I don't know."

He put the card back into his pocket and turned the attention to the notepad where I had written what Sharon Toogood told me as she died. "You've got here what you heard her say, or thought you heard her say. In the context of the moment and the rhythm of the sounds coming out of her mouth, what do you think she was trying to tell you?" He gave me the pad so I could refresh my memory.

I studied the note. *Gurgle, gurgle, gurgle ther. Gurgle, gurgle, ister. Gurgle, gurgle ill gurgle.* "Hard to say. But if I were to venture a guess, I would guess something like. 'Give my love to my father and sister,' or 'Say goodbye to my father and sister.' She could have been trying to tell me who 'killed' her, or maybe somebody is sick, I don't know."

He reread the note. "But maybe something entirely different."

"Maybe something entirely different. I agree."

3 · An idealistic moron

It didn't take P. T. Barnum to understand that a fish storm was some kind of wild story. A man caught in a hail of coho salmon? I was to become a celebrated witness, however reluctant. The inevitable horde of reporters, having learned of the fish storm, would descend on the scene with visions of interviews by network anchors dancing through their heads.

Jakes had no reason to think I had anything to do with Sharon Toogood's murder. He didn't cotton to the narcissistic talking heads a whole bunch so he let me go home—on condition that I was to make myself available if the Oregon State Police had any more questions.

When the reporters arrived at the murder scene like a pack of baying narcissists, they would find a road covered with dead salmon, but no John Denson. A cabin on Whorehouse Meadow on Jump-Off Joe Creek fifteen miles southeast of Clatskanie was vague enough to leave the reporters muttering in their microphones. An additional impediment was that Whorehouse Meadow was not listed on most maps.

I asked Lewis Jakes not to release my phone number, and he said he'd do his best, adding that it was inevitable that a starstruck moron somewhere in the system would release the number as a form of sucking up to a *deus tubus*, god of the tube.

At half past six, I pulled into my yard at Whorehouse Meadow. How long would it be until the star struck moron would release my phone number? Hours or minutes? I thought about the dead girl's eyes looking up at me. It is said that the spirit lies in the eyes. When the spirit goes, the eyes are spooky. I couldn't shake the vision of the dead girl's eyes.

The moment I opened my cabin door, my cell phone began ringing. I waited. It continued ringing. I waited, stubborn. The ringing finally stopped. Then it started again. I sighed and hit the snuff button so the phone would receive no calls whatever. The hoo hoo and nonsense of the fish storm had begun.

I was too full of what had happened to go to sleep. Besides that my face and ribs ached. I looked at my bruised face and chest in the mirror. The fish-bruise was so clear it was spooky. The storm having passed through the area, it was hot and muggy. I left the window open for some fresh air.

I poured myself some homemade elderberry wine and turned on my computer to see what I could learn about waterspouts and falling fish. I typed *fish falling from the sky* into Google and tapped the enter button. I was amazed, as usual, at the internet's ability to list hundreds of web sites that had to do, one way or the other, with the phenomenon of waterspouts sucking up fish. In the U.K. these were often sprat, whatever a sprat was. I knew about prat, as in fall, which was what this day was turning out to be.

I heard the sound of vehicles coming up Elk Creek. They were on their way, roaring toward their rendezvous with big Nielsens.

I turned off my computer and grabbed my little pipe and the last of my weed that was in a Ziploc bag. I doused the lights, and locked the door. Did I really want to go through the celebrity of the hour drill? What should I do? Taking my

Nikon and Sony with me, I hustled upstream on the trail beside the bubbling, gurgling Jump-Off Joe Creek. Willie's cabin was about fifty yards upstream from mine. I could hear the vehicles turn onto the makeshift road that followed Jump-Off Joe to Whorehouse Meadow. They were reportorial bloodhounds. Whorehouse Meadow might not have been listed on most maps, but they had somehow found it.

I retrieved Willie's key from its spot in his woodshed and opened the door. I slipped inside and pulled the curtains on his cabin windows.

Just as I settled squat legged on the floor, I could hear vehicles pulling up in front of my cabin. The pack of thrill seekers had arrived en masse to interview the man who had survived a cloudburst of salmon. What a story!

See the salmon sailing out of the sky. Marvel at the miracle. Yowza, yowza, yowza!

If I worked it right, I knew I could score a bundle off what had happened to me. But an incident of raining salmon surely lay in the domain of Willie Sees the Night. Out of loyalty and respect for my partner, I felt I should talk to him. This was intuition, a gut feeling.

I peered between the closed curtains of one of the windows and watched a group of fifteen or twenty cameramen and reporters park their vehicles in front of my cabin. The reporters were peering into my cabin, wondering where I had gone. The photographers circled my bus, recording the fishdents and dried slime. Even from the distance I could hear their oohs and ahhs and exclamations of amazement.

A woman and a photographer broke from the larger pack of media canines and headed my way on the trail along the creek. They were human bloodhounds locked on the heady spoor of sensation.

A second pair of hounds, a male reporter and his photographer, followed quickly behind. He was one of Portland's most familiar faces, anchorman Jack Hart, a lean, trim, slightly dark-complexioned man with a square jaw, who was maybe two or three inches over six feet tall. Hart had dark brown eyes and a rugged, masculine face with perfect features. I had never seen him in person, and I almost burst out laughing at his cartoon-like good looks. It was like he had stepped out of the movies or a comic strip.

I locked the door. I waited, still peering between the curtain of one of the windows. The female reporter, a blonde beauty with extraordinary long legs, strode so forcefully that her handsome bosom bounced up and down. Fun watching the rolling of her chest, but I had to keep my head down. A half a minute later she began pounding loudly on the door. *Boom, boom, boom!*

I lay down on the floor, pressing myself against the wall. Hiding like a fox before the hounds, I licked my lips.

Boom, boom, boom!

The beautiful woman yelled cheerfully, "Mr. Denson! Mr. Denson! Come out. We know you're in there. You have to be. We see your bus back there." She hammered on the door some more. "My name is Nicole Byrne. I'm affiliated with CNN. I'm offering you a world exclusive," she added. "They'll be watching you in Belgium, Italy, Japan, everywhere. Think of it!"

"I can't wait," I breathed.

Boom, boom, boom!

"Mr. Denson, please!" Her voice took on a sour note, which she was trying to suppress.

A deep, resonant voice that I recognized as Hart asked, "He here?"

Ms. Byrne pounded some more. Frustrated, she muttered, "Apparently not. He's supposed to have an Indian partner who lives near him. Willie Sees the Night, if you can believe that."

"Better than Willie Humps His Dog."

"Cute," she said dryly. "I wonder if this is the place."

"I bet it is," Hart said. "But it looks abandoned to me. Look at the weeds. Ass deep to a tall squaw."

"Whorehouse Meadow, Jump-Off Joe Creek. Now there's a classy address. Can you imagine the kind of people who live out here in all this isolation? What do they *do*?"

"They listen to the wind in the treetops. Ghosts. *Whoooooooooooooo!* That and pull their lonely little peepees." Hart laughed.

Ms. Byrne was in no mood for humor. Angrily, she said, "Did you see the pounding his bus took? Covered with scales and dried guts and blood. That had to be something else! Driving through a fish storm? That waterspout must have scooped up half the coho in the Columbia River. Whoa! A real story. He can be instantly famous if he wants. Famous! Can you imagine? But what does he do? Plays hide and seek with us, thinking he can make more money by making us wait."

"Probably thinks he can hold an Internet auction for an interview and rights to the tape."

She scowled. "What we've got here is a self-important idiot with a cash register for a brain. The worst. The very worst. Sorry luck on our part."

Hearing that, I stirred there on the floor. I was an idiot by some standards maybe. Cash register for a brain? I denied it.

Hart said, "He's probably somewhere sending an e-mail to the *National Enquirer* this very minute."

"When we find him, we'll offer him a prime-time special. That'll buckle his knees. Can you imagine the self-importance? The righteousness? The lack of respect for anybody but himself?" Her voice was as raw as sulfuric acid.

In his deep, sincere voice, Hart said, "A moron. No concept whatever of civic duty or responsibility. None. All he can think of is himself."

Listening to Hart, I was astonished. His voice made Tom Brokaw sound like a squeaky little kid.

"Totally self-centered. That's the way I see it," Ms. Byrne said.

Hart, his voice resonant and sonorous, said, "What I hate is after we run him down we'll have to sweet talk and suck up to him to get what he should have given us in the first place. If I'm forced to call him Mr. Denson, I'll do it, but it will be hard not to vomit."

"Hard to swallow being civil to such an idiot," she said. "You got that right."

With that I heard them stalking back toward my cabin.

I took a quick peek. Coming, Ms. Byrne's front had bounced wonderfully. Retreating, her behind pitched back and forth like two bags full of excited squirrels. Both coming and going, she was something, I had to admit, although my enthusiasm in that regard was tempered by listening to her call me names as she walked. A fish storm was not as good as a live shot of somebody leaping from a tall building or an airliner crashing into a skyscraper. However, on a slow day in June with the politicians in Washington unaccountably lethargic, behaving like obese, unentertaining lizards, it would have to do for Ms. Byrne and Jack Hart.

4 · Lance's advice

I had for years worked for Boogie and Olden Dewlap, sleaze-bag brothers with the clichéd hearts of gold working out of Seattle and Portland respectively. More recently Willie Sees the Night and I had been working environmental cases from a Latina lawyer named Rosalina Garza, a real cutie. Although Willie and I worked together, our relationship was unusual. Willie only worked on an occasional environmental case that engaged his fancy. He was restless by nature and was on the road weeks and sometimes months on end, hanging with his many Indian friends in the Pacific Northwest. When he was home, he was home. When he was away, he was away. He never told me where he was going or why, and I didn't ask.

It was clear to me the next morning that I needed Willie's help, and the best way to track him down was to pay a visit to Rosie Garza. I stopped briefly at a 7-Eleven and bought myself a pair of outsized shades to cover the shiner I had on my left eye. There wasn't a lot I could do about the swollen left side of my mouth.

Rosie Garza's houseboat was moored in a community of high spirited gays who intuitively sensed that I was infatuated with her. Bewildered by the complicated games we breeders were forced to play, the gays were highly amused. They over-looked no opportunity to razz me cheerfully for being such a frustrated straight.

When I arrived at Rosie's houseboat at ten o'clock, her neighbor Lance, the owner of one of Portland's most fashion-able interior design services, was lying on his deck in a thong swim suit, slathered with suntan lotion. When he saw me he leaped to his feet exclaiming, "You just missed them, Denson. They've been looking everywhere for you." He broke into his version of the song made famous in the movie *Butch Cassidy and the Sundance Kid.*

Just got sal-mon a falling on my head.

"Not all gay people know how to sing, Lance. Trust me on that. Who missed me?"

"Why, the reporters! They were here in a swarm. A star, Denson. You're going to be a star. You'll be looking out at us from the box, your face all slathered with pancake. We'll all be wanting your autograph, of course." Lance's voice dripped with sarcasm. "So thrilled we all are! So very thrilled."

"You got it backwards, Lance."

"Oh?"

"I missed *them.* Lucky for me too. If you and your pals all lie about seeing me this morning, first chance I get I'll give you all a special showing of my tape of the fish storm. If I have my way, you won't be seeing it on the box, tucked be-tween Tampax and Viagra ads. Last chance for this deal, Lance. Going, going . . ."

"Done," he said quickly. "A private showing of the fish storm! We'll be the envy of everybody in Portland. Nobody here saw you come or go. I'll see to it. You have a black eye, don't you? On *Good Morning America* they showed a photo-graph of you with your shirt open showing the cop the fish bruise on your chest. Nice chest, Denson. I like that hair. Let me see."

"I think I'll pass." Lance's sexual tastes were curious by my preferences, but that didn't prevent my liking him. He knew how to laugh, and I knew he and his neighbors would keep their word. Different they were, but I didn't care.

Lance said, "Say, Denson, you like a little advice from someone who observes the female of the species from a perspective unavailable to you?"

"You mean . . . ?" I rolled my eyes in the direction of Rosie's cabin. Rosie would have nothing to do with me romantically. She was all business. She lawyer. Me private investigator. No high emotion among professionals. It was also possible she felt I was getting a little long in the tooth as an object of romantic interest, a disheartening thought, but I was undaunted.

Lance nodded. "Females often like a little bad boy in their man. You ever think of adding a little rebel to your persona, perhaps a hint of danger or violence?"

I thought about that for a moment. "Well, I'm at least one part Henry David Thoreau. Didn't he say he 'marched to the beat a different drummer'? That's being a kind of bad boy isn't it? Does that count?"

Lance shook his head in disgust. "Heavens no! Thoreau spent all that time sitting around a pond growing his stupid beans and counting his pennies. And writing in that dumb journal of his! No woman wants Bohemian nonsense. Face it, you're an aging dork who sits around reading and drinking homemade wine."

"A dork? Gee thanks, Lance."

"You think far too much for your own good. Learn to enjoy the sensual pleasures. And that partner of yours! What's his name? Geronimo? Cochise?"

"Willie Sees the Night."

"Oh, God, that's right. I might be gay, but if you know

what's good for you on the matter of women, you'll trust me and take my advice."

"And that wonderful advice would be?"

He frowned, mock impatient. "Give them plain old predictable *bourgeois*. That's *very* manly, Denson. Spend, spend, spend! Watch football on the tube so they know you have Y chromosomes. Maybe whack 'em around once in a while, then buy them flowers so they'll stop their blubbering. When the sniffles are over throw 'em on the bed and do whatever it is that you yucky straights do. That and pay attention to anniversaries, birthdays and Valentine's day. That's the kind of romantic man that turns them on. Also don't talk too much. Grunt. Rent a tape of Marlon Brando in *A Streetcar Named Desire*. Now *there* was a hunk who knew how to treat women."

I laughed. That was Lance in the mode of parody, irony and paradox.

Just then Rosie, who had heard us talking, stepped onto deck and I hopped aboard. God, she was soulful. Cute as hell. Little she was with copper colored skin and huge brown eyes. "Denson! Look at you! Are you okay? How are you?" There was genuine concern in her voice and on her face.

"I'm still trucking, not bad for a self-important idiot with a cash register for a brain."

"Huh?"

"That's what a female television reporter called me last night when I was hiding in Willie's cabin. She didn't know I was eavesdropping on her conversation."

She said, "You have anything to eat yet? Let me cook you a bacon and egg sandwich. That's what you like, isn't it? On whole wheat bread with lettuce and mayonnaise. I got this bacon that's so good you just wouldn't believe it. Probably not good for your heart, but a little treat now and then is good for the soul."

I sighed. "The sandwich sounds good. All that fat sounds good. Yum!"

Eavesdropping on our conversation, Lance made a little noise in his throat. As I followed Rosie into her cabin, I heard him applauding lightly from the deck next boat. I reached back and flipped him the finger.

He burst out laughing and yelled, "There you go, big boy. Oooh! Oooh!"

5 · *The fate of* Ursus americanus

We settled into Rosie Garza's small galley, and I watched her retrieve bacon and eggs out of her small refrigerator. What a sweetie she was. I told her about my adventure in the fish storm. I said, "Nobody lives that far up the highway except for Willie and me. Sharon Toogood had a Denson–Sees the Night business card in her wallet, but I've never talked to her. The state cop wanted to know if she was on her way to see one of us. Willie?"

"Possibly."

"Is Willie working on a case that I don't know anything about?"

Rosie poured me a cup of coffee. "Well, yes, he is, as a matter, fact. He was in the Bitterroots fishing with some friends when I got a call from the folks at the Nature Conservancy concerned about a threat to *Ursus americanus*."

"American bear. Say again?"

She shook her head. "American black bear. There appears to be an organized ring of poachers in the Pacific Northwest who are killing black bears for their gall bladders."

"Gall bladders?"

She flopped a half dozen strips into the bottom of a frying

pan and turned on the propane heat. "Both the gall bladder and bile salts of bears are used in Chinese traditional and patented medicine. Western medicine has used synthetic bear bile, ursodeoxycholic acid, made from cow bile, to dissolve gallstones. But the Chinese don't like synthetic bile. They want the original, which they use to treat a variety of illnesses and symptoms. They use it to treat high fevers and convulsions, delirium from extensive burns, for severe cases of inflamed and swollen eyes, and for reducing the swelling and pains of trauma, sprains and fractures. That's in addition to hemorrhoids."

"That goes without saying," I said.

She turned the sizzling bacon with a pair of tongs. "The Chinese believe bear bile is a bitter, 'cold' medicine that enters the gall bladder, spleen, stomach and liver channels to 'clear the heat' and detoxify various forms of 'fire.' "

"Right."

"Western researchers say it in fact works as a poison antidote, an antispasmodic, and an anti-coughing agent." She removed the strips of bacon and laid them on a paper towel, then poured off most of the grease. She turned down the heat. "A bacon and egg sandwich is disgusting, do you know that? A giant hit of cholesterol."

"But delicious," I said. "Good for an occasional treat."

"It's your heart."

"Pining for you. Lot of good it does me."

"Shush. We've been through that. Give it up, already. By the way, at a higher dosage, a cow's gall bladder, *Fel voxus*, is used as a substitute for bear gall. The National Fish and Wildlife Forensics Laboratory ran extensive tests on 'bear' galls bought from Hong Kong medicinal shops. Only about thirty percent were from bears, the rest were from domestic animals, mostly pigs." Rosie cracked two eggs into the bacon grease. As they began sizzling, she said, "About ten years ago, the

Chinese began breeding bears in captivity and developed the ability to remove their galls while the bears were still alive. Their ambition was to raise forty thousand bears annually, only a couple of years ago they ran into the snag."

"What can go Wong, will."

Rosie gave me a look. "Please, desist. And you wonder why I don't want to go out with you!" She flipped the eggs over with a spatula. "A terrible virus hit their captive bears, drastically reducing the population. In addition, there were those picky Chinese who insisted the galls of wild bears were somehow superior to those raised in captivity. Sort of like people who want 'organic' vegetables in this country or who claim not to like trout raised in a pond."

"Partly a status thing, I take it. My gall is *real* bear gall. Your gall is just pretend."

"Correct. No self-respecting Chinese with money wants cow galls or pig galls. They want the real deal. The Chinese had pushed the population of Asian wild bears to near extinction, so entrepreneurs began looking around for another source."

"Remember, Rosie, in China to get rich is glorious. Let me guess. They turned to North America. Lots of bears over here."

She scooped out the eggs and began assembling the sandwich, ripping off some lettuce and smearing mayonnaise on a slice of whole wheat bread. She handed me the sandwich. "That's one theory. Willie's been chasing leads for almost a month. He called a couple of days ago to say he's on his way back to his cabin. You'll have to ask him what he found. Here, enjoy. Your funeral."

I took a bite. "Mmmmm. Delicious. You're really crafty, Rosie. You know the way to a man's heart is through his stomach. If you keep this up, I'll be yours forever more." I held out my cup for more coffee. "If Sharon Toogood was on her way to see me about something, I owe it to her to find out what it was." Munching on the sandwich, I said, "Only problem is that I need a legit case."

"Maybe you've lucked on that front. Your friend Bill Dennis called. Bill did the legal work for Sharon's business in Portland. When he heard she'd been murdered, he called T.G. to offer his condolences. Since T.G. is a public figure, he asked Bill to recommend a private investigator to give him a heads up if there's anything untoward on the horizon. So Bill said he could do better than that. He knew the private investigator who happened on Sharon's body."

It made sense that Bill had done legal work for Sharon Toogood. He did the legal work for six or seven Portland families with old wealth, including Sharon's mother. "Is it possible that Bill recommended us to Sharon Toogood?"

"Could have. Why don't you ask him yourself? He wants to talk to you. Says you can talk at a shooting match at Longview's new range. He'll meet you at the library at noon."

I had been shooting with Bill several times at the range Longview. He liked to drive over from Portland and go shooting with his brother Mac. "Good sandwich, really. Tastes like another."

She shook her head. "You've had enough saturated fat for one day. Just because I don't want to go out with you and endure puns and curious observations doesn't mean I want to kill you."

6 • Pleasure of shooting bowling pins

The closest library to my cabin that was worth a damn—without driving to the Multnomah County Library in Portland—was across the Columbia River at Longview, Washington. That was where I had first met a burly, ruddy-faced lawyer named Bill Dennis, whose sister-in-law, Karen, was the children's librarian. The beautiful redbrick library with classical columns at its entrance, built in 1932, was a Norman Rockwell, *Saturday Evening Post* kind of building, American at its most nostalgic: decent, good, wholesome, serving the community, offering a key to knowledge and the past, not to mention more recently fashionable videotapes, CDs, and computers. Karen read to kids every Tuesday night. On the spacious lawn outside, a ten-foot-high wooden squirrel chewed on a nut. The squirrel was a chain-saw carving, a form of Pacific Northwest indigenous art. While the cheery squirrel might not have been gnawing on the nut of knowledge, the kids loved it.

Over the previous several years, I had driven to the library at least once a week so I could sit in the lovely reading room and browse through magazines and read the *New York Times Book Review* to learn what people were writing and thinking.

Several of the magazines I read had on-line editions, but there was a certain tactile satisfaction in sitting with the actual paper in my hands reading the complete, unabridged articles. With a book or magazine article, the writer addressed a single reader holding paper. On an on-line abridgment, he addressed monitors around the planet. A big difference, in my opinion.

I parked my microbus on the street beside the library. Bill was a punctual kind of guy who considered it bad manners to make people wait on him. At high noon, with a grin on his mug, he pulled into the library parking lot in his Toyota pickup. He hopped out to take a closer look at my battered bus. "I've heard about vehicles taking a pounding from hail the size of eggs, but falling fish? This surely has to make the Guinness book of records. It'll never be broken. You'll be immortal, Denson!"

"Under what heading would that record be?"

He laughed. "How about, 'Most damage done to a vehicle by unusual objects falling from the sky.' "

He was still shaking his head in amazement as he returned to his pickup. I grabbed my .22 Ruger and hopped aboard for the ride to the shoot. We were on our way. I decided to say nothing about the business card for the moment. It was a hole card.

"Mac got hung up at work, so it'll be just the two of us. The new range is just a few minutes west of town," he said. "I got two Thermoses of coffee to keep us jacked."

"Old ready Bill. See here, a fish to the eye straight out of the sky." I lifted my sunglasses so he could see my shiner.

He winced.

Bill was a Christian, I knew. I turned and showed him the fish on my chest. "Any meaning there to your way of thinking?"

He gave me a wry look. "You never know, Denson. You want to pour us some java?"

As I poured the coffee, he said, "You're a regular fugitive. It's almost like running you to ground has a higher priority than finding Sharon Toogood's murderer. Holding out on the public's right to know. And foregoing celebrity!" He reprimanded me with a *tsk, tsk, tsk* of his tongue.

"A crime against humanity," I said ruefully. "I know. I know."

"Think of it. Getting to kick back later and watch a tape of yourself being interviewed by Katie Couric. That charming mouth once asked questions of George W. Bush! And you're saying no! Why it's outrageous!" Bill grinned broadly. "Bad form to be seen with a guy like you, Denson. My brother lives here. I'm a hotshot lawyer from Portland, a regular pillar of the community." He laughed at himself.

"A frustrated television reporter called me a 'self-important moron with a cash register for a brain.' She didn't know I was eavesdropping, but that doesn't matter. I wouldn't have turned the tape over to them anyway. I have to consider Willie's feelings. To him, those salmon weren't mere fish."

Bill looked puzzled.

"Willie will see their death as tragedy, not oddity or the grist for public spectacle. If somebody had taped a speeding truck flattening a group of children at a crosswalk, would we show that on the six o'clock news?"

"I see. Brethren of the animal spirits and all that."

"I'm not saying I agree with him especially, only that he's my partner, and I have to respect his feelings. Listening to the reporters talk behind my back last night pretty much sealed the deal, at least for the time being."

We had left Longview behind us, and Bill Dennis hung a right up a highway that flanked a creek that led up into the Coast Range of mountains.

He said, "Don Imus led with the issue on his radio program

this morning. He's with you, by the way, but there were plenty of callers who were furious. A philosophy professor at Yale said there is a case to be made that such a bizarre natural phenomenon is a form of public property. Yes, it happened to you. Yes, you taped it. And yes, by law the tape is yours. Can a scientist who discovers a law of nature take out a patent on it? No."

"Can an idiot who tapes a fish storm keep it to himself?"

"According to the professor's logic, no. Here we are." Bill pulled off the road into a gravel parking lot where the shooters were gathering. We hadn't yet discussed Jerry Toogood's need for a private investigator, but that would come. The assembled marksmen, or would-be marksmen, were those kind of sportsman and middle-America white men who had voted en masse for whatever Republican was on the ticket. To hang with them for a shooting match was not the kind of thing one admitted to polite urban company. They were mostly Christian white males, but they were not bad or evil people, certainly not racists, crypto-Nazis or any of that hyperbolic nonsense. They were guys who liked to shoot and were clinging to values and a way of life that they saw being swamped by change and what they regarded as ignoramus liberals. Being hunters and fishermen, they had a respect for the natural environment that would likely surprise a Congressman from Boston.

I said, "Last time I went shooting with you was more than a year ago." I was an awful shot, but it was still fun. The idea was to knock bowling pins off a table. Why bowling pins? The shape of a bowling pin was said to be roughly like that of a human being at so many yards away. Six pins were lined up on a table six feet wide and four feet deep. The front edge of the table was twenty-one feet from the shooter. For people firing .22 caliber pea shooters like mine, the pins were placed six inches from the rear of the table. For a medium-sized 9mm pistol, they were lined up in the middle of the table. For big boomer .357 Magnums, they were lined up a foot from the front of the table.

A perfectly placed shot in the middle of the bowling pin just below the neck, corresponding to the upper center of the human torso, would knock the pin off the table. If the shooter knocked a pin on its side, he kept blasting at it until he rolled it off.

I loaded the clip of my Ruger and waited my turn. I said, "Rosie said you talked to T.G. about me."

"You're up, Denson."

I stepped up to the line, listening carefully to the bearded safety officer's instructions. I went through the required drill as I popped the clip into the butt of the Ruger. He would shout at any shooter who deviated in the slightest from the routine. If it was a flagrant violation, say the shooter pointed a weapon at someone, loaded or not, the safety officer would stop everything and escort the dangerous fool to his vehicle and tell him to leave the premises. Given thirty or forty men and two or three women standing around with lethal weapons in their hands, I thought it was a sensible policy.

The safety officer murmured, "Why don't you just give them the stupid tape, Denson?" He gave me a reproving look.

"Can't get away with anything. Jesus!" I completed the drill, concentrating on each step so I wouldn't embarrass myself with a bonehead error. I felt the eyes of experienced shooters watching me, thinking *rookie*. Finally, I was ready.

"Fire," he said, punching the stopwatch.

I took the pins one at a time, left to right, knocking the first five off the table. I was slightly off on the sixth pin, merely toppling it on its side. It took an extra shot to spin it off the table.

I stepped back, pleased, waiting for the safety officer's instructions to unload my pistol and fire it downrange to make sure there was not a round left in the chamber.

"Good shooting!" Dennis said, although he knew it was blind luck on my part. Lowering his voice, he said, "T.G.'s first wife, Samantha, was the only daughter of Donald and Ruby Moultine."

I said, "Plywood. Lumber mills. Wooden palettes. Construction. The Moultines were killed when their private plane crashed over northern California. I remember the story."

"T.G. and Samantha had two daughters, Sharon and Mariah. When Samantha died of cancer ten years ago, Sharon and Mariah split the Moultine fortune. T.G. thinks the police might suspect Mariah of murdering Sharon because they recently had an awkward, public shouting match in which money was mentioned and threats were made. I suspect something odd was going on because Sharon recently asked me if I could recommend a good private investigator."

"Oh?"

"Wouldn't say what it was all about. I was curious of course, especially when Sharon asked me not to tell her father. She was as agitated as all getout. I gave her one of your business cards. Did she get in touch with you?"

I shook my head. "The cop who arrived on the scene found the card in her wallet."

He said, "She was killed up in your neck of the woods. Maybe she was on her way to see you."

"Seems possible, since it was you who gave her the card. Rosie says you did the legal work for Sharon's business."

"Lao Tzu's. That's right."

"What's that all about?"

"It's a sort of a combination of New Age, health food, and holistic medicine. They sell everything from healing balms to vitamin supplements and Chinese salves. Tiger balm, that sort of thing. Also North American medicinal herbs. Ye of little faith in western medicine need only go to Lao Tzu's to get your curative fix. They've got six all told, scattered in trendier areas around Portland."

"Popular with people who have more money than brains."

"That's one way of looking at it. They wanted to buy Chinese patented and traditional medicine from Hong Kong, but didn't have the foggiest idea how to do the legal stuff at this end. I did the paperwork, beginning with trademarking their business name. It's a complicated business. To avoid possible lawsuits, you have to take care not to claim too much in the way of results for the medicines but still convince people to buy them."

"And T.G. wants me to look into his daughter's murder."

"Yes, he does. He's a public figure, and he's concerned about Mariah. We both agree someone other than the cops needs to look into the murder. If it comes to that, I can recommend a criminal defense lawyer for Mariah. T.G. wants you to keep me posted on what you find. I've been a friend of the family for years. I know you and Willie."

I said, "Willie's on another case. It'll have to be just me until he finishes with whatever he's looking into."

"That's fine."

"We're talking genuine concern here."

"Mariah is an individualist, perhaps not unlike yourself, Denson. She's full of books and ideas. You might like her. You can talk to her at her, uh, summer cabin tomorrow. She's in Portland today, but T.G. tells me she's going back to her retreat tomorrow afternoon."

"Summer cabin?"

"Just wait till the tide's out and drive up the beach from Long Beach to Ocean Park, about halfway there you'll see her place on the right. It's kind of temporary." Dennis cackled gleefully. "Look for the lime green Suzuki SUV. That'll be hers. When you finish with her you can talk to T.G."

The safety officer looked at the list of names in his hand. "Bill Dennis, you're up."

Bill walked up to the line with a heavy stride that threatened to crack the earth or trigger a minor earthquake. He sucked in his mighty gut. He stroked his walrus mustache with the back of the fingers on his massive left hand. He popped the clip into the bottom of his .357 Magnum. He got into his shooter's stance, feet parted, ready to rip. He looked more like an NFL defensive lineman than a lawyer about to shoot bowling pins off a table.

I saw that one of the waiting shooters was studying me. Finally, he said, "Say, you're not the guy who survived the fish storm, are you? I seen you on TV. They're looking all over for you. Mad as hell, they are. They claim your tape correctly belongs to the public."

"I've heard that argument."

"A downpour of salmon. I know I'd like to see it. My son and daughter are both sore as hell that anybody would hold out on them like that. They're in the fourth and fifth grades. They want to see it. They don't understand why they can't."

I felt a spike of anxiety or maybe guilt course through my stomach. Of course, the kids! I hadn't thought of the kids. By giving the beautiful blonde and cartoon head an in-your-face, I was giving a raw deal to children who would be thrilled to see a tape of salmon falling from the sky. Kids were innocents. Where was the harm in letting them see the salmon fall out of the sky? What kind of jerk would hold out on kids? Even behind my dark glasses, I avoided eye contact with the man with disappointed children. I had Willie and my pride on one side and kids on the other. Were there no decisions in life that were clear cut?

Having finished his turn without a miss, Bill turned to me and said, "What do you think, Denson?"

"Not bad shooting, I have to admit. Regular Dirty Harry." I knew man with the disappointed children wanted me to lift my sunglasses. Better yet if I unbuttoned my shirt and showed him the fish bruise on my chest.

7 · Bogey man

As I drove back home, I wondered if Sharon Toogood's involvement in Lao Tzu's and her asking Bill to recommend a private investigator had anything to do with Willie's bear poaching. As I neared the small town of Clatskanie, I saw a red light in my rearview mirror. It was one of those dashboard deals in an unmarked car, a Ford sedan.

I pulled over. In the mirror, I saw a middle aged man with a stomach and rumpled suit get out of the car and shuffle my way.

When he arrived at my bus, the rumpled man turned out to be dark complexioned, with thinning brown hair. His face looked prematurely wrinkled. He had huge bags under morose brown eyes and a fleshy mouth. He wore eyeglasses. He bore a vague resemblance to the actor Humphrey Bogart. The flesh on his face drooped either from gravity or the burden of his problems. He pushed his eyeglasses up on his nose. Shaking his drooping face, looking amazed, he scoped my bus. He tilted his head, the better to see the scales and dried goo through the bottoms of his bifocals. His glasses needed cleaning, forcing him to peer through a layer of crud.

In a deep, sonorous voice, he said, "Well, if that isn't the damndest thing I ever saw. One for the books. You look like you must have driven through a fish storm, but that couldn't possibly be, could it? A fish storm? What the hell is that?" He laughed deeply, making a kind of *haroop, haroop, haroop* sound. "Mr. John Denson, I take it. The elusive gumshoe of Whorehouse Meadow." *Haroop, haroop, haroop.* For him, the world was a kick in the ass.

I nodded. "And you would be?" He *did* look like Bogart. It was amazing. Was he going to light a cigarette?

He did, yes! "I would be Alan Shearer. I am a special agent with the Federal Bureau of Investigation. Yessir, one of your basic G-men serving the taxpayers of the United States of America." With the smoking cigarette drooping from his lower lip, he handed me his boxtops.

I studied the identification. It looked real enough, but what did I know? "You look like Humphrey Bogart."

"Everybody says that. It's been my burden."

"So you joined the FBI?"

"They've loosened up since Hoover's days. What I want to know is, where is my Lauren Bacall? Bogie gets Bacall, doesn't he? You should see my old lady." *Haroop, haroop, haroop.*

I wanted to say, "A real beaut, huh?" But I didn't. "No offense, but you have a face like, a morose hound. Did anybody ever tell you that? A basset hound also comes to mind."

"You think I look like a fucking basset hound? That's a good one." *Haroop, haroop, haroop!* "And why would that be?"

I said, "The general droop of your mug. And this would have to do with what? Falling fish or dead girls? As I understand it, the investigation of a murder is a state matter unless kidnapping is involved or the killer went across a state line or whatever."

He took a puff on his cigarette, letting the smoke drift out between his fleshy lips as he sized me up. "I don't see that you have broken any law by getting hammered by falling salmon, if that's what you mean." *Haroop, haroop, haroop.* "Rest assured we're not poaching on the turf of the Oregon State Police. We've got better things to do than to look for extra work. If we didn't have a legitimate reason to be poking around asking questions, we wouldn't. I would like to have a chat with you over a cup of coffee if you don't mind. Only take a few minutes. I can follow you into town. You pick the place and the government will buy."

"Really? You won't have to dip into the social security trust fund or anything? I don't want some old fart going without because of me."

"Oh sure, the taxpayers will spring for the works. No need to worry about the oldies."

"Okey doke," I said. "No reason not to help the FBI." In my rearview mirror, I watched him shuffle back to his Ford.

When he was behind the wheel, I cranked the bus up and buzzed into Clatskanie, where I pulled into a Dunkin' Donuts. I went on inside and waited for Shearer, who paused at the door, noted the "No Smoking" sign, and took one last hit of nicotine to see him through the interview.

We got our coffee at the counter and settled into a booth by a large window that overlooked the parking lot and the highway that ran through town. He appraised me with languid brown eyes. The knot on his tie looked like a squashed horse dumpling.

I said, "J. Edgar Hoover made all you guys wear white shirts. Now you can't even tie a half-Windsor."

His hand went to the knot. "Times change. It's the new FBI," he said.

"Must be," I said. "And smoking? Did Eliot Ness smoke?"

Shearer grinned. "Aw, they don't want us to. Bad for the image and all that. Kiddies trying to copy us. But what're they going to do?" He paused, and pushed his cheek out with his tongue. "Better than Clyde Tolson, don't you think? They say he liked to suck on Hoover cigars. Little man. Big cigar." *Haroop, haroop, haroop!* "We're interested in whatever Sharon Toogood told you before she died."

"I told the investigating officer what she said. He's got it in his notes. That's what she told me. My memory was fresher then than it is now."

He took a sip of coffee. He slipped a pad out of his jacket pocket. "If you don't mind, Mr. Denson."

I said, "She was bleeding internally, so she mostly gurgled blood. In the middle of all the gurgling, I heard parts of three words. Gurgle, gurgle 'ther.' Gurgle, gurgle 'ister.' And Gurgle, gurgle 'ill.' "

"Now that you've had a chance to think about it, you have any better idea of what she was trying to tell you?"

"Ther. Ister. Ill. Gurgling in between. You've pretty much got it."

He grimaced. "You want to tell me about your partner?"

"Willie? He wasn't there."

"Where was he?"

I gave him a look. "What's Willie have to do with this? He wasn't there. He sure as hell had no reason to murder anyone. Isn't that enough?"

"He ever talked to you about Sharon Toogood?"

"Huh? No! Hell, I don't even know where's he's been the last couple of months. He's off chasing poachers."

"Poaching what?"

I shrugged. "I don't know. Bears, I think. Licensed hunters, he doesn't mind. Part of the prey-predator thing. But he doesn't go for poachers."

"Bears?" Shearer leaned forward.

I laughed. "So the FBI is interested in bear poachers, not murderers."

Annoyed, Shearer said, "Nobody said we're interested in

bear poachers. Also I'm the guy with the government boxtops, remember. I ask the questions, not a private dork with a redskin partner. I'm representing the Department of Justice of the United States of America. Jesus!"

"Whatever. Private dick."

He frowned. "So when do you expect Sees the Night to come back?"

"We each have a separate cabin about fifty yards apart on a place called Whorehouse Meadow on Jump-Off Joe Creek. Willie comes. He goes. Sometimes we work together. Sometimes we work alone. He's an adult. He doesn't need my permission to take a piss or have a girlfriend spend the night."

"Which is why they call it Whorehouse Meadow."

I said, "Hey!"

He sighed. "Okay, okay, wiseacre." He gave me a card. "Here's the number of my cell phone. If you remember anything more that might be of help, I'd appreciate it if you give me a call."

"If I close the case before you, I'll put in a good word."

He looked alarmed. "Close what case? *What* in the hell are you talking about?"

"I'm talking about Sharon Toogood."

Shearer scowled and made a sucking sound with his mouth. "Private dorks don't work for free. Who's your client?"

I thought about the girl's eyes. I said, "I'm a private investigator, part of a tradition of idealistic morons. I drive into a fish storm and discover Jerry Toogood's dying daughter. Her blue eyes look up at me, imploring. She tries to talk to me while she's choking on blood. We have a kind of moment, an odd form of bonding. I feel obliged to find her killer, a matter of honor."

"Honor? What the hell are you talking about?"

"In lieu of a client. Will that fly?"

Shearer made a noise in his throat. "You've got an imagination, I'll give you that, but you're a few centuries late with the honor horseshit. You've been reading Mickey Spillane."

I shook my head.

"No? Who then?"

"I've read a few titles by Jan Willem van der Wetering."

He looked puzzled.

"Wrote the Inspector Van der Valk mysteries. Dutch Buddhist."

Shearer pushed his eyeglasses back into place. "You Buddhist?"

I shrugged. "Don't know what I am, to be honest. But I think the Buddhists have it right when they say that unhappiness is caused by desire. It was an insight that helped Inspector Van der Valk solve a lot of mysteries."

Haroop, haroop, haroop. "What kind of insight is that?"

I said, "Unhappiness is motive for crimes of passion. To find unhappiness, sort through desire."

Haroop, haroop, haroop. "You're a real piece of work, Denson. Buddhism!" He rolled his eyes.

I smelled something foul.

Shearer was on a roll with his odd laughter. *Haroop, haroop, haroop.* "A creeper. Stealth fart. I ate eggs this morning. Eggs'll do it every time." *Haroop, haroop, haroop.*

I tried not to breathe. This wasn't the image of the FBI that the government sought so assiduously to project. Part of the general entropy of the culture, I assumed. I came up for air. "Always a pleasure doing business with professional gentlemen from the United States government."

Shearer said, "You think FBI agents don't let farts? Hell, I bet even Marilyn Monroe let real bloozers in the morning. Clint Eastwood too."

"I bet Marilyn Monroe found a way to control herself when she was in a Dunkin' Donuts with Arthur Miller," I added.

8 · He sees the night

Early that evening, a gray bank of clouds had blown in from the west and the valley of Jump-Off Joe was socked in with a light rain. The prediction had been for sun, not rain, but not even the National Weather Service, for all its satellites and Doppler radar and learned talk of high and low pressure areas, could confidently predict from one day to the next that there would be no rain in the Pacific Northwest. By that, I mean all those areas west of the Cascade Mountains. Once you got into Eastern Oregon or Eastern Washington, the sagebrush took over and your lungs expanded with clean, dry air.

There wasn't much I could do until the next day when I would drive to Long Beach to talk to Mariah Toogood. I holed up in my cabin and watched the mist swirling and floating grandly over the tops of the Douglas fir and down onto Whorehouse Meadow. The Mariners were on the box. Although I was a passionate fan of baseball—in which subtraction ruled, mimicking life—after the final out I had witnessed the previous night, I didn't feel like watching.

I poured myself a cup of elderberry wine and stared out of the window. Judging from the questions of Special Agent Shearer, there was a likely connection between Sharon Toogood's death and Willie's bear poaching case. I peered through the darkness at Willie Sees the Night's cabin, which was about fifty yards upstream from my own. The lights were on.

Willie was back. His battered old pickup was nowhere to be seen, but that was not unusual. In the late summer he often parked it in the next valley and hiked over the ridge so he could collect some watercress that grew at the top of the unnamed trickle that emptied into Stump Creek.

Willie was not given to behavior that could be described as coincidental, although coincidences by his way of thinking almost always had far-out animal spirit explanations that were by turns astounding and entertaining. I doused the lights and locked the door. Taking my Nikon and Sony with me, I walked upstream on the trail beside Jump-Off Joe Creek listening to the bubbling and gurgling of water.

As I drew closer, I could see the door was open.

Willie was squatting on the floor. He looked up at me, grinning.

"You're back," I said.

He laughed softly. "That's what I admire about you, Denson. By God, you're always logical. Nothing escapes you. Nothing. Ought to call you John Sees the Obvious."

"You got animal spirits in this room or is it just us?" What Willie called animal people, and others called the animal spirits, were like the demons in Greek mythology, an intermediary form between gods and humans, some of them tricksters and shape changers like Coyote, also known as Willie Sees the Night. At least that was Willie's story. I made no attempt to argue, a pointless exercise.

"Let me look at your bruise," he said.

I stepped up and unbuttoned my shirt. Willie lit a match and whistled when he saw the bruise.

"Pull up some floor and plop your butt," he said. He was

likely high on whatever it was that sent him on his sorcerer's trips.

I squatted on the floor. More than once I had been accused of being a poor man's Carlos Castaneda, which I found annoying. Yes, Willie fancied himself a sorcerer or shaman. But I was no sorcerer's apprentice. His conceit was that the animal people had chosen me to be Warrior, the logical white man, to help them do battle against the louts and morons who were screwing up the hunting grounds and fouling the camp. I went along with that. As an anthropologist in the manner of Franz Boas, Castaneda had been taught that, in the abstract at least, all cultures are equal. I was not an anthropologist. I was skeptical, but did my best to keep an open mind.

I left the magical, amazing hallucinogenic trips to Willie. I stayed on my own comfortable side of the metaphysical line, venturing only as far as an occasional hit of cannabis would take me. Our different ways of looking at the world were complementary; we did not compete.

"Tell me about it," he said. "The fish first, then the girl."

"The fish first." I thought a moment, then said, "A cloudburst describes it. A cloudburst of silver salmon. They were being blown by the wind and so fell at an angle, not straight down. When I looked up, I could see them hurtling out of the blue sky. The cloud had moved on. These fish came straight out of the heavens. Some were killed the instant they hit the road, but an amazing number of them had their fall broken by the tops of Douglas fir and were flopping around still alive. It was like the wind was guiding them down. You saw my chest. You should see the body of my bus. It was terrible, Willie. Truly awful. And spooky too, I don't mind telling you. Salmon hurtling out of the clear sky. Yeeeee!"

In the dim light, Willie looked stricken. There was a sad, faraway look in his eyes.

I waited.

Finally, he said, "And you got this awful business on video-tape?"

"I had a fresh tape and the light was extraordinary." I tapped the Sony. "And I got some still pictures too, but they can't be as dramatic as the tape. I think Sharon Toogood was trying to tell me who killed her. She had a hundred and fifty bucks in her handbag on the front seat of her vehicle. She ran her Explorer off the road, which suggests she was being pursued. The door was still open, so she was probably trying to escape. She had one of our business cards on her. Later, Bill Dennis told me he gave it to her. He said she was agitated about something, but didn't want to talk about it. She wanted a recommendation for a private investigator that she wanted to keep secret from her father."

"She was on her way to see one of us," he said.

"Having to do with bear poaching?"

"Could be."

I told him about my conversation with special agent Shearer.

Willie said, "The FBI's interest is no surprise. The exposure of a ring of poachers supplying bear gall bladders to the Chinese is the worst imaginable nightmare to the government and all the importers and multinational corporations doing business with the Chinese. If the American public ever learned that the Chinese are harvesting our wild bears for a medicine they could duplicate in a laboratory, how long do you think Congress would let China keep its most favored nation status?"

I shrugged. "A month? Six weeks?"

"The government wants this stopped as much as we do, only they want it to be nice and tidy, without the sorry truth sailing at them twenty-four-hours-a-day from the cable networks. The Chinese government has to be just as concerned." Willie ran the palm of his left hand down his jaw. "The people at Nature Conservancy feel that if just a couple of poachers are busted, the rest will just lay low for a while, then start up again. They want the honcho."

Willie stared at the fingernails of his left hand, a habit he had when he was in deep thought as he was now, obviously trying to make some connections.

I jarred him out of his trance. "Willie?"

"Why don't you go ahead with your trip to Mariah Too-good and see what you can find out? I'll drive to Enterprise to talk to a breed named Jonas Knowles, a game warden who works the Blue Mountains and the high country of Union and Wallowa counties. His mother is a Nez Perce, and he's hunted all his life. By the time you get back, maybe we can start piecing this together."

9 · At Long Beach

The first thing I did before I left Whorehouse Meadow was check the tide charts. To find Mariah I would have to drive on Long Beach, which was legal on a tide low enough to afford hard sand. In fact, at low tide it was legally a state highway. The speed limit was twenty-five miles an hour. Pedestrians, clam-diggers, prone lovers caught in the ecstasy of the moment, and builders of sand castles all had the right of way. At high tide the state highway turned into the Pacific Ocean.

At the Oregon end of the Lewis and Clark Bridge, a 4.1-mile-long span of the Columbia River, I started the ascent of a two-hundred-foot-high truss span that allowed outgoing freighters to deliver lumber and wheat down the Columbia River to Japan and China in return for Japanese-made cars and Chinese-made gadgets and running shoes. This was an unnerving climb for my Volkswagen minibus, a 1972 model whose engine labored so hard I drove with a dry mouth, chewing on my lower lip and with my stomach doing the twist. On the summit of the great hump, I was able to shift into third gear, and, greatly relieved, descended to twenty-five feet above the Columbia for the remainder of the drive to the Washington shore. The air cooled engine relaxed on the descent and buzzed happily along as carefree as the seagulls that floated above the bridge.

The Columbia River is narrower than the Mississippi, but deeper and with a greater flow of water. The bridge at Astoria is three miles inland from the meeting of the river and the Pacific Ocean. Meriwether Lewis and William Clark approached the mouth of the Columbia from the Washington shore and their descriptions of the harrowing encounter of river and tide are among the most memorable episodes in their journal. A sheltering jetty of enormous boulders poked northward from the Oregon shore, but the terrible bar remains a test of courage for fishermen in small boats and a storied passage for the most veteran ship's captain.

A traveler across the Columbia at Astoria faces a dramatic vista. The storms roll in from the west. Great banks of dark clouds, some trailed by streaks of rain in a slate gray horizon, followed by sunny patches of pale blue and the grandest rainbows one could ever imagine. And the water, reflecting silver at midday, turns to grand yellows, oranges, roses and purples at sunset. A little history too is in order.

The promontory that forms the northern boundary of the mouth of the river is named Cape Disappointment. Close to four hundred vessels, from fishing boats to schooners and freighters, have gone down trying to negotiate the terrible bar in the last three-hundred-odd years. Lured on by the siren of shelter and rest and respite, with surf below, wind above, decks pitching, masts groaning, pity those doughty, disappointed sailors that found their peace in Davy Jones's locker.

Meteorologists monitor ocean currents, the jet stream, the movement of Arctic and tropical air masses to predict the weather. For a weatherman, the physical properties of fluids operate according to the principles elucidated by physicists.

A private investigator deals with the fluids and currents of the human condition: intoxicants, the revealing and accusatory bodily fluids, tears, and vomit—plus various chemical and hormonal secretions, both bothersome and benign—in addition to spit, sweat, semen and the biggie that holds us all transfixed, blood. In the human body, bags of water that we are, pain and passion and joy and grief make the humors run hot or cold. This all begins in the mysterious synapses of the brain, a swirling pool of energy in a biological reservoir said by surgeons to have the consistency of soft-boiled eggs.

I have always been amazed at how much grief and passion could be expended on what were, in the end, posturing bags of water. We kill one another that we might wear fancier shoes than the next person. Odd species.

For Willie, the behavior of fluids, both meteorological and biological, demonstrated the principle of the Great Hoop. I didn't fully understand what the Great Hoop was all about, but I felt as metaphor it had wonderful charm, akin to the Buddhist belief that we all rise from a great flow of humanity and sink back again.

One thing was for sure, there was nothing akin to the National Weather Service that could track the joy and despair of the human condition.

On the Washington side of the bridge, the highway formed a T with state Highway 401 at the base of a mountain covered with Douglas fir. I hung a left and buzzed along the highway passing sturgeon fishermen sitting on huge boulders along the river.

The white sand beach on the three-mile-wide Long Beach Peninsula extended from the North Head lighthouse thirty miles north to the mouth of Willapa Bay. The shallow bay was famous for its oyster-growing industry and the large population of black bears on Long Island, site of the Willapa National Wildlife Refuge. But the bears weren't content with staying on the island. Famous for robbing dumpsters and garbage cans, the mischievous bruins also roamed the peninsula and the rain forest on the eastern shore of the bay.

The Long Beach economy was based on the summer tourist trade. In the good, bad old days before satellites, the man on the radio used a barometer to check the atmospheric pressure and maybe stick a wet finger out the window to check the wind. That was about it. A family driving to Long Beach from Vancouver or Portland just picked a weekend and took its chances. Bum luck if it rained hard every day.

As a hedge against the disaster of a wet summer, motel owners now promoted winter storms as a romantic way for couples to take advantage of off-season rates. Although it was dressed up in ten-dollar words and phrases, the pitch—a staple for seaside motels up and down Washington and Oregon coasts—was simple enough in its basics:

Imagine yourself eating overpriced thawed halibut at one of the remaining cafés still open in the winter. Afterwards, you too can cuddle by an artificial fire with a plastic glass of elderberry wine and watch the wild and stormy sea and massive breakers crashing onto the beach. Listen to the crack and boom of thunder while you do the in-out on a queen-sized bed. Lay back all sweaty with the wind slapping against the window.

Ahh, romance! The human spirit soared!

When I reached the single stop light at Volstad St., a perverse form of status qualifying Long Beach as a real town, I hung a left. This was one of the entrances for driving on the beach, a quarter of a mile to the west.

My chart was accurate. The tide was low. I drove north up Long Beach with a hard wind coming off the ocean gusting so hard against my bus that it seemed the left two wheels were coming off the sand. To the west the sun was turning orange as it settled over the Pacific. Goodbye North America. Hello Asia. Keeping my eye out for my mysterious lady, I buzzed over kelp and circled a log washed up on the sand. To the east, the beach ended in dunes topped by salt grass. The dunes extended several hundred yards to the tree line of stunted lodgepole pine.

About halfway between Long Beach and Ocean Park, Dennis had said. I kept my eye on the odometer, which still worked, having turned over two or three times while I kept replacing engines and engine parts. I regarded my microbus as something in the order of an old friend.

Then I spotted Mariah Toogood's "summer residence," for there was her lime green Suzuki. I laughed out loud. People ordinarily laugh out loud only in the presence of others. When one does it alone, it is because something is truly wonderful.

In this case it was because Mariah lived in a large hut or cabin made of driftwood erected on top of a grass-covered hump, something of an island in a sea of shifting sand. Or even call it a playhouse. It was against the law to use nails to erect such structures. Parking my bus beside it, I saw that it was lashed together out of blue-green cords that I recognized as having come from netting lost by Taiwanese fishermen who poached American waters for rockfish. Irregularly-shaped logs and boards and sticks, bleached white from the sun and rounded by being repeatedly washed up on the sand, poked out this way and that. The August resident, Ms. Toogood, a genuine loon if there ever was one, had put a sheet of black plastic over the side currently being buffeted by the wind— keeping it in place with a large hunk of orange fishing net. It was a perfectly grand cabin.

I got out of my bus, hair blowing, and circled the pile of wood looking for whatever it was that served as an entrance. I found it on the eastern side, away from the wind.

A young woman, having heard my bus, was waiting, her long black hair whipping in the wind. She had fair skin that set off her black hair, a rare combination. Her large, intelligent green eyes and dimpled chin reminded me vaguely of a young Ava Gardner, an actress whose image had faded into the dimly remembered past. But if you were old enough, Ava Gardner meant something. Mariah had Ava's sensual mouth. Her face was longer and thinner than Ava's had been, and her nose was perhaps larger, but the resemblance remained. Her face was soulful in the same vulnerable, world-weary kind of way. God, how I fell in love with Ava Gardner when I was a little kid!

"Ms. Mariah Toogood?" I said.

She smiled. "Mr. John Denson, I take it. Nice shiner."

"John Denson, yes. It's fading, thank God."

"Bill Dennis called to say I should expect you. Won't you come in out of the wind?" She stepped up to my bus and ran her fingers down the dents caused by the falling salmon. "Bill said your bus was some kind of sight. He was right about that."

In the darkness, I was subliminally aware of wings. A soundless flapping. I turned and saw a nocturnal bird darting, ghostlike, this way and that a few feet above the ground, following the contours of the grass covered dunes as it searched for prey.

10 · *Mariah's story*

I squatted and ducked inside. The sandy floor was covered with a ragged hunk of canvas tarpaulin. Mariah had stuck rags and broken chunks of plastic net floats into all the cracks in an effort to keep out the wind. It sort of worked.

She closed the entrance with another piece of canvas that contained Japanese characters.

"Hip digs," I said.

She said, "The ocean is like the past, don't you think? Stuff washes up in rags and chunks all worn from the wind and water and sand and bleached from the sun. We all build our lives out of flotsam and jetsam."

"That's one way of looking at it," I said.

"It's rare to find a net float made out of glass. You know, the green ones you see in the tourist shops. The only one I ever found was broken. It had washed ashore and hit a spike sticking out of a log. It was covered by sand, and I didn't see it. I stepped on it with my bare foot." She peeled a white sock off her left foot and ran her finger along a huge white scar. "See there. Hit a pumper. Bled like a stuck pig. I thought I was going to pass out before I could get to a doctor in Long Beach."

"You think that's what's happened to you now?"

"Something like that. I was walking along minding my own business, now this. Broken glass. I'm about to be accused of murdering my own sister. No matter how this turns out there's going to be a scar. I talked to my father on the phone this morning. I told him I'd come straight back to Portland if he wanted, but if I had my druthers I'd just like to spend another night here to just think and listen to the surf. He said no hurry. He'd take care of the details for burying Sharon after the police finish the autopsy." Tears started to well up. She stifled them, but was momentarily overcome by emotion.

The wind made a *whooooooing* sound as it flowed over the makeshift cabin. I could feel a breeze coming through the cracks that Mariah had stuffed with rags.

She blew her nose and said, "The rules are no nails, so I lashed this all together with fisherman's netting I found washed up on the beach. Most of it is from Taiwanese vessels, but some Japanese too. The Taiwanese have these huge mothers that tow a half mile of netting."

"Cutting it pretty close on the rules, aren't you?"

"I'm an artist. I lay a couple of watercolors on the mayor each summer. She likes them. The word goes down, from the mayor to the chief of police, from the chief of police to his patrolmen." She grinned.

"Not a bribe?"

She straightened, pretending to be offended. "Certainly not. I'm a bona fide tourist attraction."

"You're an attraction, that's for sure."

"I cook over charcoal. I wash my clothes at a laundromat. I shower at an RV place. I know the owners. Watercolors for them, too. Nice people. I'd offer you a cold beer or something, but I don't have a refrigerator." She opened a trunk and retrieved a large plastic jug of water. "Water isn't good here. It's the salt." She looked chagrined. "You want to tell me what Sharon told you before she died?"

I did, adding, "As near as I can figure it, she wanted to say goodbye to your father and you, although it's hard to say."

Hearing that, Mariah broke into tears again, this time weeping uncontrollably. I looped an arm around her and held her, but there was nothing to say. What do you say to someone whose sister has just been murdered?

Finally, she recovered and wiped the tears from her eyes with the back of her arm. "By the way, Bill also said the police have searched my apartment in Portland."

Oops! "You want to tell me what the Portland Police Bureau told the judge in order to get a search warrant?"

Looking resigned, Mariah took a deep breath and exhaled slowly through puffed cheeks. "When our mother died, she left Sharon and me a substantial inheritance."

"The Moultine family fortune."

"Correct. A couple of years ago, our stepmother Janine talked us into investing in a store selling homeopathic medicine and organic vegetables."

"That would be Lao Tzu's."

She grimaced. "Right again. Janine then hired a cosmic witch named Luci Douglas to manage the store, and Tommy Hilfinger, a moron in combat fatigues, to be a 'buyer.' "

"Buying what?"

"Natural medicines in the Pacific Northwest. He's got a company pickup and a Hummer. Soon that one store turned into two, then three, until there are now six of them. Six! My God!"

"Ambitious."

"Yes, using Sharon's inheritance and mine as collateral to borrow the money they needed. My stepmother is okay, I guess. I have no reason to distrust her. But she had obviously been conned by Luci. And Tommy Hilfinger. There's a real piece of work. He had a girlfriend who was a dancer at Mary's, but someone beat her to death, obviously him in my opinion, but he sailed serenely on without being charged with anything. Finally, I had had enough. I asked for my money back. I was told that was impossible. It was all tied up in loans."

"I bet you were thrilled by that."

"Thrilled? Right. Sharon and I had a confrontation on the sidewalk outside the main Lao Tzu's store on Barbur Boulevard. A thieving witch using our inheritance as collateral to borrow money for those stupid stores. And a likely murderer as a 'buyer.' It was crazy. Honest to God! I asked her, whatever was she thinking? She said she was as upset as me, but she had learned something that needed to be settled before we got into a public row that would only hurt my father, him being a television weatherman and all. 'What was it that needed to be settled?' I asked." Mariah fell silent, chewing on her lower lip.

I was insistent. "What did she say?"

"She said there 'would come a time' I would understand. When, I asked? When would that time come? She said she was going to hire a private investigator to look into the matter. She said Bill Dennis recommended one."

"That would likely have been me. She was headed in the direction of my cabin when she was run off the road and murdered. She had my business card in her handbag. I say 'my' card. I have a partner, Willie Sees the Night."

"Sees the what?"

"Sees the Night. He's a Cowlitz."

"I see. Good name. I had had enough of the doubletalk and games. We proceeded to have a knockdown, drag-out brawl. We both got hysterical and were screaming at one another. At this point Luci and Tommy Hilfinger showed up. I had a .22 pistol that my father had given me, and I lost my head and screamed that if I didn't get a cashier's check the next day, I was going to by God come back and blow holes in anyone who got in the my way!"

"You threatened to kill her."

"I was talking about the fat murderer, although I suppose, yes, what I said could be interpreted as threatening Sharon. Unfortunately, there were witnesses. But I would never murder Sharon. That's ridiculous. She was my sister. I loved her. I just wanted my money out of the clutches of Luci Douglas and Tommy Hilfinger. The police must have interviewed the neighbors."

"Where is your .22 now?"

"It's in my apartment in North Portland, a Browning Buckmark."

"You're sure about that?"

"Why yes. My father gave it to me for 'protection,' but I've never learned how to shoot it. I don't know why I keep the damned thing around."

"And you have no idea what it was that Sharon was going to hire a private investigator to look into?"

"None whatever. Part of what made me so sore was that she made it sound so mysterious. It threatened our father's reputation, she said. *What* exactly was at stake? I was her sister. Why couldn't she tell me?"

"Is there any possibility that Luci or Tommy might have killed her to shut her up and are now trying to frame you?"

She blinked. "Frame me? I can't imagine why. They already have my money. Where's the motive?"

"With a murder charge on the line, it's not smart to rule anything out. Would you feel offended if I suggest we search your cabin here just in case? If we find nothing, no harm done."

"I wouldn't feel offended at all."

"Just in case," I said.

"I agree. Just in case."

11 · Kee-eau! Kee-eau! Kee-eau!

Mariah Toogood and I set about searching her diminutive driftwood cabin. There wasn't much to search, there being little in the way of hideaways in the tangle of driftwood around the interior that was no more than six feet long and four feet wide. But when we began poking into the sand with a knife, I hit something. I dug down and there it was. A .22 caliber Browning Buckmark in a plastic freezer bag.

I sighed. "What's this?"

Mariah's jaw dropped. "It looks like my pistol. How did it get there?"

Whether or not Mariah had buried it there, I had no doubt that it was hers. "You didn't stash it there?"

"No, I didn't. I swear!"

I fell to my knees on the sand. Handling the plastic bag with my fingernails, I opened it and dug the gun out with the scaling blade of my Swiss army knife. The scaling blade had a notched end for removing hooks from a fish's gullet. I sniffed the muzzle. Recently fired. I said, "If the police searched your place in Portland, this place is next."

"What do we do?"

I grimaced. Would Mariah have been so stupid as to murder her sister then drive back to Long Beach and bury the pistol under the sand of her beach hut? Any sane person would have thrown the damned thing off the bridge between Astoria and the Washington shore. Stupid she wasn't, but there was no accounting for what went through the mind of somebody who had just committed murder. Maybe the fish storm had rattled her. "We get rid of the pistol," I said abruptly.

"I didn't bury it there. You have to believe me. Besides, I'm not that damn dumb." She made a face.

"Quick, quick. We do it now. I'll need a rag or piece of plastic."

She pulled a wad of black plastic that she had used to fill a crack in the wall of her hut. I used the plastic to hold on to the bag with the Browning. I took an expense receipt from my wallet and wrote the serial number on the back.

Mariah grabbed a flashlight.

I said, "Leave it. We can see well enough without a flashlight. We don't know who's out there watching. If you've got a shovel, grab it."

She had a folding camp shovel. "How about this?"

"Perfect."

I followed Mariah outside into the wind, uncertain of what to do next. The geography of the beach was constantly altered by the wind. First from the north. Then from the south. Nothing remained the same from year to year. Where to bury the pistol presented a problem. I said, "Take me to a stump or log that's unlikely to get washed out to sea with the next high tide."

"Got it. Follow me."

We set off negotiating islands and ridges of sand covered with dune grass, separated by gullies cut through the sand by high winter tides. As we struggled through the sand, the wind picked up, stinging hard against our faces. At last we came to a pile of enormous logs washed up by what must have been a tide that would have startled Noah. There, among the logs, clearly visible in the moonlight, was a huge gnarled stump. Should I wipe the pistol clean of prints? If Mariah had buried the gun, she had likely had the brains to remove her finger-prints. If somebody else had stolen her gun, used it, and bur-ied it to frame her, they likely used gloves and left the gun dirty with her prints. But suppose they had made a mistake and there was a partial there somewhere. I decided to leave it the way it was.

As I dug frantically, the night bird I had seen earlier—or one just like it—floated by, skillfully riding the night wind. I scooped out a hole nearly three feet deep under the stump and buried the pistol. Mariah and I returned to the cabin in thoughtful silence. I was not comforted by the thought that I had likely committed a felony, but at the time I had done what I thought I had to do. I could only hope that it was the right thing.

When we got back to the cabin neither of us knew what to say. We stood in the wind for a moment, awkward. Finally, she said, "I thought I wanted to be alone tonight, but I'm grateful you showed up, so I have somebody to talk to. Helps me take my mind of Sharon. You smoke?"

I knew she didn't mean tobacco. I said, "If you've got some. What do you say we spend the night in my microbus." I hesitated. "Out of the sand and sleeping over the spot where we found the buried pistol."

"For me it would be like a night in a fancy motel. Be right back." She ducked into her hut and emerged a half minute later with a bag of pot in hand. As she did, the ubiquitous night bird darted silently by.

We sat squat-legged in the back of the microbus. She unzipped the top of a plastic freezer bag. I smelled the smell.

"Mmmm. Sticky green," I said.

"Smells good, huh? Grow it myself from Dutch seeds a friend gave me. At least she said they're Dutch seeds."

A gust of wind rocked the bus.

Mariah took a hit and said, "If ever there was a night to get high, this is it. South wind means good kite flying tomorrow. Sunny and with a stiff breeze sending the sand scurrying up the beach." She loaded a small wooden pipe with a ceramic bowl and passed it to me. "Go for it."

I took a hit and held the smoke in my lungs.

She said, "I knew you'd smoked pot before. Guy like you. How old are you, by the way?"

I slowly released the smoke, studying Mariah in the dim light. "Forty-seven."

She looked me straight on. Her lower lip hung languidly. "Hard to believe Sharon is gone."

I didn't know what to say to that. I knew changing the subject wouldn't alleviate her grief, but I didn't know what else to do. "When I got here there was a bird out there riding the night wind, quicker than hell. Soundless. A regular phantom. I saw it again at the stump and when we got back from burying the pistol. What is that, do you know?"

"It's a short eared owl. I'd seen it out there a half dozen times, and so I looked it up on the Internet. Short eared owls are either diurnal or nocturnal, hunting at night or early in the morning or just before dark. They fly a few feet above ground looking for prey. Insects, mice or whatever. They like open territory, but will hole up in a forest if they have to. They like to ride the wind. They're good at it. Silent as shadows."

I said, "As a matter of fact, an owl hangs out in the meadow where we live. Maybe it's the same species. Your dad teach you about the wind, did he?"

"Is a pig's ass pork?" She laughed. "Air is cool and dry in a high pressure area. It compresses and warms as it descends. In a low pressure area, the air rises and cools, forming clouds. Wind moves from a high pressure to a low pressure area. The greater the difference between the high and low area, the faster the wind. You get a lot of wind at the beach because of the difference in temperature between the air over the water and the air over the land."

I looked mock impressed. "I see." I was already feeling drifty. My God!

Mariah liked it. She was getting stoned. "The earth rotates under the moving air. In the northern hemisphere the rotation pushes the wind in a counterclockwise direction. In the southern hemisphere it pushes it in a clockwise direction. This is called the Gustave-Gaspar Coriolis effect."

"Well sure." I pretended to fumble for a pencil and pad. "I'll have to take notes."

She laughed. "It sounds like a rare disease, I know. You should know that the toilets do not flush in the opposite direction in Australia. The Coriolis effect applies only to large air masses. Speaking of which, aren't you getting cold? I know I am."

"Time for the fart bags," I said.

We set about unrolling our sleeping bags. The smell of her beside me was intoxicating. That plus I was getting thoroughly stoned. The combination on my imagination was something on the order of combing nitro with glycerin or a lit match with high octane gasoline. Unfortunately, Mariah was still recovering from the death of her sister. I was determined to keep my hormones in check. This was the time to listen and let her talk, not put a move on her.

Restraining myself wasn't easy. We lay in our sleeping bags, side by side. I could feel the warmth of her body. Or could I? The sleeping bags would likely have kept us warm in a

Siberian winter. Or maybe it was my imagination. I likely just thought I could feel her, a form of inchoate longing.

She said, "What are you thinking about?"

"The pistol." That was a lie.

"You think I murdered my sister?"

In the dim light, I peered into Mariah's green pools. No way I that believed this young woman had murdered her sister. "No."

"Why not? Because we just had a moment?"

"You said you didn't kill her. I believe you." Should I tell her I thought bear poachers most likely killed her sister?

She looked bewildered, yet hopeful. "You believe me? Even with the pistol and all?"

I paused. She was right. Under the circumstances that had been an unusual declaration. "I said, 'The pistol,' but that was a lie," I said.

She rose, resting on her elbow. "Huh?" She was genuinely alarmed. "You think I killed her. My God!"

"I wasn't thinking of the pistol. To tell the truth, it's hard for me to concentrate on much of anything right now except . . ." I let it drop.

She didn't say anything.

I waited.

Finally, she said, "Except what? What were you thinking about? Concentrate."

My mind drifted. I had lost track of what we were talking about. It was the pot, of course. I tried to retrace the sequence of the conversation. I was in the rear of my bus side by side by a walking wet dream who had been accused of murdering her sister. I had found a .22 caliber Browning Buckmark pistol stashed in her driftwood cabin. But anybody could have stashed it there. If somebody was trying to frame her, there had to be a motive. There was. Bear poaching. She had asked a question. What was it? My mind raced. "Say again?"

"I said, 'What were you thinking about?' "

"Remind me of where we were. I'm lost."

She laughed. "You're stoned. A stoned investigator. I'm supposed to trust you with my life! Sah-weeeeeet Jeeeeeeeeees-sus!" She laughed even louder, a broad, deep throated the-hell-with-modesty *har, har, har.* "I asked you what you were thinking about. You said the pistol. Then you said that was a lie."

What had I been thinking about? Her lying there beside me. That was it. Her eyes. "I was imagining I feel your body warmth, even though the sleeping bags. I was wondering if you could feel me too or if it was just my imagination."

She smiled. "Your imagination, hotshot. I can't feel a thing."

I slipped my hand down and straightened myself out. "Doesn't take a whole lot to flip the switch."

She looked puzzled. "The switch."

"To the mind pump. Sends the blood south to jack up the apparatus. That's how it works, you know. That's why it gets hot and hard and everything. It's blood that does it."

She looked amazed. "Really? Is it still pumped up?"

"Oh yeah," I said. "It's pumped. The mind switch is not an intellectual thing. It's chemical. You have to understand the principles of hydraulics to appreciate how it works." I thought about that for a moment. "No, I take that back. It's both chemical and hydrological and more than that too. A kind of thunderstorm in the synapses. In any event, rigid as a marine at attention it is. Unyielding in pursuit of duty."

"You just going to leave it that way?"

"Probably better. At least for now anyway. I've always won-dered if the process of pumping blood to the south means that the cells in the uppermost north might not function properly."

She giggled. "Brain cells starved for oxygen."

"Something like that. Somebody is trying to frame you for murder. Smart to concentrate on that."

"Can you do that? Just leave it all pumped and ready to go and do nothing."

I laughed. "I won't be able to sleep for a while, that's a fact. I'm facing a bad case of blue balls."

"Really?" She giggled again. "Now you flipped *my* switch."

"Isn't life a bitch?"

"Is sure as hell is." She wiggled closer. We were like large worms in our separate insulated cocoons. "Here we are having fun with the flirt. You wondering whether or not I murdered my sister. Neither one of us was tracking straight on account of the cannabis."

I could smell her. Jesus!

She kissed me softly. "Good night to you and your pal down there."

We both lay there. What was she thinking about? My eager marine declined to relax. He didn't understand why he wasn't getting any action. He was not to be confused with a quitter. He refused to give up. Such frustration! "You could look at it as a high pressure area," I said.

We were silent for a moment, then I said, "I'm something of a fugitive myself."

"Oh?"

"From television reporters."

"I bet. Why don't you just give them what they want?"

I sighed. "There are kids to consider. I understand that. And science. Bizarre natural phenomena and so on. But you have to understand that my partner is a sorcerer, or so he claims. Thinks he's Coyote. Salmon falling from the sky is clearly his thing. Not good to go on the tube without talking to him first. Elementary respect."

"I see."

"Maybe public television is the way to go."

"Hmmmmm. Public television, I agree."

"Tomorrow I'll talk to your father and see what he has to say. Maybe he knows something you don't. And he is my client, after all."

"By the way, I'm going to help you run down my sister's murderer. We'll do it together. Whatever it takes, I'll do it," she said. "Well, no. I take that back. There are some things I won't do. I have limits. If we don't have limits, things come apart. On the other hand, some limits just don't make a whole lot of sense. You know, John, I've just discovered something. These sleeping bags of yours are designed so you can zip them together making one double bag that two people can share. Very cozy. Easy to do."

Zzzzzzzzzzzppppp!

I groaned.

"*Kee-eau!*" she called. "*Kee-eau! Kee-eau!*"

"What's that?"

Mariah giggled. "The mating call of the female short eared owl. They had that on the Internet too. I thought you said there was one in the meadow where you live."

"There is. I've heard that call many times before. I just didn't know what kind of owl."

Zzzzzzzzzzpppp! Both sides were unfastened. She was simultaneously getting naked and working zippers.

On my side, I began shucking clothes with abandon. I said, "You don't know what the male of the species sounds like by any chance?"

"Kind of a pulsing, *voo-hoo-hoo-hoo!* I'm probably better at doing the lady."

Zzzzzzzzzzzpppp! She mated the bottoms of the bags.

"One side to go," I said. "Almost joined." I tried my luck with the call of the male short-eared owl. "*Voo-hoo-hoo-hoo! Voo-hoo-hoo-hoo!*"

"Whoa there, partner. Turn me on!" She giggled again. "*Kee-eau! Kee-eau!*"

Zzzzzzzzzzzpppp! She joined the sides of our bags.

We came together in our mutual nest. So soft she was. I shuddered from the touch. The wind beat against the side of my bus.

12 · The answer, my friend

The next morning I told Mariah she should get herself a lawyer and recommended Rosalina Garza. I then called Jerry Toogood in Portland and made an appointment to talk to him, after which Mariah took over the cell phone. She seemed upbeat and confident and reassured her father that she was doing just fine and that she was glad he had secured my services. She liked me and trusted me. She added that she would likely secure Rosie's services. T.G. said it was up to her, and that I would be reporting the results of my investigation to Bill Dennis.

After his daughter's murder, T.G. had taken some time off his work at the station and was at his home in Northwest Portland. After admonishing her to say nothing but the truth to the police, should they come calling, I gave her a goodbye kiss and I set off to Portland to talk to her father.

As I drove back across the bridge to Oregon in a light mist, I struggled to recall what it was about her name that had a special meaning, she being the weatherman's daughter. There was something, I knew, that I couldn't remember. Then it came to me. An old song made popular by the Kingston Trio that I barely remembered from my childhood where it was

said folks in California's Big Sur had a name for the rain and
for the wind and for the fire. Rain was Tess. Fire was Joe. And
the wind, Mariah, blew the stars about. She set the clouds
afire and made the mountains sound like folks was out there
dying.

I wondered if Jerry Toogood, then likely studying meteor-
ology or beginning his career as a television weatherman, had
heard that song and so named his second daughter Mariah.

Jerry Toogood lived in a grand art deco home on the hill
overlooking Portland, which lay to the east, dissected by the
Willamette River. Covered with rose colored stucco, the house
had arches over the doors and windows. I stood for a moment
at the edge of the street looking at the city of Portland sprawling out to the east. At the foot of the hill lay Northwest Portland, where the yuppies with bucks had gentrified an area
formerly the haunt of writers and artists. Beyond that, a free-
way cut through the city, then came Old Town, a former in-
dustrial area transformed into a tourist area featuring
restaurants, bars and jazz clubs in addition to Portland's Chinatown. To the right of Old Town, the copper-colored U.S. National Bank high-rise marked the northwestern edge of the
business and financial district at the heart of the city.

Beyond Old Town and the business and financial district,
the Willamette River split the city between east and west. And
finally, forty miles to the east, Mt. Hood, having lost most of
its snow cap to the summer sun, rose splendidly in the clear
blue sky. What a view! Only the oldest and wealthiest of Portland families could afford it.

I walked up to the handsome front door and rang the bell.

A good looking young blonde woman about thirty opened
the door. She had a nice way about her. "Mr. Denson?"

"Yes, ma'am," I said.

"I'm Janine Toogood."

"Mr. Toogood's wife?"

"Jerry's a big television star and all that. Isn't a young wife one of the perks?" She laughed.

I was slightly embarrassed. "Sorry."

"No need. I'm used to it. Also the age thing cuts both ways. As far as I'm concerned, older men are far sexier than young twerps. Won't you come in. Jerry is expecting you."

I stepped inside the door, to be greeted by a little blond girl about three or four years old who had Shirley Temple curls, cornflower blue eyes, and a great big smile. A real charmer.

"And this is our daughter, Carrie."

I stooped and shook her tiny hand. "Well, I'm pleased to meet you, Carrie."

Carrie said, "Daddy's crying."

I blinked.

"He's very sad."

I looked at Janine Toogood.

To her child, she said, "You run along now and watch your Barney tape now." She gave Carrie a gentle push, and the child did as she was told. To me, Janine said, "Jerry's not in a very good mood, it's true. He's just received some terrible news."

"Oh?"

She said, "He just got a telephone call from the police in Long Beach. About twenty minutes ago, somebody heard a gunshot in Mariah's little hut there on the beach They called 911 on a cell phone. The police checked and discovered Mariah's body. She had committed suicide."

My mouth dropped. "She what?"

"Her gun was in her hand. Clear cut, they say. Jerry is stricken. First Sharon, now Mariah. I told him he ought to phone you and cancel his interview, but he's in denial. He says there's no way that Mariah committed suicide. She was murdered, he thinks. Framed for murdering her sister then murdered herself. All the more reason to talk to you."

I took a deep breath and exhaled through puffed cheeks. "I think your husband is likely right on both counts, Mrs. Toogood. I don't think Mariah committed suicide either."

Janine Toogood led me into the living room where Portland's famous weatherman stood at a huge window looking down at the city of Portland sprawled out in the late morning sun. T.G. was tall and lean. He had hair that was too black for his age. Ronald Reagan hair it was, down to the pompadour. His voice wasn't the best. But he had a charming way about him that people liked.

His wife placed a hand on his shoulder. "Jerry, the detective is here to see you."

T.G. turned, his face morose. He looked older than he appeared on television. It was the makeup, I supposed. He looked exhausted and profoundly sad. "Glad that you're here, Mr. Denson." We shook. To his wife, he said, "I'd like to talk to him alone, Janine."

She looked uncertain. "Are you sure? Maybe I can help. I'd like to help if I can. It's possible that I can remember a detail that you've forgotten. Something crucial."

T.G. shook his head. "You take care of Carrie. Let me take care of this. It's something I have to do. I've lost two daughters. I can't bring them back alive, but I can help find out who killed them and why."

She frowned briefly then perked up. "Well, whatever. Would you like some coffee, Mr. Denson?"

"Yes, please."

She looked at T.G. "Dear?"

"One for me too, please." When she was gone, he said, "I

know I must look like hell. I have these recurring bouts of insomnia after which I sleep for half the next day. Now this. Last night I had another bout."

"Did the police find any sort of note?"

He shook his head.

"I spent last night with Mariah. She was with me when I called this morning to make this appointment. You heard her, she was with me. She was in a cheerful, upbeat mood. No way would she commit suicide an hour later."

He stared down at the city, saying nothing. Then he started to speak, but closed his mouth when Janine came back with a tray containing a silver pitcher of coffee and two cups plus a creamer and sugar.

When she had disappeared a second time, I told him what Sharon had told me in her dying moments. Whatever I had told the police, I told T.G. straight how Sharon told me to say goodbye to him and Mariah. "She wanted you to know she loved you," I said.

"That's what the police said." He fell silent for a moment.

I poured some cream in one of the cups and took a sip. "Mariah said she had advanced Sharon her half of her inheritance to invest in the business, but then Sharon wouldn't give it back. That's why they fought."

"That's what Mariah said."

"That means they both have a huge stake in the business. Who gets it now?"

He looked surprised. "Why, their sister, Carrie!"

"Leaving you to sell the business."

"No, no, Janine and I have decided to keep it for the moment. Foolish to sell it until we know what's it's really worth."

"You're going to run it?"

"No, no, that would be Janine. I've got far too much on my hands as a weatherman to do that also. Janine didn't want any part of it either. She said she doesn't know anything about running health food stores, but I insisted. She studied business administration for two years at Portland Community College, and she's smart as hell. She'll do all right if she has the right people running the stores for her. We've got Bill Dennis to make sure everything is on the up and up. Maybe we'll keep it. Maybe we'll sell it."

I saw Janine out of the corner of my eye.

She said, "I was wondering if there is anything else I can get you. I wish you would let me help."

"The coffee is fine. We've got everything under control." As she disappeared, he said, "I don't know what I would do without Janine. So much can go wrong when you get married. I lucked out with her, I have to say. Right now I don't know what I would do without her, that's a fact. Every man needs a young wife, Mr. Denson. I . . ." He wanted to say something more, but thought better of it.

"What?"

He cleared his throat. "Mariah called and offered to come home, but I told to her to spend another night at the beach if she wanted. Was her last night a good one? Foolish question, I suppose, she being my daughter and all. But she was a grown woman."

If I had been her father, I would have wanted to know the whole story too. "We spent the night together in my microbus. We talked. I did my best to comfort her over the loss of her sister. Mariah and I had a very good night, Mr. Toogood."

He seemed pleased that Mariah had not spent her last night alone mourning the loss of her sister. He said, "Call me T.G."

"I will find whoever it was who killed her," I said. "I guarantee. She did not, I say again, did not commit suicide. No. By the way, Mariah told me something that struck me as odd. She said Sharon intimated that something odd was going on with Lao Tzu's, but she wouldn't tell Mariah what it was. Did Sharon ever mention anything like that to you?"

Looking surprised, T.G. shook his head. "No, she didn't. Of course, I don't have anything to do with those stores. The fact is, I've never even been in one of them. All that natural food hoo hoo is female nonsense as far as I'm concerned."

"I'll look into it. Wherever it takes me."

"Bill Dennis tells me you're a very good investigator indeed, Mr. Denson. And if Mariah liked you that cinches the deal as far as I'm concerned. I don't want to know the details of your fee, Mr. Denson."

"I'm in this case because of Mariah and her sister, not the money. A new suit costs money. The maintenance of one's soul ordinarily comes at a higher price. But I won't turn down a fee. I have to eat and buy gas for my bus."

T.G. said, "I'm a public figure, Mr. Denson. My career depends on people liking me. The police in both states are honorable enough, but my public reputation is not their highest concern. Take those silly health food stores, for example. Like it or not, I'm connected to them. I can't afford the wrong kind of surprise. If they're involved in any way, I need to know it as soon as possible so I can deal with it. I can afford whatever it is you ordinarily charge. Let Bill Dennis know what you're finding out, and he'll take care of your fee and expenses."

Settling the detail of the bill was T.G.'s signal that he had had enough talk. He wanted to be alone again. Under the circumstances, it was hard to blame him.

I finished my cup of coffee. "I'll start with Lao Tzu's. I have a cell phone. You have my number. If you remember anything you think I should know, just call. I'll keep in touch. And you might be getting a call from my partner, Willie Sees the Night."

"Bill Dennis mentioned him. A Cowlitz, he says."

"A protean Cowlitz. A man of many mysteries and unusual abilities."

T.G. managed a smile. "If Mr. Sees the Night calls, I'll do everything I can to help him." We shook again. "Find the truth, Mr. Denson. Please."

"I'll do my damndest." At the front door, Janine Toogood appeared again. "If there's anything you think I can do to help, please don't hesitate to call."

"I'll do my best to find out the truth." With that I stepped outside and returned to my microbus. Mariah and I had buried her pistol together. Were the police going to tell me she went back and dug it up after I left? I didn't believe that for a second. I used my cell phone to dial up a friend in the Oregon State Police. I asked him if the State Police been given the serial number on the gun that Mariah Toogood had used to kill herself in Long Beach. Yes, they had. The serial number was no state secret. It matched the one in my wallet.

I asked him if there was physical evidence of a third party being present. He said that was a tough one. If Mariah had been murdered and her killer escaped down the beach in a vehicle the tracks were washed away by the rising tide. There were footprints in the sand in and around her hut but those were just indentations, no proper impressions for a forensics lab. And even those were smoothed out by the blowing wind. The gun was in her hand. It was her pistol. She had powder burns against her head. She was under suspicion of murder. The conclusion: suicide.

Mariah! Charming, sweet Mariah! Sitting there behind the steering wheel, I gasped in disbelief. The suggestion that Mariah had committed suicide was infuriating. She had not killed herself. No. That was just plain wrong. I was determined to nail whoever the son of a bitch was who killed her. I fired up my engine. Time to talk to Willie Sees the Night and see what he had found out.

13 • Willie's offer

Willie Sees the Night and I sat cross-legged on the floor of his cabin with the door open. Outside crickets trilled, and we could hear the trickling of Jump-Off Joe Creek. Through the open window, moonlight, and stars as white and dazzling as diamonds over the silhouettes of Douglas fir. We had glasses of our homemade elderberry wine. This was from a bottle that we had corked two years earlier, which was, by our dubious standards, vintage stuff.

I told him about my visit with Mariah and with Jerry Toogood. "The murders of the Toogood sisters are connected with Lao Tzu's and bear poaching. Have to be."

"I agree, Chief."

"Mariah's 'suicide' was too much, Willie. It doesn't follow from anything I learned about her. She loved life. When I left she was upbeat and confident. There was a total lack of evidence of any sort of intruder. She didn't kill herself. Yes, yes, I know, somebody had to dig that pistol out of the sand. Just two of us knew where it was buried. Who else but Mariah dug it up? And yet I know she did not commit suicide. I know it in my bones, but I can't prove it."

"It's a puzzler, I agree."

"And your talk to what's his name, Jonas Somebody. How did that go?"

"Jonas Knowles. Jonas said there has been a startling rise in bear poaching the last few years, and the FBI has been poking around asking questions. He said the feds are not interested in occasional poaching by survivalists, but guys who are regularly popping bears. Most of these are apparently working out of northeastern Oregon, northern Idaho, and western Montana. One of Jonas's suspects is a mountain man named Wintertime Wallace, a notorious recluse. One morning Jonas pulled into a café for breakfast and saw Wintertime emerge from the High Country Tavern on the outskirts of La Grande and lean against the door of a dark blue Toyota pickup. He had an animated conversation with whoever was inside."

"What was suspicious about that?'

"Wintertime is not known for being especially talkative or for having a whole lot in the way of friends. In fact, he's downright laconic. All Jonas could see was the back of the head of the driver of the pickup, a man, and the passenger, a younger woman. Finally, the pickup went on its way, and Wintertime disappeared around the back of the tavern. Jonas waited. A Budweiser beer truck emerged, but not Wintertime. Where had Wintertime gone? Jonas was curious. He cruised the street, thinking he likely missed something obvious. He found Wintertime's Jeep Cherokee parked two blocks away. The blue Toyota pickup was parked a half block up the street. Jonas had no idea where the man and woman went."

"A little mystery there," I said.

"Jonas talked to the bartender, who said Wintertime regularly came in late Friday afternoons, had one beer by himself and disappeared outside. Jones ran the pickup's plates through the Department of Motor Vehicles. It was registered to Lao Tzu's Inc., of Portland."

"Bill Dennis does the legal work for Lao Tzu's. He took me shooting in a dark blue Toyota pickup."

"Which raises the question of how many dark blue Toyota pickups do they have? More than one. By the way, on the mystery of Mariah's death, you say you've hit a logical wall. Why don't you let me send you on a trip flying out of your skin? Maybe you can see over the wall." Willie looked amused. Over the years every time I got seriously stumped, scores if not hundreds of times, he had made this offer. Each time I turned him down. It was a standing joke between us. I was Mr. Logic. Willie was Magic Man. Never the twain shall meet. No, I would not go flying. That was out. Nein. Nyet. No. Nay. Non. Whatever.

This time it was different. I cocked my head. "Say again?"

"You never know, Chief. Leave your body. Fly. Experience the magic."

"Are you sure?"

"Well, you know I am. How many times have I made the offer?"

"I'll do it," I said.

I had obviously taken him by surprise. He laughed nervously. "What on earth are you talking about?"

"We know that rats have a limited ability to negotiate a maze. At a certain point their cognitive skills fail them. We humans think we can know everything, but maybe not. We know that a worm has limited cognitive ability. So does a fox. But we fancy ourselves different. We think we can know everything if we just try hard enough and refine our observation and logic. But can we really? Is it possible for us to know the limits to our own cognitive ability? Maybe I'm a fallible human caught in a truth I can't accept and a puzzle I can't solve. I've run into a logical wall. You're right. I need to be shaken up."

Willie thought about that. "A crisis of confidence for the logical warrior?"

I shook my head. "No, no, no. Not at all. It's entirely logical that the most likely route outside the maze lies in my subconscious. Why not go there and see what I can find? No good to keep on bumping into the walls."

"It's dangerous for a novice to travel with the animal spirits, you know that."

"You've said that many times."

"Not just dangerous. Sometimes travelers don't come back. Nobody knows what kills the unprepared traveler. Or even a veteran. Maybe the substance that releases their spirits. Maybe the shock of what they learn. A veteran can go down just as easily as a beginner. Also, whether you later believe or deny what you saw, you run the risk of encountering something that will haunt you. After that, your spirit can leave your body and fly on its own, often when you least expect it. This is a clear danger, Chief. It is not to be underestimated."

I sighed. "I want to go. For years you've offered to send me. Now that I've accepted, you can't back out."

Willie took a sip of wine. "I won't send you flying out of your skin on any kind of spur of the moment impulse. That's out. I won't do it. I want you to think about it some more."

I said, "Fair enough. I tell you what, Willie. I need to get this fish storm behind me. I can't work and be hounded by reporters at the same time. What do you say I call PBS and offer to allow them to interview me and show the fish storm tapes? The reporters and producers there are halfway civilized and will help me put what happened in context. When I'm finished with that, you can send me flying."

"Public television is entirely fine by me," Willie said. "In one of the plagues the Lord visited on the Pharaoh, He smote the border of Egypt with frogs. The animal spirits want people to know that something terrible has gone wrong, but we Indians want a respectful reporting of the rain of salmon, not a circus."

"You want to appear with me?"

He shook his head. "A shape-changing coyote in human form? Not even public television could prevent that from becoming a freak show. I'd be hounded, pursued. With you it's different. You got caught in a fish story. They're after you, but once you show them your tape and answer questions, that should pretty much be the end of it. I'll brief you for the interview. You can attribute the explanation to me. People can accept or reject it as they please. Public television is the best solution, I agree. And it'll give you time to change your mind."

"I appreciate your caution, Willie."

Willie Sees the Night looked at me, his eyes dancing as though something else had just occurred to him, some kind of flash or insight. "And you think this change of heart of yours is entirely logical? You're stumped, so it makes sense to try a new way of experiencing reality."

"That's it."

"After all these years. Suddenly, 'Let's do it, Willie.' No other explanation."

"I don't know what it would be."

"The fish."

I furrowed my brows. "The fish?"

"You get knocked off your feet by a salmon falling out of a clear blue sky and wind up with the bruise of a fish on your chest. Now all of the sudden, you tell me you're all hot to go flying in the world of the animal spirits to see what you can find out. You're the one who's always telling me you don't believe in coincidences. Don't you think that's bit of a coincidence?" Willie gave me a wry grin, his eyes dancing.

I frowned.

"When the animal spirits choose to enter a human, they're

rarely timid. In fact, they can be dramatic as hell. You know what I really think, Dumsht?"

"What's that? You tell me, Mr. Sorcerer."

"I think the animal spirits have taken the next step with you. I was wondering if they might not do that some day. The bruise salmon left on your chest is where he physically delivered an animal spirit into your body. It doesn't have to be salmon's spirit. You'll just have to wait and see which animal, but from now on, like it or not, you'll be inhabited by that spirit. You'll be its host."

"What?" I was disbelieving.

Willie ignored me. "When this is over, you'll be the same old skeptical John Denson. That's who you are. Or who you think you are. You can't change your nature. The animal spirits know that. I know that. But if in the end flying helps you solve this mystery, it's my bet that from now on when you get stumped, you'll fly again. You won't be able to help it. You'll become a regular flyer, just like me."

14 • He smote Egypt with frogs

Wilma Amundson was one of those quiet, well-mannered television reporters who gave public television a good name. A thoughtful, intelligent woman in her mid-forties, with a civilized way about her, Amundson was the antithesis of the narcissistic airheads like the one who had called me a self-important idiot. She was polite without being obsequious. She was charming and respectful without being fawning, forceful when she had to be, but in a civilized manner. She was no narcissistic airhead scrambling for higher Nielsen ratings. It was reassuring to know that at least one place remained where grownups reported the news.

Wearing an unostentatious but attractive gray dress, womanly yet professional, Amundson interviewed me by remote from Washington, D.C. I sat in the studio of the public television station in Portland watching her familiar face on a monitor in front of me.

Before the interview started I told her why I had chosen public television to release my tape of the falling fish and why Willie Sees the Night wanted me to offer a shaman's explanation, not him. "You know some of these animal spirits have the ability to travel in and out of the human world. They're shape changers. Willie's supposed to be Coyote in human form."

We decided that the interview would come first, followed by my videotape and then the still photographs of me and my bruised face, including those Sgt. Lewis Jakes had taken with my camera and with his police camera.

After she introduced the story, including the nature of my unusual partner, she asked me where I was and what I was doing when the fish started coming down. I told her about the ominous black cloud and wind and rain and lightning and broken radio. "Willie says the animal spirits caused the rain of salmon. He says that the raining of fish in Oregon is not so different from the plague of frogs the Lord visited upon Egypt, although I'm not sure of the point of drawing the parallel."

"Frogs?"

"I'm not an expert on the Bible or anything. The story is found in Exodus beginning with chapter 8, verse 1. God tells Moses that he is God to Pharaoh. His brother Aaron will be his prophet. Aaron is to tell Pharaoh to let the Israelites leave Egypt." I paused.

She smiled, my cue to keep talking. Time for a leisurely telling of the story, a rare television luxury. Of course, in the showing of the tape of the rain of salmon, Wilma Amundson was likely sitting on the highest ratings all year, and she knew it. No way her viewers were going to change stations before they got to see the fish storm.

"Aaron went to Pharaoh and threw down his staff, which turned into a snake. Pharaoh's magicians did the same thing, so he was not impressed—even when Aaron's snake swallowed the staffs of all the Pharaoh's magicians. Still Moses said, 'Let my people go so that they might serve the Lord.' The Pharaoh refused. To get his attention, the Lord then visited a series of plagues upon Egypt. In the first plague, He changed the water of the Nile into blood. In the second, he vowed to 'smite the borders' of Egypt with frogs, which is sometimes interpreted as a 'rain of frogs.' How else could the Lord 'smite' the borders other than to send frogs plummeting from out of the heavens? They came up out of the lakes and rivers until there were wretched, smelly piles of them. Frogs everywhere. The Lord followed this with plagues of gnats and flies, a plague on the Pharaoh's cattle, and plagues of boils, hail, locusts, darkness, and the plague of the death of the firstborn. The Pharaoh finally yielded, and the Lord instructed the Israelites on the ceremonies the Jews now call Passover, after which Moses led six hundred thousand Israelites on a journey by foot from Ramses to Succoth in Israel."

"I see. And the point of the parallel?"

"Willie says that obstinate Christians and Jews have a way of ignoring everything without a precedent in the Biblical texts. People are like hogs, he says. You have to whack them on the snout with a stick to get their attention. He says the Lord visited the many plagues on Egypt in order to get the Pharaoh to listen up. It worked. In order to get us whitefaces to listen up, the animal spirits did the same thing with the rain of salmon on the Oregon highway." I considered telling her about Willie's notion that when the salmon smashed against my chest, it delivered an animal spirit into my body. But I thought naw. Better leave that one alone.

"To get our attention?" Amundson laughed. "If that was their intention, they surely succeeded. And why that particular place and time?"

"The salmon fell on the bend in a country highway where a young woman, Sharon Toogood was murdered. Willie and I both think Sharon was murdered by someone other than her sister Mariah. We believe that Mariah was framed then murdered herself."

"I see. But as I understand it, the evidence seems clear that

Mariah murdered her, then committed suicide."

I shrugged. "That's what the police say, but they like to close cases. Can't blame them for that. Sharon talked to me in her dying moments, and I think she was saying goodbye to her father and sister, not telling me that her sister murdered her. If Willie and I think something smells with a police conclusion, we can be pretty damn stubborn. We think the stink of the murder-suicide theory is strong enough to knock a dog off a gut wagon."

Ms. Amundson grinned. "But why would the animal spirits cause a rain of salmon because somebody murdered Sharon Toogood? Where's the motive?"

"Willie says the animal spirits are fallible. Sometimes they don't have any idea what they're doing, just like us humans. Willie and I both agree that the public should see my tape. Willie asked me to point out the parallel between the fish and the frogs. So here I am. When we prove who really murdered Sharon Toogood, Willie says, it will be clear to those who see this program why the animal spirits got so upset."

"Well! I see! Stay tuned then."

"Or maybe it won't be clear. Maybe we expect too much clarity in a world filled with ambiguities. Ambiguity and uncertainty give us the space to be comfortably sloppy."

She looked impressed. "Is that what Willie Sees the Night says?"

I shook my head. "It's what sloppy John Denson says. That's why we wear clothes, incidentally."

"Oh?"

"To preserve the ambiguity and allow for a little creativity. That's not to mention the mystery. Who knows what lies beneath the fancy surface? More fun for everybody, don't you think?" I gave her a mischievous grin.

She laughed. "I see. A sorcerer and his philosophical partner. Do you believe in shamanism, Mr. Denson?"

"I believe in the likelihood that the Chicago Cubs will always fold in August and the teams with the highest payrolls have the best chance of making it to the World Series. Beyond that doubt in one form or another almost always sets in."

"Shall we look at the tape then? We'll start with video of the waterspout itself, then switch to the rain of salmon."

I said, "Sure. I would like to add here that I was moved to show this on public television because a beautiful young woman from a commercial network called me a 'self-important idiot' for not giving it to her right off the bat. I *am* an idiot sometimes, it's true. I hope all your viewers enjoy the tape. Fun to share it, but I don't need the money badly enough to sell it."

On the monitor, I watched the huge waterspout move slowly up the Columbia River. Here the salmon began their unhappy journey.

Then a switch. Fish began splatting onto the highway.

In the Portland studio, the technicians let out of a collective gasp. "Whoa!" a young man shouted. I didn't blame him. The sight of so many salmon hurtling out of the clear blue sky and crashing *whap, splat, whop, splot* onto a narrow mountain highway was nothing short of astonishing.

Soon the highway was covered with salmon, twisting, leaping and flopping about in their death throes, a sad and unsettling sight. The way I saw it, the salmon had been sacrificed to the capriciousness of fate, a tornado settled onto the Columbia River at the wrong time. To Willie, the fish had fallen as a kind of omen and to give salmon an opportunity to deliver an animal spirit into my body through a bruise on my chest. As I watched the dying salmon on the highway, it was fun to imagine the emotions experienced by Nicole Byrne when she explained to the CNN people in Atlanta how it was she had so pissed me off that I gave the tape to public television.

15 · *The mortality of detectives*

The rain earlier in the night had cleared and the cool air smelled clean and pure with a hint of pine needles. I poured myself a glass of Oddball Ale, watching the foam well up. I took a sip, savoring the flavor of hops mixed with juniper berries, the mark of Oddball. I leaned across the table. "A deal is a deal, my sorcerer friend. You say you know magic. I say yes, let's fly."

Willie sighed. "You're sure you want to go through with this. You've thought about it."

"I've had two days. I'm positive. It's logical for me to experience the illogical if for no other reason that I might be better able to understand it."

"Its opposite, the logical, being what, exactly?"

I chewed on my lower lip, thinking. "A system worked out by Aristotle a couple of thousand years ago. A logical syllogism contains three propositions. The hypothetical, *modus ponens*, says if p then q. If I observe p, I conclude q. The disjunctive, *modus tollens*, says either p or q. If I do not observe p, I conclude q. The categorical contains four premises. All x are y. No x is y. Some x is y. Some x is not y. Suppose that I assert that 'all thought comes from the brain.' That's the major premise."

"They say our cocks sometimes do our thinking."

I grinned. "Our cocks being connected to our brains. Nice try, Willie. I add a minor premise: All brains are material. My conclusion? All thought is material. See? Whether you're awake, asleep, or under the influence of a drug, you never escape your brain. Never. Not even in so-called near-death experiences. Here I have a human partner who claims he can fly out of his skin. Not logical, Willie."

"Your minor premise isn't valid."

I grinned. "Another nice try."

"Please, Chief, uncle! I give up. You say you hit a logical wall. You want to tell me where your logic failed you this time out?"

I thought about that for a moment. "Suicides are tough to understand on a rational level. Mariah left no note. Can one assert that all people who commit suicide leave notes? No. Some do not. Can one say that all suicides are irrational? No. Some people kill themselves to relieve unbearable suffering or to avoid punishment for committing a crime."

"Possibly Mariah's motive."

"Yes. Only I deny it. Can one say that all questionable suicides must have alternative explanations? Yes. The only trouble with that is Mariah helped me bury the gun. Only she could have dug it up."

"Unless somebody watched you bury it."

"Correct. But there is no physical evidence of an intruder. She had the means, motive and the opportunity. All things considered, it is both logical and illogical to conclude that Mariah Toogood committed suicide. Which brings us back to my story of the rats in the maze that I told you the other day. I want to fly out of the confusion that I don't understand and look down on it. Maybe I'll see something I missed because I just wasn't smart enough."

Willie laughed.

"Something that will open my eyes."

"Is that a logical conclusion?"

I shook my head. "At best, a definite maybe."

Uncertain whether I should continue, I stared for a moment into my glass of Oddball Ale. Perhaps I should pay attention to his warning. The dangers lay both in whatever it was Willie had used to spike the Oddball and whatever visions and revelations that I encountered on my journey. And yet I wanted to make the trip. I wanted to experience the magic. I wanted to be jarred out of my rational zone.

Willie said, "No shame in changing your mind, Chief. In fact, I'd recommend it. But a man has to do what he thinks he has to do. Nobody else can decide for him."

I held up the Oddball. "You're still not going to tell me what you put in this."

He shook his head. "Carlos Castaneda wrote that Don Juan gave him jimson weed. Then a bunch of nutball kids went out and killed themselves taking jimson weed. They're still doing it. Peyote is dangerous too. Add to that the wrong kind of mushrooms. Emergency rooms are sometimes too far away, and the stomach pumps and antidotes don't always do the trick. So no, I won't tell you what I'm giving you. Maybe one of the above. Maybe none. All I can say is that it is dangerous, but I have guided novices before. If I think you're in danger, I'll give you something to make you vomit it up."

"Tell me what will likely happen."

"There's no telling. You'll most likely leave your skin and fly. It's remarkable how often these adventures take the form of a trilogy of episodes. A beginning. A middle. And sometimes a confrontation with one's creator."

"Sometimes?"

"Not always. No matter what happens, Chief, we both of us have a long night ahead of us. You take the journey. I have to watch out for your safety. If it goes truly bad, you might not live to see the sunrise. That's the terrible risk. And there's one other drawback that you might find disconcerting. Not saying it will happen, mind you, but it could. It oftentimes does."

I swallowed. "And that would be?"

"Sometime in the future, when you least expect it, you'll leave your skin and fly again. And the second experience will not be diminished in any way. It will be just as clear and real and compelling as the first time. No, I take that back. It is oftentimes more vivid and dramatic than the first time. There is no explaining this, but might happen."

"Whoops!"

"Yes, something to think about. If you find your first trip revealing and don't mind a repeat, it will be cool. But if you were spooked by your first trip and are frightened by what you saw and learned, you sure as hell won't want a sequel. It's a risk you take, Chief. I have to tell you."

"Sort of like the side effects listed on a bottle of prescription medicine."

"Yes, something like that."

I took a deep breath and emptied the glass of Oddball in a single pull. "Decision made," I said. "What now?"

"You lie back and close your eyes and wait."

Willie began drumming, mimicking the insistent rhythm of the human heart, got louder and louder: *ba-bum, ba-bum, ba-bum.*

The room began to spin lazily. "Whoa there!"

Ba-bum, ba-bum, ba-bum.

Willie laughed. "Be patient." Even as he said that, his voice was fading.

Ba-bum, ba-bum, ba-bum.

16 · Night flying

I rise up above the bed. I look down and see myself lying there with Willie at my bedside. As I'm drawn into the vortex of the unknown, the slow, insistent drum beat turns high, fast and pushy.

I yell down at him. "Willie! Willie!"

He looks up, drumming furiously, grinning mischievously. "Well, this is what you wanted, isn't it, Chief? Go. See what's out there. Find out for yourself."

I'm momentarily confused. Go. How? Through the door? Then I have the feeling of being sucked or drawn into the darkness, like I'm caught in a riptide tumbling into a deep, violent sea. I'm suddenly afraid. I want to go back. This is all stupid, dangerous silliness. I call out to Willie, or try to call. My mouth moves, but no sound comes.

Then it's too late. I'm floating above the bed. I have magical powers, don't I? Wasn't that what Willie had said?

I step though the window like the glass wasn't even there. I whoosh upward in the moonlight until I'm well above Willie's cabin. In the moonlight I see Whorehouse Meadow with Jump-Off Joe Creek meandering down the center and the Douglas fir on the surrounding ridges. Even as I fly, I know it is impossible. Can't be. And yet there I am, flying in the night. This is no dream. Can't be. It is vivid and real, immediate. I am, in fact, flying.

Where am I going? And why?

I hear the roar of surf. I am flying a few feet above dunes covered with the salt grass. To my left, I see the long, white sand beach. Out at sea beyond the beach, I see the running lights of a fishing boat. Up ahead, I see the driftwood cabin where I visited Mariah Toogood. I see my bus. I fly down and settle easily onto the sand by my bus. I crouch on the sand with wind blowing through my hair. I see that I have wings, but I think nothing of them. They're entirely natural. There is light coming through the cracks in the driftwood cabin. I hear a voice, my own and Mariah's.

The makeshift door opens. I see my human form, naked, walk outside to take a leak, leaving the door halfway open. This is precisely what I did the previous night. It is like seeing a replay, watching myself. It is immediate and real. I want to see Mariah Toogood. Is she too the same? I peer between the tiniest of tiny cracks in the driftwood wall. I see that Mariah is naked, waiting for me to get back. The same Mariah. Yes. And a beauty she is too. I am revisiting my night with Mariah.

I see an agile bird fly through soundlessly through the open door into the cabin. It is an owl. It settles onto Mariah's shoulder and blends into her body except for her head. Mariah's body has the owl's head.

The owl occupying Mariah's body looks my way and blinks. Its huge eyes, evolved for night hunting, are yellow with deep, black purple. To me, the owl calls out, *"Kee-eau! Kee-eau! Kee-eau!"*

Then the human Denson, me the previous night, returns from relieving himself. He is oblivious to the owl's head on Mariah's body. When I say "he," Denson, I say again: I am him, and he is me. I now have wings and feathers. I am an owl. Willie believed salmon had likely delivered the spirit of an animal through the bruise on my chest. Is this it then? Am I forevermore to carry the spirit of owl?

In this zone or space outside my, or his, body, I fly! In such place, I observe myself spending the previous night with Mariah Toogood.

When I leave this state, will my human form remember?

When Denson starts talking, the owl's head atop Mariah's body changes into Rosie Garza's head. Denson continues talking to Mariah, flirting with her. He's clearly infatuated with Mariah, only the head atop her neck is Rosie's. He doesn't notice that it is Rosie's head any more than he had been aware of the owl's head. The body is Mariah's. The voice is Mariah's. As far as he is concerned, nothing in the hut is unusual. The human Denson sees Mariah's head; I, Denson as an animal spirit, a bird of some kind, see Rosie's head. Human Denson is blind to the truth. I see it clearly.

Sweet, sweet Rosie looks up at Denson with admiring eyes, and it is clear that she loves him. She gives him the grandest, sexiest smile imaginable. Wow!

Then Rosie looks straight at me, the traveling, night-flying voyeur, peering in through the crack at my human form, lover boy John Denson. She knows I'm here. She knows I'm watching and listening. I'm amazed and bewildered by the truth behind my wonderful night with Mariah Toogood.

The Rosie Garza head on Mariah's body winks at me. She talks to me, "Well, what do you think? Denson has no idea whatever that I'm in Mariah's body. None. And he has no idea whatever that I'm talking to you right now. Pretty wild, huh?"

Mariah runs her left hand over her breast. Her Rosie Garza head says, "She's got a great body, don't you think. She's tall. I always wanted to be tall. And she's got real cleavage. And that skin. So white!" Mariah's Rosie voice sounds wistful. Does

Rosie think her human body is not as attractive as Mariah's? "He likes Mariah's body, I can tell. When I put Mariah's arms around him, I feel him shudder. When I pull him into her body, he moans out loud. Human males are all the same. For him first time sex is the most mysterious and exciting. The best. It's likely what compels some men to be unfaithful to their wives. Fun to see him all turned on. He loves the Rosie Garza he works for, I know, so it's okay. No harm. No foul."

I say, "Rosie, please, don't do that."

She says, "A great deal for him, if you think about it. He's single. He's on the road all the time with his investigations. He gets lonely. He seeks the warming bed. No getting tired of the same old Rosie time after time. If he knew I was really an owl, that would be the end of his being in love with me, wouldn't it? He'd try to be all liberal and say it doesn't matter. But this is not a racial thing. It's between *species*. No, more than that. Between an animal spirit and a mortal human. Never mind that I've assumed a human form. It wouldn't be the same. Couldn't be. You can understand that, can't you?"

I try to say, "Please stop, listen, you're wrong," but it comes out as "*Voo-hoo-hoo-hoo! Voo-hoo-hoo-hoo!*"

"But after tonight he'll *know*, won't he. He'll remember what you're seeing tonight and this conversation, but whether or not he can accept it is another matter. He's in love with Rosie, so he'll want to think, yes, she's a shy, feathered lover, Rosie's *thymos* slipping into the skins of every female he meets, carrying on a passionate, secret romance with giddy, first-time sex each time out. Then he'll think no, that can't be. It's impossible. It runs contrary to everything he believes. He'll be stuck in a zone of doubt, tormented."

I cry, "*Voo-hoo-hoo-hoo! Voo-hoo-hoo-hoo!*"

"You shouldn't have made this trip tonight. You know that. It was a mistake. Willie warned you. Remember he said that some travelers die not from the substance they take, but from the shock of the truths they find."

I want to object. I want to tell Rosie to knock it off. I don't care whether or not she is an owl. She ordinarily occupies a sweet little human body. So what if it's only a vessel. She should use that. I'll take what I can get. Give me the animal spirit occupying the vessel of the lawyer Rosie Garza. That's fine by me. I want to swear to her that her Rosie's body will never get boring. That I will always look at her as fresh and exciting. I don't care if she is an owl or not. I'm not in love with her human exterior. It's the Rosie inside that I desire. It's the *thymos* that matters. The spirit.

But then I'm off again, flying silently, darting this way and that over the grassy dunes. I leave the driftwood hut behind me.

I'm going for a walk in the Coast Range of mountains in my human form when I'm sucked up by a terrible wind and hurled into the night sky. In the grip of the howling, I tumble wildly through the darkness. In the starlight, I am aware that I am not alone. I'm rolling, arms and legs askew, in the middle of hundreds if not thousands of large fish. Salmon.

Just as I realize what was happening to me, that I'm caught in the tornado, the wind abruptly ceases.

I plummet to the earth, hurtling downward with the salmon.

Falling, falling, falling . . .

Down, down, down . . .

As I fall, I see that what I had thought were salmon are not fish at all. They are humans. Friends and acquaintances of mine. Pamela Yew, the prostitute turned private investigator that I had met in one of my early cases. Willie Sees the Night. The lawyers Boogie and Olden Dewlap, who for years had sent

Willie and me out on cases. Willie's cute little cousin, Melinda. The Sasquatch expert Dr. Sonja Popoleyev. Dr. Jenny MacIvar, the lady who counted spotted owls. Bobby and Whitefeather Minthorn, who had gone with us on our trek up Mt. St. Helens in search of Bigfoot. Leiat Podebski, the retired English teacher in Enterprise. Rosie Garza. Mariah Toogood. All of them. They are beside me doing a free fall into the blackness, hurtling to their doom.

I look below and see the forest rushing up. What were weeks and months and years suddenly turn into nanoseconds, each more precious than the one preceding it.

My emotions are also compressed. I want to call out to my friends to say goodbye and to tell them how much I appreciated their company and how much I will miss them. I grieve that my turn is up. I try to call out to Willie. I want to hear him call me "Chief Dumsht" one more time. But he is a fish. My friends have all turned back into salmon.

The trees coming up.

I hit the top of a Douglas fir.

Highway rushing at me.

I am in a house. I am barefoot, walking on cool tiles. There is a fan overhead, spinning lazily. The room is full of Asian women jabbering in a language I don't understand. They each have a can of Coca-Cola. They are eating what appear to be chunks of caramelized, fried banana stuck on small bamboo sticks.

I open a door and step into a small room that has shelves of books on the walls. There is a ceiling fan here too. The single window has glass louvers that are open. Outside, past a screen and metal bars, I see a concrete block wall with shards of glass and beyond that, the top of a palm tree and a house with a corrugated tin roof. I'm in the tropics.

A Caucasian man with gray hair and a mustache, naked save for walking shorts, sits at a computer. He has books and piles of paper by his bare feet, surrounding him like a large bird's nest. There is a bottle of San Miguel beer on a small table beside him.

Concentrating on the screen, the man pulls at one end of his mustache, twisting it. He looks right at me, but can't see me. I circle around behind him, picking my way through the paper and books on the floor. I want to see what he's writing. He seems oblivious to my presence. I know his writing has something to do with me. Why else would I have traveled here on my trip? There is meaning here somewhere. He takes a swig of beer.

He begins writing again, his fingers hopping on the keys. He writes in quick bursts, then stops. Another burst. He seems unable to get a sentence down that pleases him. He scrolls up and down in whatever it is he is writing, going tap, tap, tap, on the left side of his mouse. Concentrating, he continues to twist the end of his mustache. Judging from the clutter of his work space, he is indifferent to physical order, but as a writer, he is an anal compulsive. He reworks the sentences again and again, deftly using his mouse to cut and paste. He does not like clutter in his prose. His sentences are imaginative sweat, the sheen of obsession.

Finally, I get into position so I can read over his shoulder.

I read about rising above my bed and looking down at Willie. I read about soaring above the valley in the moonlight.

I read about my flying above the dunes and seeing the running light of a fishing boat at sea. I read about my encounter with the shape-changing owl that was Rosie Garza become Mariah Toogood. Even now, as I watch over his shoulder, the author pops back to that episode and recasts a sentence. He obviously likes the idea that of having Rosie, the insecure animal spirit, fall in love with a human but afraid to let him know it. A devious, if not slightly sick author, he forces me to witness Rosie occupying Mariah's body. He has set me up as a self-deprecating skeptic, but now has Rosie tell me the details of her secret so that I will forever twist slowly, slowly in the winds of ambiguity and doubt.

I read about getting caught in grip of the terrible wind and plummeting to earth with the salmon morphing into my friends, with years compressed into seconds, and changing back into salmon again.

Suddenly, I am in the room with the Asian women drinking Coca-Cola and eating chunks of fried banana.

The man at the computer, my creator, is writing what I am seeing and feeling and thinking. His whim is my fate. He is me and I am him.

He looks up at me, grinning mischievously. He doesn't see me, of course. He imagines me standing over his shoulder after flying out of my skin. He says, "What do you think, Denson? There she is, sweet Rosie, inside every female you meet, forever yours. What is this experience going to do to you? Jolt you out of your skepticism? What comes next?"

He twists the end of his mustache. He enjoys the sick thrill of taunting me with doubt.

17 · Major premise

I woke up, wet with sweat. The sheet on the cot was soaked. The pillow was sodden. Through the east-facing window, I could see a rose-colored sky. It was dawn and a little chilly. My stomach was a grinding pit. I was so hungry it was unreal. I was also exhausted.

Willie walked through the front door, zipping his fly. "Well, Chief. Back among us, I see. The flyer returns. How'd it go?"

I sat up. I could smell myself. My mouth was dry.

"Hungry, are you?"

I grinned. "Hungry isn't the half of it. I could eat the south end of a skunk going north. But the first thing I need is a good hot shower. I smell like a goat."

He laughed. "I didn't want to send you off. I worried the whole time. It's a relief to have you back, I admit. I'll cook us a big breakfast, and you can tell me about it. Some biscuits. A little bacon maybe. Some fried potatoes. And some fried eggs cooked the way you like 'em."

"That sounds great. To hell with the cholesterol." While Willie started breakfast, I went into the bathroom and turned on the hot water and stripped. I soaped off the sweat and stood with the hot water beating on the back of my neck. I changed into some clean jeans and a shirt and padded bare-foot out to Willie's kitchen. I poured myself a cup of coffee and started loading up a plate. Saying nothing, I proceeded to wolf down the food.

Willie was curious, I knew, but I said nothing.

Finally, he said, "Well?"

"Well what?" I spread some more huckleberry jam on a biscuit.

"Come on, Chief."

Munching on the biscuit, I told him in detail about flying to Mariah Toogood's hut on Long Beach and my encounter with the shape-changing owl who was my secret lover, Rosie Garza.

He took a sip of coffee and grinned. "Mmmm. That's an interesting turn of events. What do you think about having an animal spirit fall in love with you?"

"It was all real enough, that's so, but it was all a dream."

"Was it?"

I told him about tumbling in the fierce wind with the salmon who turned into my friends and back into salmon as we plummeted to the ground.

"That's pretty wild too. What else?"

I slid another egg and some more fried potatoes onto my plate. I snagged another biscuit. I was ravenous. I felt like I could load up on food and sleep for a week.

"I'm curious. Did you meet your creator? Sometimes that happens. Sometimes not."

"Boy these biscuits are good, Willie. You outdid yourself this time. I could eat a couple of dozen, I swear."

"Ahh, so you did meet him. And?"

"And what?"

"Are you going to tell me about it?"

I shook my head. "Naw. Believe me, Willie, you don't want to know."

"Where's the harm? I thought it was all a dream."

I gave my eggs a solid hit of Louisiana hot sauce. "My alleged creator is a novelist living somewhere in Asia. I saw Filipinas or Vietnamese women frying bananas. They could also have been Indonesians or Malaysians. Cambodians maybe. Laotians."

Willie looked interested. "A novelist. That's one kind of creator, true enough. And if he created you, he very likely created me. Interesting."

"I didn't meet any kind of creator, Willie. Major premise: all human awareness originates in the brain. Minor premise: all brains are material. Conclusion?"

"All human awareness is material."

With my mouth full of biscuit, chewing, I said, "It was an hallucination, face it." Having said that with so much assurance, I still couldn't help but wonder. What if it was true about Rosie Garza? Worse yet, what if it was true that I was the product of the imagination of a demented author holed up somewhere in Asia? A guy twisting his mustache and having a giggle at my expense. His stupid grin made him look like I'd caught him sucking on a turd. No way in hell I was going to admit my doubts to Willie. I said, "One thing I'm damned sure about."

"And that would be?"

"That's the last trip for me. And I hope to hell I don't have a spontaneous repeat. No sequels for me, thank you." I shoveled in a forkful of fried potatoes. Chewing on the potatoes, I asked one more question, couldn't help myself, "Tell me, Willie, not all animal spirits are angels or saints, are they? From what you tell me, they're gripped by the same gamut of passions as we screwed-up humans."

"Correct. What are you thinking?"

"Would it be possible for an animal spirit to murder a human being out of envy or jealousy? I mean, if the spirits experience the same emotions as humans, that would at least be theoretically possible, wouldn't it?"

Willie's eyes widened. He leaned forward. "*What* are you thinking?"

I dug out the last of the huckleberry jam from the bottom of the jar. "This is good stuff, Willie. You got any more in your larder?

Willie cocked his head, studying me intently. "Tell me, Chief, do you really think an animal spirit murdered a human? That's a serious charge."

Munching on a biscuit, I said, "I only asked if it would be theoretically possible. Since there are no animal spirits, as far as I'm concerned it's a moot question. As an animal spirit yourself, you might want to look into it further. I assume you have some way of policing yourselves. Far be it from me to extract justice from something I don't believe in." I gave Willie a knowing smile. Let him wonder. Fun making him twist. The only problem was that I wondered too. Couldn't help it.

Later, back in my cabin with a glass full of elderberry wine, I contemplated my wild journey. I regarded the brain as a kind of biological computer. The output depended on the input. Visions, hallucinations, and dreams were shards and loops of remembered experience. We were prisoners of our brains. When our brains died, our *thymos* evaporated.

If I flew outside of my skin, it was in my imagination only, a chemically-induced interior journey, a vision arising in my subconscious from shards of personal experience. Nothing we know of how the universe works supports the possibility of spirits traveling outside of the skin. While my journey seemed real enough at the time, I only *thought* I was flying. I *imagined* that I was talking to an animal spirit who was Rosie. I *thought* I met my creator.

The source of the first part of my flying, that of watching myself with Mariah and talking to the animal spirit Rosie Garza, was fairly straightforward. I had long been infatuated with Rosie and for years had listened to Willie's stories of shape-changing animal spirits. Easy enough for my subconscious to come up with that fun little scene. The source of the second part of my adventure, that of falling with the salmon who were my friends, was also clear.

The third part, confronting my creator in a house in tropical Southeast Asia, was more complicated. That scene, I assumed, had most likely been inspired by my reading.

Wine in hand, I settled back and scanned the spines of the books that I had liked well enough to keep. Thomas Carlyle once wrote that "A good book is the purest essence of a human soul." I felt strongly that was true. And in spite of the vast repository of knowledge that was the Internet, it remained true. The tropical setting might have come from my love of Eric Ambler's thrillers. It might also have come from reading George Orwell's descriptions of his experiences as a young British bureaucrat. But the notion that I was the soulful creation of a novelist was more obscure.

It escaped me. And as long as I couldn't figure the third scene, I knew, I would be nagged by the troubling possibility that Willie's conceit of flying out of one's skin might also be true. One thing that troubled me was that I had not asked for my creator's name. Surely he had one. What was it?

The seventeenth-century French philosopher Blaise Pascal, in his famous wager, concluded that logic compelled the skeptic to believe in God. If eternal life existed, the skeptic gained everything. If eternal life did not exist, he lost nothing. In short, a prudent bet.

Pascal's logic had always fascinated me because it was incomplete; it did not acknowledge the pleasures of intellectual pursuit and the achievement of personal integrity. If a skeptic chose to turn his imagination over to the yoke of religious dogma, did he not, as Carl Sagan argued, lose the remainder of a luminous life of inquiry? Earthly lives were too short to give up on the question of what comes next.

On the other hand, if one agreed with Pascal, it followed that the choice of religions was of paramount importance. If all religions were logically equal in that they all depended on faith, one should choose that which offered the greatest reward.

I was infatuated with Rosie Garza. I coveted her. I found it hard to keep my mind off her. If believing in Willie Sees the Night's shamanism and the world of the animal spirits offered me Rosie in the body of every woman I met, shouldn't I, following Pascal's logic, turn my imagination over to shamanism? What did I have to lose? If Willie was full of nonsense and I was wrong, no harm done. Christians looked forward to salvation and heaven. I was offered the prospect of having a romance with Rosie's *thymos* occupying other women's bodies. Under the circumstances, I understood how passionate desire could turn into faith, or how the practice of habitually professing to believe often turned into actual belief.

18 · *The lady is always right*

The second I stepped through the door of the main branch of Lao Tzu's on Broadway in downtown Portland, I heard a weird, high-pitched, thin voice. It was such a strange and unattractive voice as to be a form of birth defect, yet there was no easy simile or metaphor that I could think of that accurately conveyed what it sounded like. Maybe a stoned female impersonator after a binge of drinking rubbing alcohol. Or something.

I drifted down an aisle pretending to be interested in a display of Chinese herbal medicines. The woman with the weird voice, a stoop-shouldered woman perhaps five foot ten inches tall and in her late thirties, was tending to the wants of a largish lady who wore a print dress stretched over immense buttocks that jiggled with the slightest movement. The customer turned, and I saw that she had a truly beautiful face, plump yes, but flat beautiful. There were truly those men, including a friend of mine, who preferred a handsome helping of meat with their potatoes, but it was not likely that this lady believed for a second that men could be attracted to her.

Weird Voice had a wide jaw and an extremely high forehead just short of the sort popularly imagined by people claiming they had been abducted by aliens. Her lips were so thin they were nearly nonexistent. The middle of her face was dominated by a narrow plowshare of a nose that had a humped ridge and deformed, slightly twisted base. Her ears stuck out like pink spinnakers filled with wind, giving her the appearance of being forever at full sail.

She glanced my way. The anorexic little worms that were her lips, said, "I'm Luci Douglas, the manager. I'll be with you in a minute." She was clearly proud of her name and position. Luci Douglas. Manager. Important stuff.

The message Luci sent by her demeanor and body language was unambiguous. In her mind, she was born to be in charge, a fact she wanted everyone she encountered to know from the start. Although her body drooped like a wet mop from stooped shoulders, it radiated arrogance. That might sound incongruous, but it was so. I was grateful for the gift of a minute because I needed a little time to fully appreciate Her Grand Importance. The human zoo contained some curious specimens, of which this lady was certainly one.

Owing to her outsized ears, Luci did not turn her head. She tacked it. If she got hit by a stiff gust of wind, she surely risked damage to her spinal cord. She had ugly bags of wrinkles below her tiny feral eyes, an indeterminate gray in color, which were constantly active, as though searching for a morsel of food or an exposed throat.

If Luci was concerned that her face appeared to have been imagined by a demented cartoonist, she compensated it for by applying makeup in abundance. The vast expanse of her forehead was tracked with so many deep, parallel lines it appeared to have been harrowed into a kind of cranial north forty. She might have planted and harvested mung beans or African violets in the makeup. One wondered, did Luci buy these chemicals in bulk at Costco or Sam's Club? Rouge by the barrel. Mascara by the hogshead.

In a doomed attempt to fill in the furrows of her summer fallow forehead and the baggy wrinkles beneath her eyes, she had slathered her face with goo of an off-flesh color. She had used so much of the foundation, if that's what it was, that she left a clear line on her neck—sort of a chemical mask. In places she had troweled on the gunk so thickly that it had dried into tiny cracks that looked like dried mud. Her eyelids were covered with eye shadow the color of green pond scum.

A tall, short-legged woman, Luci wore a lime green jumpsuit that accentuated the unsightly lumps of fat at the tops of her thighs and clunky sandals with cork soles. She had thin, straight, off blonde hair that hung limply down the back of her excessively long, drooping torso.

With a buck on the line, Luci was in her charming mode, exuding concern and attentiveness. Her strange, thin voice said, "Oh my yes. How many generous Chinese women do you see? I've yet to see one. Some of their slender figures are due to genetics, yes, but a lot of it is diet that respects the time-honored principles of yin and yang. Balance. A properly balanced diet keeps the weight off." When she talked, Luci revealed small, narrow, rodent's teeth.

By "generous," the charming Luci meant fat.

The beautiful large lady overlooked the euphemism. "Balance," she said.

"That's right," Luci said. "The Chinese have discovered the principles of balance over thousands of years of traditional medicine. Too much yang and your body is overwhelmed. Americans are totally ignorant of the need for dietary balance. You need to counter yang with yin. That's why we have fresh burdock flown in from Canton Province. Properly dressed with a light vinaigrette, it makes a delightful salad. A trifle spendy, it's so, but it is a rich, sophisticated source of yin."

The beautiful, large lady leaned over a refrigerated display of burdock, no doubt contemplating the need to balance yang with yin. She had small, delicate hands.

Luci said, "I know a generous lady from Woodburn, an aide in a nursing home, whose family has been afflicted with too much yang for generations. She drives up two or three times a week so she can maintain a fresh supply. It works for her. She said two weeks ago a man followed her around in a Safeway store. Couldn't take her eyes off her." She laughed a high pitched, thin laugh. As near as I could tell her alleged mirth was entirely bogus, an unembarrassed affectation that was entirely devoid of humor.

But the beautiful large lady wanted desperately to believe and so did. She was caught in Luci's odd spell. Her exquisite little hands fluttered over the burdock like indecisive butter-flies. She could have been a hand model. She examined the leafy vegetable with pale blue, hopeful eyes. Many is the skinny woman would have killed for such stunning eyes.

I watched as the beautiful large lady bought a large bag of burdock at $19.95 a pound.

After she had conned her mark, sweet Luci headed my direction. All charm she was. What was she thinking when she saw me? Overpriced "Siberian" ginseng for this earnest creep who likely has trouble getting it up and is too cheap to buy Viagra?

"Hello, may I help you with something?" Her voice was warm and inviting. She was so very, very charming, a classy lady. Thoughtful. Considerate. My, my, my, such a sweet person. When she talked her hyperactive little worms did their best to impersonate real lips.

"Yes. My name is John Denson. I'm a private investigator . . ."

"A what?" Luci showed rodent teeth. Her nostrils flared. She compressed her anorexic worms. Her mean little eyes, narrowing, peering over the unsightly bags of wrinkles, bore on me with unconcealed animosity. She was pissed and then some. Boy oh boy was she ever! Her transformation from charm to fury and raw hatred, a kind of psychic tilt, was instant, casual, and complete. The tilt was unnerving. But of course she counted on that. It was a practiced tilt that she'd probably been using since she was a child controlling her parents.

Trying to maintain my composure, reminding myself that zoos contained cobras and ferrets as well as soulful pandas and cuddly koalas, I said, "A private investigator looking into the murder of Sharon Toogood for . . ."

She cut me off a second time, her voice sharp and admitting of no reply. "Why would I want to talk to you? We have police to investigate murders." She looked at me with cold, controlling eyes. She was in charge. I would do as I was told. Any other response was out of the question.

I was determined to finish my sentence. ". . . for Jerry Toogood. I just have a couple of . . ."

Again she declined to let me finish a sentence. "You can tell the famous T.G. that the police have concluded that his daughter Mariah murdered her sister then committed suicide. He might be a weatherman, but he can't control the storm. Case closed. He can read the details in the *Oregonian* or the *Seattle Times* if he wants. If you want to buy something do so. Otherwise leave or I will call the police. I do not have to put up with casual intimidation."

"But . . ."

"I believe you heard me. You can investigate all you want, but you'll do it without my help. If the police ask me a question, I am obliged to answer, but not you. *Get out!*" Her weird voice rose malevolently.

"If . . ."

She cocked her head appraising me. "Before you go, know one thing. If you continue to poke your snout into my business, you'll have to deal with me. Believe me when I tell you that's something you don't want. If you cross me, you'll quickly learn that I'm smarter than you, guaranteed. I get what I want. I always win. Always. I never lose. Never. Remember that. Now goddamit, get the hell out of my store! How dare you come in here and presume to interrogate me!" She glared at me, showing poisonous little rodent teeth.

I wondered if the confident Ms. Douglas was half as smart as she thought to make a casual enemy of a stranger before giving him a chance to be a possible friend. If she took a swig of bear bile she'd probably think it was sweet as Kool-Aid on a hot summer day.

I exited Lao Tzu's wanting desperately for Lady Lucifer Douglas to be Sharon Toogood's murderer so I could have a hand in throwing her into the slammer. I had remind myself to be cautious. It was my job to pursue the evidence, not my passion or personal dislikes, in addition to which people like Luci Douglas were ordinarily cowards whose primary skill was in calculating self-interest, which rarely included doing hard time in the slammer.

19 · The man with two moving parts

There were two bartenders in Leonard's, a slender young man with a shaved head and a hippie with a red bandanna around his forehead. Shaved Head disappeared into the kitchen. I waited while the hippie said goodbye to his girlfriend, a cute little Asian girl, then I told him I was looking for a man named Tommy Hilfinger who was supposed to be a regular. He said that when Hilfinger was in town he ordinarily showed up somewhere between six-thirty and seven. As he said this, he grimaced slightly. It was clear that he did not look forward to the daily appearance of his estimable customer.

"You're not a friend or anything?" he asked.

I shook my head. "Never met him. Do you know what he does for a living?"

The Hippie shrugged. "He hunts maybe. Or guides. Or something macho. He periodically disappears for a week or two, a blessing. Claims he's traveling. Who knows? He's gotta be pulling in the bread to afford a Hummer that probably cost fifty thou."

I nursed a beer and waited. Sure enough, at the appointed hour the hairy-chested he-man Tommy Hilfinger, sporting an outsized Emiliano Zapata mustache, swaggered through the door with a self-important, splay-footed stride. He wore combat boots and starched, bloused combat pants with deep pockets on the thighs. Over his massive belly was stretched a camouflage-green T-shirt with an American eagle emblazoned on the front. He topped off his costume with a jaunty Aussie hat, one of those Crocodile Dundee numbers with the brim snapped up on one side. He had matching tattooed rattlesnakes wrapped around his biceps. The dotted line tattooed around his neck came complete with instructions: *cut on the dotted line.* The message of his persona, from stride and mustache to costume from boots to hat and his tattoos was clear: *Me hot damn stud. You dog turd. Stay out of my way.*

Hilfinger had a wide, porcine face with huge jowls separated by the tiny, dimpled island that was his chin. His head rested on a disgusting bulge of fat that surrounded his neck like a pink inner tube. Tiny pink ears stuck out from the fat like deformed mushrooms. His mouth was small and mean, lacking only tusks to qualify him as a mascot for the Arkansas Razorbacks. His little pig's eyes peered out between rolls of fat. His face was a sheen of sweat. He mopped the perspiration with the back of his hand, flipping it onto the floor with disdain.

His combat fatigues were clean and neatly pressed. It was not like he had emerged from a long day of fighting in the jungle, but more like he was prepared for an inspection from an anal retentive drill sergeant. That was also part of his image. He was no fat slob. He was just big as hell, see. Stout. Strong. Quick and aggressive. Disciplined. Proud. It was my bet that he likely hadn't spent a day in any military service.

He yanked up the bottom of his T-shirt, and clapped a massive hand to his hairy belly with a loud pop and yelled, "Draw one!"

The hippie bartender briefly caught my eyes as though to say: *Here he is. Good luck.*

For the moment I held back, content to observe Hilfinger's annoying entrance as I imagined an anthropologist might assess the triumphant arrival of a cannibal, species *Dumbus shitus.*

Hilfinger took the stool next to mine and looked through me as though I didn't exist.

"Fuck's the game?" he shouted, his voice indignant.

The bartender waved a remote at the tube above the bar. Seattle Mariners manager Lou Pinella popped onto the screen, emerging from the dugout giving a wad of gum a workout.

Hilfinger said, "Mariners are on the tube, and you stand there with your thumb up your ass. You think people come in here to watch some faggot interior decorator. Fuck's the matter with you. Jesus!"

The hippie bartender put a frosty mug of draft beer in front of Hilfinger. Dryly, he said, "Hepatitis C, I think. The health department's been nagging me to come in for a checkup."

"You better lay off that fudge packing, you know what's good for you," Hilfinger said.

The bartender looked indifferent. His bald colleague emerged from the kitchen.

Hilfinger said, "You got that little Chink girlfriend. Forgot. Errol is the faggot." Watching the bald bartender, he laughed *haw, haw, haw.* To the hippie, he said, "The little Chink sprinkle MSG in her pussy, does she? Enhance the flavor. If I were you, I'd watch it. They say eating too much of that stuff will give you a headache." He laughed again, *haw, haw, haw.* It was clear what Hilfinger's game was. He intimidated people and mocked them, daring them to do anything about it. When he was in the room, it belonged to him. He was in charge. He wanted that made abundantly clear.

Still not acknowledging my presence, in fact intruding on

my space, Hilfinger pulled on one tail of his Zapata mustache, as though it was a hirsute gear shift that engaged his dubious brain. His mean little mouth snarled, "Peanuts. Two bags."

The bartender fetched two plastic bags of peanuts and flipped them onto the bar in front of him. He grabbed one between his teeth and ripped it open.

How on earth was I going to open a conversation with a self-important moron like this? Should I tell him I was a writer for *Soldier of Fortune* magazine? That I was recruiting mercenaries for the President of the Central African Republic? I thought no, I better play it straight. "Mr. Tommy Hilfinger?" I asked.

His eyes focused, as though seeing me for the first time. "Fuck's it to you?"

"I . . ."

"I don't do no business in no fuckin' bar."

I said, "My name is John Denson. I'm a private investigator . . ."

"Fuck you say. You hear that, everybody? A private dick!" *Haw, haw, haw.* Unlike Luci Douglas, Hilfinger did not send me packing. More fun to intimidate me so that I would remember what a jerk he was and regret that I hadn't somehow stood up to him. Same personality types. Different tactics. "Ain't never talked to a private dick before. This has to do with what?"

"I'm investigating Sharon Toogood's murder."

He looked surprised. "Her sister killed the stupid bitch! You think I murdered her? Don't you suck up to me! Can't stand flatterers." *Haw, haw, haw.*

"I'm talking to all her former friends."

"You think I was her friend?" *Haw, haw, haw.* "Listen, pal, I know why you're here and it ain't got nothin' to do with Sharon Toogood. You've been hired by little Alice's family to want to nail me in a wrongful death suit. If the cops can't get enough evidence to charge me with murder, what do you think a private dick is gonna accomplish? You're a dick all right. You think I'm stupid. Give it up!"

Did I think he was stupid? Not necessarily. Uncivilized, most certainly. And who was Alice? Wrongful death suit? I cleared my throat.

Hilfinger had me on the run and was enjoying it, going so far as to answer my questions before I could ask them. "Alice Overman was a slumming slut liberal. Alice Underman was more like it. She was a dancer at Mary's, for Christ's sake. She come on to me, not the other way around, then turned out to be a nosy little bitch, always butting into my business and asking questions. Questions, questions, questions. I gave her the mighty Hilfinger sausage." He grabbed himself by the crotch. "Just picked a hole and let her have it hard as I could. Skinny little thing she was. A bag of bones. But like they say, the closer to the bone the sweeter the meat." *Haw, haw, haw.*

"I see."

"No you don't. You don't see shit. She wasn't especially good at fucking. Or being buggered for that matter. She laid there like two holes with legs. Don't know why I bothered. I knocked her around now and then, which was kind of fun, I admit, and she seemed to go for it. Showed real emotion. All that weeping and wailing and blubbering, saying how much she loved me while she wiped the blood from her mouth. Then it was back to the questions. Can you imagine?" He looked bitter. "Stupid cunt!" he snarled. He twisted one of his weird little hamster's ears.

Hilfinger narrowed his eyes and clenched his teeth, although the drama of the latter display, a favorite among more primitive simians, was diluted somewhat by the jowls that overwhelmed his jaw line. "If you want to leave this joint in one piece there's something you gotta get straight. I did not kill the silly bitch. I kicked her whimpering ass, that was so, but nobody ever tried me for murder. No evidence." He emptied his mug in a single pull and banged it on the bar. "Beer here!"

The Hippie, glancing at me to let me know he was pleased that I had shown the moron up, set about pouring Hilfinger another beer.

I said, "You a military man? A veteran?"

He took a swig of beer. "I've been around. Here and there. I don't talk about it." He sniffed, pretending to be offended that he be asked to talk about his mysterious past.

In other words he was a posturing clown. A wannabe. With the slightest movement of his head the Hippie bartender gave me a *right on, man!*

Hilfinger stalked off to take a leak.

I watched the Mariners on the tube, aware that the bartender was watching me. After a couple of minutes he drifted over to my spot at the bar, and said, casually, "Tommy Hilfinger murdered that young woman and everybody with half a brain knows it. Beats the hell out of me why he was never charged. You know, rumor is that he has a tragic birth defect."

"Oh?"

"We probably should feel sorry for the poor bastard. He only has two moving parts." He watched me, amused, waiting.

I grinned. "Okay, I'm game. And those would be?"

"His mouth and his asshole, and they both work the same."

As he said this, Hilfinger emerged from the can, zipping his fly. He wiped his hand on the thigh of his trousers. "What? What's that?" he bellowed.

The bartender said, "I was telling this gentlemen about our specials of the day. Meatloaf and ham sandwiches. They both cost the same."

20 · Sometimes me sits and thinks

My Volkswagen bus, which was now old enough to qualify for exemption from Multnomah County's clean air standards, was perfect for surveillance duty—a few hours or an all night, it didn't make any difference. I had a cot in the back. I had a miniature refrigerator and hotplate, both of which ran off a squat jug of propane. Thus equipped, I could fix myself a cheese sandwich. I could have hot coffee or a cold beer. I could take a cat nap. I could even relieve myself in my plastic and porcelain Portla-pot, an efficient little model made by a local company. If I had to live in my bus for a few days or weeks, I could do that, no problem.

I loved my bus. The moving parts of its engine had been recycled so many times that I had lost count. Although its exterior was now as dented as a wad of crumpled tinfoil from the impact of the salmon, I had washed the blood and fish scales from it. No way I could afford to have the dents fixed. I would have to find a decent body in a Volkswagen graveyard somewhere, and Willie would help me move the engine and my interior gear into the new body.

I once read a short story by the Japanese science fiction author Komatsu Sakyo about a little boy going to school one day. He passed an abandoned car in a field of weeds. The next day, he stopped to clean the windshield of the derelict vehicle. The day after that, he began polishing the exterior. With the passing of weeks, the car became grand, looking almost new. One day it followed him home from school.

That's how I felt about my Volkswagen bus. It got me to where I wanted to go. It shielded me from the elements. I took care of it in return.

Since I had a pair of overpriced night binoculars, I parked the bus in the shadows of a sprawling tree a block from Luci Douglas's house near Reed College, one of the loveliest parts of Portland with quiet streets rowed with trees and grand old houses. Owing to the layout of the streets, it was unlikely that any but the most paranoid visitor stopping by for a midnight chat with Luci would pass by my bus. Or maybe a cop. If a cruising cop spotted my bus, guaranteed I'd be hustled out of the neighborhood.

As was my usual practice, I drew the curtains around the bus's rear window so I could peer out undetected. As I watched, I remembered a quote I had read somewhere. Attributable to whom? A peasant? A shepherd watching over this flock? I couldn't remember. "Sometimes me sits and thinks. Sometimes me just sits."

I often thought there must be a sweet tranquillity in being able to just sit with a completely blank mind. I could not do that. I did not listen to the radio while I was on surveillance. Music took up the space better occupied by speculation. I sat and thought—most often about whatever or whomever I was detailed to watch. When I was a kid, I had a friend who loved to tear machines apart to see how they worked—a windup clock, an electric fan, it didn't matter. He grew up to be an airline mechanic and loved the work. I remembered a line by the actor Peter Boyle in the movie *Taxi Driver*. He told the taxi driver played by Robert De Niro that people are changed by their jobs. They became their jobs. It couldn't be helped. It was the way the world worked. I was curious about the illusions of the human *thymos*. In my current case, monitoring the activities of two reprehensible individuals whom I suspected of double murder and of being involved in the wholesale slaughter of bears for their gall bladders, I was faced with twisted *thymos* run amok.

A popular cultural delusion was the belief that one could buy "class," as though "class" was somehow an exterior thing available on an installment plan or bought by the pound like potatoes. A Mercedes-Benz meant "class." A pair of overpriced Nike running shoes equaled "class." A huge SUV meant "class," never mind that the owner had no use whatsoever for a four-wheel-drive vehicle and had been forced to buy it on a seven-year contract at a usurious rate of interest. Being the engine of the economy, the snare and delusion of conspicuous consumption was widely encouraged by the advertising industry. Alas, the more one thought one could buy class, the less one actually had. Being willfully, if not obstinately blind to this irony was the defining quality of the hopelessly bourgeois.

Judging from the house she had bought and the neighborhood that she had chosen, Luci Douglas believed that consumption on the grand scale was class on the grand scale. The exterior "show" was what mattered. Everything else was drek.

The area just east of the Willamette River where it cut through Portland had been developed by old money and the city's pioneering families. It was a genteel, languorous neighborhood, resonating luxury. The lawns, greener than green, were always freshly mowed, the hedges neatly trimmed. There was so little traffic in some of the streets that one could almost imagine the trilling of crickets and buzzing of lawn mowers on a hot August afternoon. This all in the heart of a bustling city. Here was the jumping-off place for old folks with family money. Sipping lemonade on the front porch of an inherited house one July afternoon. A nursing home come September.

These people and their families had lived here for generations. The idea of someone who hustled ringwort and Ginkgoba moving in on their turf must have been as disconcerting to them as having to eat French's hot dog mustard instead of Dijon, a lack of taste as revealing as the stupid Russian who ordered red wine with fish in *From Russia with Love*. Elegant James Bond had been hip to his pretense immediately. So too the residents to this aspiring interloper. Luci Douglas might live among them as she tacked up the sidewalk with her spinnaker ears billowing before a fitful wind, but never as one *of* them. Although she would deny that she would never be accepted, she would know it, and the knowledge would grind at her.

In a way it was amusing that Luci had so crassly interrupted the grand solitude of their isolation. Made me smile, I had to admit. But I did have a question. How in the hell could the manager of a chain of health food stores afford a million-dollar house? She had popped for that excessive wad on the assumption that, in the eyes of others, she would have maximum class, never mind her rodent teeth and north forty forehead, not to mention her crass greed and vile temper. Here was a neighborhood that might have been imagined by F. Scott Fitzgerald. Ahh, I thought. That was it: Luci Douglas was a female James Gatz. No, that wasn't it either. Although Gatz grew up poor, and despite his posturing, he had a natural class that Daisy's rich husband, Tom Buchanan, lacked because he behaved like an asshole. As far as I could tell, ambitious Luci was devoid of any form of redeeming qualities.

Both Luci and Tommy were examples of ego gone haywire. Perhaps they both looked in the mirror and hated themselves. They wanted Hegel's recognition. They wanted Plato's respect. They believed power was one of the perks of money. If they had money, the respect of others was mandatory. To that end, they became control freaks and chronic bullies. That they owed any form of recognition or respect to others or that recognition and respect were in any way reciprocal did not occur to them. *They* were the important ones. Only *their* feelings counted. The feelings of others, their inferiors, were irrelevant.

Sometime in the middle of the night, I nodded off. I woke up with a start. Two people were getting into a dark blue Toyota pickup parked in front of Luci Douglas's house. The driver, a man, was closing the door. The passenger was female, but I just caught a glimpse of her head as she disappeared inside the cab. The Toyota pickup somehow looked familiar. Swearing at myself for falling asleep on the job, I grabbed my infrared binoculars, too late in time to make out the license plate number.

I checked my watch. It was 5:00 A.M. I'd lucked out not to have been rousted by a cop. I had been awake at 3:00 A.M. Who on earth would come calling at that hour of night, and why, unless it was because they didn't want nosy neighbors to see their coming and going? Willie's game warden friend had observed his reclusive mountain man talking to someone in a dark blue Toyota pickup that was registered to Lao Tzu's.

Had the mountain man been talking to Bill Dennis? Was this him again visiting the evil Luci? I knew Bill was doing the legal work for Lao Tzu's, but why on earth would he call on Luci at home in the middle of the night? And who was the woman with him? It was Bill who had recommended that Jerry Toogood hire me. I was supposed to share with him whatever it was I found so T.G. wouldn't get caught by any surprises.

Was it really Bill Dennis who didn't want to get caught by any surprises?

21 · Tête-à-tête at Wong's

I missed seeing whoever it was in the Toyota pickup who had visited sweet Luci in the middle of the night, but the day wasn't finished yet. I stayed put. It was a Saturday morning, but that didn't mean Luci wasn't going to work. The weekends were presumably big days in the business of hustling traditional medicines, and besides, it didn't strike me that Luci's main pleasure was selling. It was the accumulation and exercise of power, an obsession not limited to either gender. The lady liked being in charge.

But eight o'clock came and went, then nine and ten. I made myself some coffee and waited. This was rather like bank fishing. One sat. One watched. One waited. Finally, at eleven o'clock, the door to Luci's garage rolled up and seconds later, a huge cream-colored Mercedes-Benz 450 SL rolled out. Milady did like show. No question. First the real estate. Now the honking big German sedan. No way in hell she made that money hustling Ginkgoba.

I gave her a couple of blocks head start, then pulled onto the street behind her. After a while one develops a sixth sense about whether or not a rabbit thinks a hound is somewhere behind him, nose to the ground. I don't think Luci Douglas was concerned in the least that somebody might following her. There could be two reasons for that. One was that she didn't have anything to hide. After the middle of the night visit by her mysterious visitors, I didn't believe that for a second. The other was that she was so arrogant as to believe nobody would dare follow her. That was my bet.

I followed her north up Martin Luther King Jr. Boulevard, formerly Union Avenue, then west on Burnside Street. I got caught in the wrong lane and nearly lost her on the Burnside Bridge crossing the Willamette River, which bisected the city. Then, ahead of me in the sea of blues, silvers, reds, a flash of cream.

She turned right at Broadway, the entrance to Portland's modest Chinatown. I got hung up by a red light, but I wasn't as alarmed as I had been on the Burnside Bridge. I suspected Luci wasn't going far. When the light turned I also went north on Broadway, and almost immediately spotted her Mercedes. I wasn't so lucky finding a parking spot, but after some cruising, I found one. I loaded my Nikon with 400 ASA film just in case and hiked back to Chinatown with the camera slung around my neck. She was likely here for lunch. But where and with whom?

I hiked past my favorite spot, the Hung Far Low, a longtime Portland Chinese restaurant named by a distant Chinese with a sense of humor or by his fun-loving American backer. Either way, pointing out the Hung Far Low was always a pleasure for Portlanders giving visitors a tour of the city.

I stepped into several restaurants and found nothing. Finally, at Wong's, a dim sum place, I stepped into the foyer spotted my rabbit in the dining room to my right. Luci Douglas was having lunch with a immaculately dressed Chinese man in his fifties.

I started to retreat but Luci spotted me. She glared at me with hatred. No, not just hatred; her eyes blazed like a professional wrestler determined to top last week's ratings.

Before Luci could do anything more, I snapped a quick photograph of the table and retreated. I returned to my bus and checked my Portland telephone directory. Never mind that I only had one used frame on the roll, I found the nearest shop that offered one-hour developing and drove there.

22 · Mary's rules

That night I returned to my spot, ready for another night of monitoring visitors to Luci Douglas's pretentious house. I say pretentious. At the risk of sounding snobbish, I'll say that it is more accurate to say it just didn't fit her. An old, retired couple with money earned over decades, yes. Luci Douglas, no. At about ten o'clock a Hum Vee drove up, one of those smaller, $50,000 jobs as opposed to the full-sized $100,000 versions driven ostentatiously by Hollywood movie stars. For a suburbanite interested in show, driving even the smaller job was absurd show. But if one was a hunter or had business in the mountains in the winter, it made sense.

I wasn't surprised when Tommy Hilfinger hopped out. He was wearing a getup similar to the one he had worn at Leonard's—camouflaged fatigue trousers, T-shirt, and baseball hat. About a half hour later, the he-man warrior emerged, seemingly energized, and got back into his Hum Vee.

Follow him or stay put?

I was a sport. I decided to follow him. He took pretty much the same route that Luci had taken earlier in the day, only he wasn't headed for Chinatown. He parked on Broadway a couple of blocks off Burnside. I followed him on foot south on

Broadway. He crossed Burnside and stepped into Mary's.

When I saw him do that, I had to smile. For the truth was
that however much a person could be a jerk, there were few
people without redeeming qualities. To the casual person, to
assert that Hilfinger had taste in skin bars might sound curious. But Mary's was the classiest of classiest skin bars because it was totally unpretentious. It had been around
Portland perhaps forty years, so that among discerning aficio-
nados of the city, it ranked right up there with the Rose Gar-
dens or the Hoyt Arboretum as a must-see. The best time to
go there was on a lazy afternoon when there were just a handful of customers. At night, it got crowded and its ambience
suffered.

Should I follow him inside? No point in doing that if he
was by himself. No sense tipping him off that I was following
him. On the other hand, suppose he was meeting somebody?
Who? Hard to keep an eye on Mary's from the outside, because it shared its toilets with an Asian restaurant to the rear,
and it was easy to slip out that way unnoticed. When it came
to making a decision as to whether or not to go inside Mary's,
logic was hard to come by.

Finally, I thought to hell with it and stepped inside Mary's.
I had heard people talk about comfort food. Mary's was a
comfort skin bar. It was the same always. Quiet, unpretentious, welcoming. There was a grand painting of a reclining
lady with outsized breasts behind the short bar on the right.
Then came the small stage surrounded by stools for those
gentlemen who liked to watch up close and extremely personal. Opposite the bar and the stage there were maybe a
dozen small tables. To the rear there were two pool tables,
and beyond that the toilets. In the afternoon, in the silence
between songs or dancers, one could hear the clicking of ball
against ball and the occasional clicking and clacking of a spirited break.

That was Mary's. It was a beer and wine place, and the price of that was kept as modest as possible. No jackass five-dollar draft beers in Mary's. The dancers selected the jukebox music on stage, and it was tradition for them to solicit quarters for the music. The beer was cheap, the least the customers could do was spring for the music. Fair enough.

One did not get drunk or behave boorishly at Mary's. It was not done. Contrary to the portrayals of skin bars in the movies, the customers at Mary's were restrained and civilized in their behavior. Hookers understood that this was not a place to hang out.

The female of the species delivered succor and hope and a kind of soulful, primal beauty that went beyond the ability of language to describe. The dancers were in their sensual prime and contrary to being humiliated, they were proud of their bodies. The men were appreciative.

I was always bewildered by those critics of both genders who found such pleasure, by both dancers and those who enjoyed the dance, somehow sinful or disrespectful. It was in fact a joyous, celebratory coming together of the yin and yang of the human imagination. No amount of suppression, guilt, jealousy, bitterness or resentment, cant, or dogma would dissuade either the watchers or the watched from enjoying the extraordinary power and the glory of the sweetness.

I immediately spotted Tommy Hilfinger. His attention was riveted to the stage where a lithe young brunette, down to her pubic hair, was on her back, undulating directly in front of the gentlemen with the seats at the edge of the stage. Their rapt attention was not gynecological. It was humble. They were paying tribute to the miraculous power of the softness rising and falling in front of them.

I took a seat at the bar. Hilfinger wasn't paying any attention to the bar, guaranteed.

Then the dancer, having finished her turn, gathered up her

clothes and collected the tips from those she had given mind-blowing close-ups and retreated from the stage. She was replaced by a slender blonde, who leaned over and said, "Gentlemen, we need quarters for the music."

In Mary's, all men were equal. An aged, yellowing sign on the wall, tucked in with placards giving the price for cellophane wrapped hot dogs and hamburgers reheated in the microwave, said, "No touching the dancers." That sensible limit was in fact a city ordinance. But beyond that the unspoken rule of the house was that the dancers were to be treated with civility. There was no city ordinance demanding that dancers were to be respected. That was enforced by the patrons.

The state of Oregon had a house rule against murder. There were statues defining the various degrees of homicide, from involuntary manslaughter to first degree murder. But the limit was clear. In Mary's the responsibility of one's fellows to maintain the limits of acceptable behavior was also clear.

23 • Should she kiss it?

After three dancers had taken their turns, I grabbed a chair and joined Tommy Hilfinger. Hilfinger looked at me annoyed. "What are you doing here, Denson, following me around?"

"Naw," I said. "Mary's has been a favorite of mine for years. I pop in here once in a while."

"Fuckin' liar," Hilfinger muttered.

I ignored him. "Wonderful place. A kind of church or temple."

He looked puzzled. "Fuckin' church?"

"Of wistful admirers," I said. "Worshipful we are. We pay homage."

"Shit too."

I said, "Sharon and Maria Toogood were like these young ladies. Alert. Fun loving. Beauties. In their prime. Full of life. Their ration ahead of them. Husbands to love. Kids to bring up. The full deal."

Hilfinger made a noise in his throat, then said, "Quiet now. Annie's going to dance. She calls herself Kammy Sutra, but she's actually plain old Annie Dancer."

Kammy Sutra strode onto the stage. She was in her late twenties or early thirties and was long and lean, just short of being bony, with short, strawberry blonde hair. Kammy had a narrow face, Brigitte Bardot lips, and playful green eyes. She was, well, spirited. She was having fun driving the johns nuts, or if she wasn't, she was doing a helluva job faking it. She got quickly down to a thong bikini hardly larger than dental floss and a silver chain between two clamps on her nipples. They weren't meant to suggest pain or anything like that, just enough to keep the chain in place. She flipped the chain, giving us all a teasing. She raised an eyebrow. *You like that, big boy?* Then she turned quickly, rotating her rump, knowing that the bikini bottom didn't cover a whole bunch.

Hilfinger said, "Ain't she something?"

"She sure is," I said and meant it.

"She's as sexy as Alice used to be. Packed 'em into Mary's. Got that way about her."

"That would be the Alice you were suspected of murdering."

"Bullshit! All bullshit!"

On the stage, Annie turned her back to us, spread her legs and bent over and put her head between her legs so that she was looking up at her rump and crotch. Thus positioned, she shook her head sadly and said, "My God, is that what you guys are buying that overpriced beer to see? Amazing! What do you say? You want me to kiss it? I can if I want."

Everybody applauded enthusiastically.

"Come on now. Applause doesn't cut it. Gonna cost you."

Everybody dug for their wallets while Annie, looking upside down at the money piling up at the edge of the stage, looked amused.

When the round of tithes was finished, she pretended to give herself quick peck and unwound. "You guys!" She was having fun.

"Whoa," I said.

Annie lay on her side and demonstrated her remarkable

spine. She had the remarkable ability to make her slender body roll like the surf, starting with her feet and ending with her head. She demonstrated her flexibility by putting herself into the most extreme yoga positions imaginable, chatting amiably at the amazed spectators as she did. The sculptors who rendered the Kama Sutra statues in India would have come up with even more amazing stuff if they had had a model like her.

"Double jointed," Hilfinger said. "Ain't that somethin'? Never seen that before. Can you imagine what she could do in bed? Whoa, Nellie!"

He had a point, I had to admit. She was extraordinary. Kammy popped to her feet smiling. She said, "What do you think, guys, would you like me to turn the other way and do that? I can if you want." She grinned mischievously. "No? You don't care?" She looked down at the upturned faces directly beneath her feet. "Come on, you big tippers, you want to see it? Don't be bashful now. You know you do."

Everybody in Mary's wanted to see it. The hands went up and the tips began accumulating. The guys at the tables went forward to add to the kitty. There wasn't a male on the planet who didn't want to see her pull that trick. Even I was a sport. I took a ten spot from my wallet and went forward to lay it on the edge of the stage. Looking down at me, she gave me a wink, murmuring "Thank you, dude."

I went back to the table, and we all watched, including the guys at the pool table, who called a break in their game.

Kammy lay down on her back, spread her legs, and once again her joints went both ways as her body with its remarkable joints and spine moved forward and backward in waves, the most erotic thing I had ever seen.

She loved every moment of it. She hopped to her feet grinning mischievously. "You guys like that."

We burst into spontaneous, enthusiastic applause.

"You want it without the thongs?"

We applauded louder.

"Then let's see the green."

Kammy Sutra was a double-jointed bandit. Once more, the bills piled up on the edge of the stage. I gave her another ten spot. As I did, she said, "Pretty hip, eh?"

She put more music on the box and went through her double-jointed drill again and it was, well, wow.

Kammy was replaced by an auburn haired girl who offered large breasts for the discerning gentleman. But there wasn't a man in Mary's who wasn't still thinking of Kammy Sutra doing her yoga thing.

As the auburn-haired girl began her drill, Kammy emerged from the diminutive dressing room at the rear of the bar. Twirling the silver chain with the nipple clamps, she circled toward our table on her way to the bar to wait for her next turn. She paused by our table, "Yo, Tommy. Who's your new friend?"

"Ain't no friend of mine. He's a dick."

"Oh?" Grinning, she arched a playful eyebrow.

"No, no, no, not that kind. A private dick. Mr. Butts-in-where-he's-not-wanted."

"Like Sam Spade or somebody?" she asked.

"Only dumb," Hilfinger said. "Too many questions for his own good."

She laughed. "Ahh, I see."

"You like the dance?" she asked me, her eyes teasing.

I said, "Lady, a person would have to be brain dead not to like that dance. You should have become a contortionist. Also I like your stage name. Kammy Sutra. Hip."

She laughed. "I figured to hell with that Jade or Amber nonsense. Being double jointed is inherited, by the way. My mother was just like me."

"Annie works for us now," Hilfinger said.

"Us?"

"Lao Tzu's. She's our new buyer for Chinese stuff. Does Korea and Thailand too."

She answered my unasked question. "I'm saving up to buy my own shop."

"Huh?"

"Not natural medicines, though. Gourds. Make more money here than at Lao Tzu's. I figured I have something more entertaining to offer than a big pair. Fun, huh! Gotta go. We're not supposed to jabber too long with the customers at the tables. Okay to talk to them at the bar while we're waiting our turn." With that, the remarkable Kammy Sutra was off.

I could understand why Annie Dancer put her unusual physical skills at work in Mary's. As Kammy Sutra, she likely made several hundred bucks in tips for one turn on stage. Gourds?

24 · *Pleasures of Fat Fred's*

Ever since the horror of September 11, 2001, the security of all federal buildings was jacked to the extreme and the one in Portland was no different. The next morning, I was one of the first people into the building at 9 o'clock. After going through a security search, I was allowed to visit the local field office of the Federal Bureau of Investigation.

I asked the receptionist, a pleasant middle-aged woman, if I could please talk to the special agent in charge.

She said, "That would be Special Agent Gregory Dunsmuir. And you are?"

"John Denson. I'm a private investigator."

"And this would be in reference to?"

"Murder and possibly bear poaching."

"One moment, please." She rose and disappeared into an office. A half minute later, she emerged saying, "Mr. Dunsmuir will speak with you."

"Thank you," I said and went inside the office, which had a nice view of the Willamette River with Mt. Hood rising in the distance.

Special Agent Dunsmuir rose to shake my hand. He was a trim man in his late thirties and wearing a suit that while pressed, wasn't so perfect as to pin him as an anal compulsive. Two primary movie stereotypes obtained when it came to FBI agents. They were arrogant jerks who looked down on local cops. Or they were know-it-all supermen good guys. Dunsmuir didn't appear to be either of those. He seemed rather like an okay guy, good enough to be made special agent in charge of the Portland field office.

That was not to say that he wanted a private investigator underfoot. I understood that and didn't resent it. I introduced myself, which was hardly necessary because I got the feeling he already knew who I was. I said, "A man who looks like Humphrey Bogart is running around with boxtops identifying him as FBI Special Agent Alan Shearer. He talked to me in a Dunkin' Donuts in Clatskanie. Hard to believe he's really an FBI agent, although I suppose he could be."

"He's a fraud," Dunsmuir said simply. "The boxtops are bogus. We know it, but for the moment are ignoring it. We have a reason to be watching him."

"But you're not going to tell me what it is."

He smiled. "I don't think so."

"Or even who he really is."

He shook his head. "I think we'll pass."

"I'll just bet you money, marble or chalk that this had something to do both with the murders of Sharon and Mariah Toogood and with the slaughtering of bears for their gall bladders."

"I can neither confirm nor deny what we're investigating. You know that."

I said, "Can you imagine what would happen if the public found out that the Chinese are ripping off our bears for their gall bladders? If you're an American farmer selling durum wheat to the Chinese for noodles, or a multinational corporation selling telecommunications equipment to them, it's a turd in the punchbowl of free trade!"

He grimaced. "I suppose I've got a nerve since I won't tell you anything, but you want to tell me what Shearer was after?"

I smiled. "Sure. Don't anybody say I'm not a regular kind of guy." I told him about my conversation with Humphrey. "My partner Willie Sees the Night and I are both determined to find out who really murdered Sharon and Mariah Toogood. If we can lay hands on them, we also want to bust the jerks who are poaching bears."

Dunsmuir leaned across his desk. "Tell me, Mr. Denson, do you have a paying client, or are you just out there like Don Quixote driving a Volkswagen bus?"

"Two paying clients. I'm investigating the murders of the Toogood sisters for their father. The Nature Conservancy is our client in the poaching investigation."

He pretended to study a paper on his desk.

I waited.

Finally he said, "Believe me, it is not good for you and your partner to get involved in this. There are issues involved in which you are unaware. It would be dumb as hell for you not to pay attention."

I showed him the photograph I had taken in Wong's that morning. "Who is the Asian gentleman having lunch with Luci Douglas?"

He didn't want to say.

I said, "Come on now, we both know if Willie and I keep at it, we'll find out for ourselves."

Dunsmuir studied the back of his left hand, then said, "Okay, what the hell? His name is Win Ho Eng."

"And he would be?"

"He sells Chinese homeopathic medicines to stores on the West Coast. A wholesaler."

"Anything more?"

"Not that I want to tell you," he said.

I said, "I thought I should tell you about the bogus boxtops. Not good. Public duty and all that. I'm not all bad, truly."

"Thank you for telling us about that. We appreciate it."

I extended my hand. "I'll find my way out," I said.

"Before you go," he added quickly. He handed me a business card. "The number on this card will get me twenty-four hours a day. Same with the e-mail address. If an e-mail comes in, I'll be alerted immediately. I don't like you and your partner poking around a case that's important to us, I admit that. But legally I can't do anything to stop you. Please, if you find something you think we should know, or if you need help, contact us immediately. Never mind the time of day, just do it. Ultimately, we have the same goal."

"And that would be?"

"For starters, the truth, and maybe such amount of justice that we can squeeze in."

I slipped his card into my wallet. I said, "That puts us on the same side, I agree. And I bump into something that I think you should know about, I'll let you know soonest."

He looked relieved. "Thank you much, Mr. Denson."

"No problem."

Back in my cabin, I rarely ate breakfast. Just drank coffee. But when I was buzzing around on a case, I liked to have a breakfast. For some reason loading up on lethal cholesterol, a form of farm boy comfort food, helped me concentrate. The best places for breakfast were those old fashioned little places my mother used to call "greasy spoons" with thick mugs that were much beloved by lumberjacks, truck drivers, and construction workers. Yes, and nostalgic nitwits like me. With most of their aging customers having eaten their last Denver omelette and joined their generation in the obits, many of those little cafés had gone under, replaced by the bulldozer of fashion.

One of these fast-disappearing places, Fat Fred's, had been a favorite of mine for years. It was on the eastern end of Powell Boulevard, which happened to be a couple of doors down from a Lao Tzu's. That's where I went to have a late breakfast and to call Bill Dennis, on the assumption that he had made it home after his early morning rendezvous at Luci Douglas's grand residence. That's if the Toyota pickup had actually been Bill's.

I wasn't the only fan of Fat Fred's. It was packed, mostly with older people savoring small pleasures of the past. Fat Fred's was Americana as it once was; it might well have been celebrated by Norman Rockwell in the *Saturday Evening Post.* I was lucky to find a stool at the counter, onto which I gratefully slipped. A plump waitress wearing a black skirt and white blouse with a name tag telling me she was "Doris" appeared immediately with a pot of coffee and a cup in hand. In an age when little girls were being name Ashley, Savannah, and Summer, it was nice to know that there were a few old-fashioned Dorises still left. For this Doris, it went without saying that I would want one of Fat Fred's bottomless cups of mud.

"Coffee?"

I nodded. "Gotta have mud in the morning."

"Breakfast, this morning?"

"Short stack plus two fried eggs, plus a Mariners victory tonight."

Doris grinned. "Ain't them Mariners something!" She moved on to another customer.

To be completely classic, such a place as Fat Fred's had to have clear glass salt and pepper shakers with a checkered pattern on the glass, plus stainless steel napkin dispensers and little bottles of Tabasco sauce for their customers' eggs. Fat

Fred's was class. Gone however, were the heavy glass ashtrays. While that tip of the hat toward fashion might have been mandated by Oregon law, the new smoke-free Fred's was fine by me.

While I waited for my hotcakes, I called Bill Dennis, who was in his usual amiable mood.

"Denson, you've been on the job, I take it. Where are you?"

"Having breakfast at Fat Fred's on Powell Boulevard."

"I know that place. Good spot. Give me a second to pour myself a cup of coffee."

I waited. I heard him pick up the phone again. I said, "I paid a visit to Lao Tzu's in an attempt to talk to Luci Douglas. Hot tempered lady. Told me to take a hike."

Bill laughed. "I could have told you that. Saved you the time."

"I did get to talk to Tommy Hilfinger at his favorite bar. He was all decked out in combat fatigues like he was a Navy SEAL or something."

"That's his usual costume. We all have our little fantasies, I suppose."

"The bartender said he spent his time driving around the Pacific Northwest to buy medicinal herbs."

"Tommy buys North American medicinals, correct."

"Who buys your Chinese traditional medicines?"

"That would be Annie Dancer, a young woman who grew up in Hong Kong and speaks both Cantonese and Mandarin Chinese. She works in the branch out at Eighty-second and Powell, just down the street from where you're having breakfast."

He was talking about Annie of the remarkable body. "She's your chief buyer of things Chinese then?"

"That's it. Hasn't been on the job long. Three or four months maybe. She has contacts in Hong Kong. She keeps a good set of books. Nothing gets by her."

"Who used to buy the Chinese medicines?"

"Luci."

"From?"

"From a man named Win Ho Eng."

"But no more."

"No more," Dennis said. "Annie Dancer now buys directly from Hong Kong. Established her own contacts. Cheaper than Win Ho Eng."

There was no law against Luci Douglas having lunch with her former supplier, although it was hard to imagine anyone wanting anything to do with her outside of business. "Why doesn't Annie work in the main branch with Luci?"

"Would *you* want to want to work in the main branch with Luci? My God, man!"

"You got a point there."

Bill paused and I could hear him take a sip of coffee. He said, "If we hadn't moved her to the store on Powell, we'd have lost her. I can't imagine how Annie could be of any use to you. What could she possibly have to do with the murder of the Toogood sisters? That's if they both were murdered."

"I agree, Bill. Hard to imagine. I know you want an occasional progress report. Just checking in."

"You're a man of your word. Good man. T.G. doesn't want any surprises."

Doris appeared with my breakfast. "Gotta go, Bill. My hotcakes and eggs have arrived." I hung up and took a bite of egg mixed with hotcake, one of life's genuine pleasures.

I bought a copy of the *Oregonian* from the newspaper rack and read about the Mariners as I ate. Doris, knowing that her tip was likely dependant on her attentiveness to my cup of java, kept it filled. As I ate and read, the number of people at the counter began to thin.

After a while, a female voice said, "Hey you, hippie man!"

I glanced up. I was being addressed by Annie Dancer, a.k.a Kammy Sutra, who had settled into the booth behind me. She wore an off-yellow Beavis and Butt-head T-shirt, faded blue jeans, and Adidas running shoes. She had a necklace made out of polished koala nuts around her long neck. There was a Seattle Mariners baseball cap in front of her, a good sign.

I put down my paper and pointed my left finger at my chest. "Me?"

She laughed and said, "Yes, you. You *are* John Denson, aren't you?" She had a playful, coltish way about her. She was an enthusiast and a natural tease.

"How do you know my name?"

"From Tommy Hilfinger, the fat slob at Mary's. My heavens, do you have Alzheimer's?"

I laughed. "It's not so advanced that I remember that he introduced me scornfully as a private dick. He never did mention my name."

Doris arrived at Annie's booth and poured her some coffee. Annie took a sip of coffee, eyeing me over the rim. "You're right, maybe he didn't mention it. Let's see how is it that I know your name? You're a private investigator. How many guys who look like you have appeared on public television after having gotten caught in a fish storm? Then you show up at a girlie bar to hang with Tommy Hilfinger. It doesn't take Sherlock Holmes to deduce that Hilfinger is not the kind of guy you ordinarily hang with. On the tube you said your partner is a shape-changing animal spirit who believes he can leave his skin and go flying. Now *that* is interesting company."

"You a regular here?"

"Come here all the time. I work in the Lao Tzu's just down the street. We got a memorandum from Luci saying you might be around asking questions. We're not supposed to give you the time of day. Give you the bum's rush, in fact. You want to join me? You can ask me about Sharon Toogood if you want, so long as I get to ask you how it felt to be slammed by salmon falling out of a blue sky."

Better to ask my questions over coffee at Fat Fred's than standing in the aisle at Lao Tzu's. I said, "Sure, I'll join you, why not. I'm told the Arabs say it is a sin to turn down the invitation of a good-looking woman. I take it that would be especially true for a young woman with your remarkable, uh, physical skills."

Her eyes widened. She pretended to be indignant. "Hey, hey, this invitation is to join me at breakfast and talk only! My God, I don't believe I've ever seen such ambition! Control yourself, please."

I folded my *Oregonian* and moved to her booth, cup of coffee in hand. I raised an eyebrow then lowered it, looking chagrined. "No need to worry. Not a whole lot ever comes of my ambitions."

"Easy to imagine why," she said dryly. "No offense," she said quickly, her green eyes dancing.

Annie Dancer's breakfast consisted of whole wheat toast with orange marmalade and coffee. As she spread some marmalade on a piece of toast, she said, "Man, I love orange marmalade. They have one here at Fat Fred's made with pineapple and apricot that's good too. Mmmm. You want to try some?"

I took a sip of coffee. "I overdid it with eggs and hotcakes."

"Ahh," she grinned. "He says hotcakes instead of pancakes. Is it supper or dinner with you?"

"Supper," I said.

"I knew it," she said with approval. Watching me, she said, "You know they say a man makes his own face after age forty. I think it was Orwell who said it. Or somebody. He was right."

At that moment the clapper rigged to the door banged, alerting Doris that she had two more customers. They were young men in their early twenties, wearing Portland Trail Blazers T-shirts.

Chewing on toast, Annie nodded towards those the two young men. "You take those two dudes there. They're likely okay guys, but you can't tell from their faces who they really are. They could be real creeps, and a person would never know it. They haven't really done anything yet. Couldn't have. They're too young. Little boys still. Bland, uninteresting faces. When they get old enough, their faces will change, and they'll look sour, cheerful, soulful, or whatever."

"Good point," I said.

"There are some young actors, pretty boys, who make a couple of movies then disappear. Think of the faces that lasted: Clint Eastwood, Donald Sutherland, Gene Hackman. Now there's some men with real faces. Character. *Gravitas*. Keifer Sutherland's face isn't as interest as his old man's. You ever notice that?"

"Michael Douglas has got a good enough face," I said.

"But not until he got older. It took him a while to compete with Kirk."

"I always liked the face of the character actor Slim Pickens. For most people he was a one paragraph obit. For me it was a real loss. Who can ever forget him as Major Kong riding the atomic bomb out of the hatch in *Dr. Strangelove*?"

"He had a memorable face, I agree. You've got a good face too." She glanced at the two young men who had taken seats at the counter. "Hard to imagine either of those two running into the fish. It would have been a waste."

"And you don't think it was with me?"

"A guy like you, with a mustache like that and wearing a ponytail and driving thirty-year-old VW bus around? Naw. So what if you got knocked nearly senseless by a falling fish. You've likely been pondering its meaning ever since. Salmon falling out of the sky? Why me?"

My cell phone rang. It was Willie. I listened while he told me that he had lucked out and found a new body for my bus at a small farm about fifteen miles from our cabins. The owner, hoping to swap the body for some goats or a washing machine, had been running an ad in a throwaway. Money was cool too. He wanted a hundred bucks. "It's been sitting in a barn in the old Bunton place, Denson. Engine and clutch shot, but no rust. We'll have to move your engine, clutch and interior gear into it."

"What color?"

"Kind of an off yellow."

"We'll have to repaint it."

Willie laughed. "That goes without saying, Chief. Blue with white trim it will be."

"Buy it. We've got good weather. No sense waiting. We can tow it this afternoon and get a jump on it. If we work hard maybe we can finish it off in a couple of days."

"My sentiments exactly," Willie said and hung up.

"I should be on my way in a few minutes." I put away my cell phone with Annie watching me, curious.

I said, "That was Willie. He's found a bus that's been stored in a barn. We'll tow it to our cabins this afternoon and begin the chore of moving my engine and running gear into it. You knew Sharon and Mariah, didn't you?"

"I knew Sharon a little. I went out with her for a drink after I got the job. We went to a Greek place in Old Town. We had big old gyros dripping with yogurt and drank too much retsina. She didn't want me to quit after my first encounter with Luci, which is why she and Bill Dennis connived to have me work in another store."

"How did you learn the details of importing medicines from Hong Kong?"

"Understandable question," she said. "My mother is a citizen of the U.K. who was raised in the United States. My father is an American who ran a business importing Chinese-made goods into the U.S.—Christmas tree ornaments, kitchen doodads, children's clothes, running shoes, whatever. I'm an American citizen born overseas. Got a fancy certificate to prove it. When the Chinese took over in 1997, my parents emigrated from Hong Kong to the United States and retired. They bought themselves a place in Brookings down on the coast. You know where that is?"

I nodded. "Near the California border. Warm spot on the coast. Lotta fog though."

"I'm a graduate of the University of Hong Kong. I speak both Cantonese and Mandarin. I worked for my father long enough to learn the details of the importing business."

I sat up straight. "Impressive. Who do you think killed Sharon Toogood? Mariah?"

"As I understand it, Mariah loved her sister, and they got along just fine. They might have quarreled over the money Mariah loaned her, but those things happen. Do I think Mariah murdered her sister? No. I suspect the same person might have murdered them both. Why, I have no idea." She gave me an odd look. "Did you know Mariah?"

"I drove to Long Beach to talk to her about her sister's murder."

She said, "I suspect that sweet Luci and Tommy have involved the stores in some kind of illegal scam and Sharon somehow tumbled onto it."

"Oh?" I tried to sound casual. Doris arrived with the coffee pot. I was taking in far too much caffeine, but still I held my coffee up for more.

Watching me, Annie said, "You're wondering why I'm telling you all this?"

"The thought had occurred to me."

"I cannot abide Luci. As soon as I can save enough to open my gourd business, I'm outta here. Lots of places can use someone who knows how to order shipping containers and fill out customs forms."

"You want to tell me about the gourds."

She leaned forward, her face alive, eager to tell me about gourds. "Gourds are just wonderful. They've been used to make pots for thousands of years. They come in all sizes and shapes. Tall skinny ones. Short fat ones. If they're decorated properly they can be beautiful. Now you take Oriental lacquerware. That takes months of applying alternate layers of a kind of sap with a thin layer of clay, building it up until you get that shiny, hard surface that we all associate with lacquerware. Now the Chinese have come up with a far quicker way to get the same effect and in some wonderful colors in addition to the traditional black and a few others. We're talking burnt orange, turquoise, wonderful greens and so on. I know of a cooperative of female artists in Canton who can make fabulous lacquered gourds. I want to have my own shop here in Portland."

"Which is why you're working two jobs at once."

"Correct. Tell me something, do you and Willie need another hand in renovating your bus? I'm not any kind of mechanic, but I know the difference between a ratchet and a Philips screwdriver. If you're going to paint it, I can mask off the headlights and whatever."

If Annie Dancer was the young woman who had visited Luci Douglas in the early hours of the morning, she had likely been dispatched to find out everything I knew. If she was straight up honest, she was a high-spirited charmer and a delight. Taking chances was what gave life its fizz. I said, "Sure, but it'll be a long day, guaranteed, and we'll probably be working on it all day tomorrow."

Annie grinned from the clichéd ear to ear. "All right! What's a couple of days playing hooky? I'll call the store and tell 'em I've got a horrible case of PMS. Luci will be sore as hell, but she needs me more than I need her. If she wants to sack me, she can be my guest. I make more money at Mary's anyway, and the work is a whole lot more fun. You should see the looks on the faces of those guys looking up at me when I send my spine into a wave." She burst out laughing. "God, it's wonderful. You cannot imagine. You just cannot imagine."

"Yes, I can."

She laughed even louder. "You've got me there. You should have seen yourself, your mouth was wide open."

"You were watching me?" I was incredulous.

Tilted her head, her eyes teasing. "Sure, good-looking guy like you. Big tipper. Enough to curl a girl's spine." She laughed again.

25 · *The shack of the rising sun*

Beside me, Annie Dancer was pumped with excitement and a sense of adventure, however mundane the chore ahead. I wasn't as sanguine. I had been towed several times—one gets used to that on my kind of budget—so I knew what the drill was all about. People living in the city generally avoided the experience on the grounds that it was in some way revealing and humiliating. If they had a breakdown, they called an overpriced "professional," ranging from a kid with tattoos to a middle-aged eighth-grade graduate, who drove out to do the job for them at an extortionist fee levied by all fixers of emergencies, from plumbers to lawyers and heart surgeons. The iron law of the market, not taught in economics 101, was elegantly simple in its basics: the more you had to have something, the more the supplier was going to charge. But out in the country, folks towed wounded vehicles all the time. It was a form of redneck touring.

Being towed was an dicey experience. It was up to the driver being towed to keep the rope taut; to do that he had to work in tandem with the towing driver. When the towing driver had to slow or make a turn, it was his responsibility to warn the trailing driver with a hand signal. The brake lights wouldn't do it. By the time they went on, it was too late.

If the driver being towed didn't pay attention and ride the brakes when he was given a hand signal, the rope went slack. This, alas, was followed by a spine wrenching jerk.

The rope went slack.

"Shoot!" I said.

My neck snapped.

Annie laughed.

"Hold on," I said. I got the rope tight again.

Ahead of me in the pickup, Willie held his left hand down by the side of the door, indicating that he was going to slow.

Annie braced herself.

I put on the brakes. I did it right. The rope remained tight.

She said, "Good job! First time being towed for me. I didn't know it was so involved."

"The smart thing to do is hire a proper tow truck, but Willie and I are far too broke and cheap to pop for that. He's slowing for the turnoff. It won't be long now."

Concentrating on the pickup in front of me and waiting for Willie to give me a hand signal, I said, "Do you know anybody who owns a newer model dark blue Toyota pickup with an aluminum canopy over the bed?"

"Luci bought six identical models for company use."

"Company use. That would be?"

"Bill has one. He doesn't have to drive every day but Luci got him a deal on the pickup, so why not. One of the perks of being a lawyer. Tommy uses his to collect the medicinals he buys from women gathering them around Oregon and Washington. That would be mostly Indian women, Yakimas, Umatillas, Nez Perce and so on. Vera is Luci's friend. She wanted one, so she got one."

Willie signaled that he was going to slow for yet another curve in the road. I put my foot on the brake. "Luci's friend?" I couldn't help but sound surprised.

"It takes all kinds I guess. Good for Luci that she has someone who will put up with her. There are rewards in it for Vera. Luci made her the manager of the store in Beaverton when there were more qualified people. She was the only store manager to rate her own pickup."

We entered the curve, then sped up. The rope stayed tight. A nicely executed maneuver. I said, "She knows which side of her bread is buttered."

"You reap what you sow."

Nobody was going to beat me in a cliché challenge. "What goes around comes around."

Annie giggled. "A real pair we are. Boy, it's beautiful up here."

Twenty minutes later, we pulled into Whorehouse Meadow through which Jump-Off Joe Creek meandered and where Willie and I had our separate, neighboring cabins. The meadow was colorful with wildflowers, some blue, some yellow.

I said, "Here we are. Home. The first little cabin is mine. The second is Willie's. The first thing I do when I meet a new female is bring out here and impress her. I've never met a woman yet who didn't have her heart set on isolation and boredom in a pathetic shack."

We passed by my cabin and continued on to Willie's. He had all the tools, and that's where we would begin the renovation of my bus, or more accurately, the construction of a new bus. After a final jerk, we eased to a stop and Annie popped out, lean and light and ready to go.

She took a deep breath and slapped herself across the chest with the palm of her hand. "Mountain air! Cool and clear and wonderful! Wildflowers. The trickle of a creek. A red-tailed hawk floating above the meadow. Wow!"

"The mountain air gets pretty damn cold at night," I said.

Eyeing her, Willie said, "I bet if you two use your imagination, you can find a way to keep you warm."

All innocence but with a sly grin, Annie said, "I see you two guys have chimneys. Maybe we can build a roaring fire and drink some of that homemade elderberry wine Denson told me about on the way over." A regular little pistol was Annie Dancer. Quicker than all getout.

While Willie and I set about removing the engine from the rear of my old bus, Annie Dancer set to work inside, industriously removing the carpet, window curtains and my storage cabinets. By the time we got the engine unfastened and ready to move, she was inside the new bus removing the seats so she could lay the carpet. I was pleasantly surprised that she didn't insist on listening to the radio while we worked, being content to listen to the trickling of the stream, the clicking of grasshoppers, and the occasional call of a meadowlark. Well, that and either Willie or me at the back of the bus swearing when we barked a knuckle.

There wasn't a whole lot that was useful in the engine compartment of the new body, so we yanked the works while Annie was laying carpet inside. After a couple of hours work, we took a break and sat squat-legged in the late afternoon sun, chewing on jerky and drinking bottles of cold homemade beer that Willie and I had made. It was Oddball because Willie and I threw in a handful of juniper berries along with the hops blossoms to give it flavor. I had designed a label on my computer that I had run off in number and that we had placed on each amber stubby:

> **Denson and Sees the Night's**
> **Oddball Ale**
> **It makes you drunk**

We all took a swig of Oddball.

"Different, but good. I like it," Annie said.

Adventurous, she was! I said, "I gotta hand it to you Annie. You're great date! Hard worker. Indefatigable. You never stop. And you like our Oddball."

She took another hit of ale. "My, my, you sure are a sweet-talking man, John Denson. What's the deal, Willie, he get a different woman in his cabin every night?"

Willie liked her teasing and high spirits. He was up to the challenge. "Oh, hell yes. Sometimes he takes them outside to cavort around in the moonlight. Buck nekkid! Weeds up to their rumps."

Her mouth dropped. "Buck nekkid? Really?"

"Oh yes. Then there's all that rolling and thrashing around on the ground. Kind of unnerving having to listen to them carrying on all night."

"My heavens!" Annie made a remonstrative clicking sound with her tongue. *Tsk, tsk, tsk!*

We watched a jet lay down a vapor trail from horizon to horizon in the thin blue sky high, then went back to work. Willie and I moved the engine from my old bus to the new and began connecting everything up. Inside, Annie put the cabinets in place and began marking the spots where she had to drill holes. As I lay on my back ratcheting bolts into place, I could hear the buzz and whine of the drill inside the bus. She was a hard worker, more than keeping up her end of the chores to be done. All in all, it was a bucolic, romantic kind of afternoon.

When the sun settled low in the western sky, cooling to a dimming orange orb over the tops of the Douglas firs, we were pooped. Time to quit. The next day, if we got an early start, we stood a chance of getting everything hooked up and running, although we might have to wait for the day after to paint it blue. We adjourned into Willie's cabin, bone tired, but feeling good. Fun to step back and admire what we had done, almost turning two wrecks into one good bus in one afternoon. Sweet!

After we had all showered down, Willie popped the caps on more cold bottles of Oddball Ale, and I helped him rustle up a supper of smoked salmon, smoked razor clams, elk jerky, and three kinds of pickled vegetables: chanterelle mushrooms, milkweed buds, and cattail shoots. That's in addition to Willie's special treat, deep-fried meatballs, about the size of golf balls, made of dried, reconstituted venison and seasoned with sea salt and wild garlic. After we cleared the supper dishes, we switched to elderberry wine and played several games of gin rummy.

At close to eleven, with a white three-quarter moon rising in the sky, we folded the cards. We had a long day ahead of us. It was time for Annie and me to take the hike back to my cabin. It suddenly hit me. It was dark outside.

Annie immediately picked up on my change of mood. "What's the matter?"

I inadvertently licked my lips. "Nothing. Would the lady like to accompany the gentleman back to the shack of the rising sun?"

"Against every word of advice my mother ever gave me," she said.

"Early start in the morning," Willie said.

26 · A stroll along Jump-Off Joe

I held out my elbow for Annie Dancer and, amid the trilling of crickets, we set off down the trail in the chilly mountain air. Beside us, on our right, Jump-Off Joe Creek serenaded us with its trickling, gurgling song.

Annie said, "Easy, easy, what's the hurry, nice night like this? Everything in good time. Time for a leisurely stroll through Whorehouse Meadow. Oh, I know, you're thinking about my, uh, being so limber. Got your imagination working overtime, did it? Got you all hot to trot."

She misunderstood why I walking fast. It was not out of anticipation of maneuvering a double-jointed young beauty into bed, although that prospect had its charm. It was something more elemental and spooky. I slowed down.

As we walked, I told Annie about my night with Mariah Toogood and burying the pistol in the sand. "She was in good spirits when I left her, as upbeat as she could be, considering the fact that somebody had just murdered her sister and she was apparently under suspicion. Does it sound to you like Mariah killed herself?"

"No, it doesn't," Annie said.

"She was murdered and framed. Had to be."

"Judging from what you're telling me, you're right."

"But by whom, and why?" I asked. "If she had known about the bear poaching, she would have said something."

"Maybe the murderer thought Sharon might have told her."

I took a deep breath. "But why did Mariah go back and dig up the pistol?"

"Maybe she got scared and thought she needed it to defend herself. Maybe somebody had followed you there without you knowing it. There are lots of black bears around Willapa Bay. The island in the bay is thick with them. Bears are largely nocturnal. You have a pair of night binoculars. A bear poacher would almost certainly have them. He could see that you were burying something. He was curious. When you and Mariah went back to her little hut, he dug the pistol up."

Somewhere, out there, I heard the call.

Kee-eau! Kee-eau! Kee-eau!

"What's that?"

"Probably the owl that hangs in this meadow. We hear it all the time," I said.

"What kind of owl?"

I continued walking. "A short-eared owl. They're nocturnal. Out and about looking for rodents and insects on a night like this."

Kee-eau! Kee-eau! Kee-eau!

I said, "On the other hand, it could be Willie."

"Willie?"

"Willie's good at doing birds."

"He must be." Annie looked around. "Why would he be out imitating an owl?"

"To have a little fun with us. That's the call of a female looking for a mate." I searched the meadow through the dim night light, but couldn't see anything.

Annie looked about too. "Giving us the razz, is he? Wait till I get ahold of him in the morning."

I said, "If that's a real owl. It's rare to actually see one. They're soundless, like shadows in the night."

I waited for another call, but there was none. I was suddenly gripped by a disconcerting thought. At Long Beach, Rosie Garza had changed shapes with, well, a feather's touch. In the batting of an eye, she soundlessly entered and assumed Mariah Toogood's body. An owl could turn its head a hundred and eighty degrees. As a stiff necked primate, I didn't have that kind of a vision. No matter if I looked left or right, the deft flyer could silently enter Annie behind my back. It was entirely possible, without my knowing it, that Rosie had already touched down and occupied Annie's body. That's if there were such things as animal spirits.

"You okay?" Annie asked.

"I'm fine," I said, grateful that we had arrived at my cabin. Willie had warned me against traveling out of my skin. He said whether or not I believed what I saw, the memory of what I saw would haunt me. He was right about that. I knew I had to confront the possibility head on. As I stepped inside, I said, "What do you want? Lantern or electricity."

"Lantern," she said. "Who needs all that light?"

"Oddball Ale or elderberry wine?"

"Elderberry wine. The Oddball was okay when we were working hard and sweating."

I lit the wick of my kerosene lantern. I poured us each some wine. As we sipped it in the flickering yellow light, I looked Annie straight in the eye. "Willie and I hear that owl out here every once in a while. I taped the call of the male and female off the Internet. Would you like to hear it again?"

"Sure," she said.

With the light of the lantern sending shadows dancing against the cabin wall, I punched on my tape recorder. *Kee-eau! Kee-eau! Kee-eau!*

She grinned. "Nice!"

Voo-hoo-hoo-hoo! Voo-hoo-hoo-hoo!

"And that would be?"

"The call of the male."

"Also looking for a mate." She arched an eyebrow.

"Correct."

If the self-conscious Rosie Garza was inside there looking at me through Annie Dancer's eyes, pulling her animal spirit ruse, she had a better poker face than Nevada Slim, I'll give her that. "I'm curious," she said, "have you ever heard of the contortionists and gymnasts called the Cirque de Soleil in Paris?"

"I think maybe," I lied.

"The original cirque billed themselves 'the four little girls who fold.' That's me, a girl who can fold. True double-jointed people, mostly females, are less than five percent of the population, and even then their degree of 'hypermobility,' as it's called, varies greatly."

"Depending on?"

"In the case of the spine it has to do with the discs between your vertebrae. If they're longer than the vertebrae themselves you can bend both ways. The longer the discs in relation to the vertebrae, the more supple you are. I'm easily in the top five percent. Or used to be. When I was fourteen or fifteen, I could really twist myself into knots, but then little by little, year by year, I began losing it. Still . . ." She grinned wickedly. She tested my bed with her hand. She pulled back the blanket.

With the bed waiting, I put my arm around her, and we stood at the window looking out at the white moon. I lacked faith in animal spirits. Or did I? Haunted by the memory of my night flight, I was trapped in an ambiguous zone. Which was it to be, Sagan's skepticism or Pascal's sensible bet?

Annie smelled sooooooo damned good. I kissed her lightly on the neck. She was intoxicating. If Rosie was inside her, calling the shots, I suppose a man in my position, giving my long-standing infatuation with Rosie, could have regarded it as an answered prayer. Not me. I didn't want that. No dream lover for me. I wanted Annie Dancer and nobody else.

Annie took my free hand and guided it to her breast. Even as I felt the exquisite softness of her breast, I couldn't help but wonder if it was really Rosie's hand covering mine. Logic or faith? To believe or not to believe? Which was the blessing? Which was the curse?

Eyes never leaving me, Annie peeled off her jeans and T-shirt and the rest of it. She hopped lightly onto the bed. There was little doubting that this wonderful, slender, beautiful, happy little dancer wanted me. She arched her back until, head upside down, she looked back at her rump. "What do you think? Do I have a good butt? For a contortionist, I mean." She gave herself a slap on the behind. "No bird calls."

Boy, she was fun. "Absolutely everything but bird calls. We can howl or yowl or cry out as loud as we want. Free speech rules!"

"Four letter words, anatomical references, and stuff like that?"

"Nobody out here to hear us or to give a damn."

"Ooooh. You wicked man. Nasty!"

I gave her a gentle push with the back of my fingers and sent her toppling.

No more words. Our soulful tongues a tangle of desire, we tumbled onto the waiting sheets and there joined, writhing and twisting skin to skin.

27 · Ambush on Whorehouse Meadow

Annie and I got up early the next morning, feeling so damned good it was impossible to put into words. We walked up to Willie's cabin, had a good breakfast, and set to work for the second day on reinventing my VW bus. Willie and I had the engine and transmission pretty much in place, although we still had to finish hooking up the fuel line and electrical system. After that we had to install the clutch and decide whether or not the brake drums were worth moving. Annie had to complete the interior hookups and tape the windows so we could use our rented sprayer to paint it later in the day.

As Willie and I worked on the engine at the rear of the bus, Annie attended to her chores inside. The chorus of bugs and grasshoppers began clicking, buzzing and snapping as the sun rose and the air got warmer. Above us a red-tailed hawk circled lazily. As we worked, we talked about the puzzle of who murdered Sharon and Mariah Toogood? Were the murders linked to bear poaching? Who was behind it all?

From above us, inside the bus, the sound of Annie's drill. *Zzzzzzzzzzzz*. The drill stopped. Annie said, "You know, a lot of people would think you two lead screwed lives. Look at you, back there struggling to put a reconditioned engine into the rear of a bus that's thirty years old. If you really had any brains, you'd have something. You don't have anything." *Zzzzzzzzzzzz.* "Too much Henry David Thoreau for you, John, and the wisdom of Chief Runamok for you, Willie." She laughed. *Zzzzzzzzzzzz.* "Eating pickled milkweed buds. And drinking Oddball Ale. Yuck!" *Zzzzzzzzzzzzz.* "Okay, okay, so you two have got it made. Don't rub it in. Do you think I want to be in the back of the Lao Tzu's working at a computer all day checking the prices and inventories of our suppliers? How much for fifty kilos of dried sheep's penis? How much for twenty-five kilos of zizyphi semen?"

I said, "What?"

"You don't want to know. Borrrriinngggggg! I want to be out here with you and Willie figuring this all out."

Willie said, "Give me the fifteen millimeter ratchet, will you, Kemosabe?"

I gave him the wrench. To Annie, I said, "If you really want to help us you should go back to work and stay alert. Good to have somebody on the inside. You never know what you might overhear."

Zzzzzzzzzzzz. "Easy for you to say. While you're out here taking a nap in your little cabin with grasshoppers clicking outside, I have to deal with Luci. You met her. You know what she's like." *Zzzzzzzzzzzz.* "Such a bitch!"

I laughed. "Luci's a real sweetheart, I'll give you that."

"Those ears of hers, and she could use that nose for an ice cutter." *Zzzzzzzzzzzz.* "But her mouth is the worst. Not the fact that she has those little teeth and no lips, but the pushy hateful words that come out."

"Let me tell you how our business works, and maybe you'll understand why we need you to stay in place for the moment. We chip away at the edges of the truth, Annie. We get a detail here and a detail there until a pattern emerges. Historians, scientists, private investigators. We all work the same way. We all want to know. *Not knowing* what happened or how something works drives us nuts. Sometimes we luck out and tumble onto something unexpected. Sometimes we get lost in a maze of dead ends."

Willie said, "Need a flat-blade screwdriver, Dumsht."

"Dumsht?" Annie asked.

"Willie's shorthand for dumb shit, as in Chief Dumsht. Got it, Willie." I handed him the screwdriver.

Zzzzzzzzzzzzz. She said, "Not a lot of difference between Poirot and Pasteur if you look at it that way. How do you like those Ps, John? Alliteration!"

"Or between Spade and Salk. There you go."

"I know stuff like that. I'm a well-rounded person. Metaphors. Similes. I was an English major." *Zzzzzzzzzzzzz.* "There. Got the holes drilled."

"You're well-rounded all right," I said.

"Well-rounded and now I get to screw. A whole bunch of screwing. Turn you guys on down there? Getting all sweaty, are we?"

"It's a hot day."

"You'll just have to control yourselves. Personal discipline."

"Sixteen-millimeter ratchet," Willie said.

I pawed through the tool chest. "Okay, you say you want to help. Let's go through a drill, and see if we can't figure out what it was that Sharon was trying to tell me as she lay dying. First question, what if 'ther' was not the end of father? What else could it be? Give me some 'ther' words."

She said, "Leather, heather, gather, blather, lather, slather, dither, hither, father, mother."

I said, "This screwing is hard on my wrist. I wouldn't have expected that."

"Hard on your wrist?"

I ignored her. "Any of those words strike you as having possibilities?"

"Mother," she said.

"Sharon's mother is dead."

"But not her stepmother," she said. "Same t-h-e-r ending."

"I can't get a grip on the nut. Could you hold it for me?" Willie asked.

Annie said, "What *are* you guys doing down there? Listen to you! My God!"

"Okay, Janine Toogood," I said. "And your reason for including her?"

"Lao Tzu's was apparently Luci Douglas's idea, but she didn't put up the initial money. Jerry Toogood did. Sweet Janine talked him into it. I take it you're tracking with me."

"Oh, yes, I'm very much with you. You're making the case for 'gurgle, gurgle stepmother.' It was not just Sharon and Mariah's inheritance at stake, it was T.G.'s money too. Why did Luci go to Janine in the first place? She surely didn't pick her out of the telephone directory. What was their connection?"

Annie squatted beside me, shaking the cramps out of her wrist. "That I don't know. But I think it's possible that Janine might have worked in a health food store before she moved to Portland and met T.G. She's been in the store a few times with evil Luci, and she seemed to have more than a passing knowledge of what the business was all about. Where did she learn that?"

"Good question. From Luci?"

"That makes sense too, I guess."

From under the bus, Willie said, "I've got some cold water in the refrigerator."

"All that business with the nuts makes you thirsty, does it? Be right back."

When she was gone, I said to Willie, "Assume that Luci

knows the basics. She also knows Janine. She talks Janine into pitching Sugar Daddy for the bucks. T.G. can't say no to his young wife."

Willie said, "The Chinese can't run a poaching ring in the United States without the help of Americans. At a minimum people running the Lao Tzu's stores are fencing gall bladders. That asshole Tommy Hilfinger deals with the poachers. I want the gall bladder of whoever is in charge."

Annie was back with a plastic pitcher of cold water and three plastic glasses.

Looking grateful, Willie stood to stretch his legs.

Annie poured us water, admiring the pitcher as she did. "I know class when I see it. Genuine Tupperware. Wow! Nothing but the best for you two."

The cold water was good. "Tell me, Annie, where do you think Luci learned the health food business, and how long has she known Janine? If you don't know exactly, take a guess."

Annie was thirsty too. After she finished gulping down a glass of water, she wiped her mouth with the back of her arm and laughed. "Hey, hey, wait a second. You're the detectives. I just got off the boat from Hong Kong. I were to make a bet, I'd say Luci learned the health food business at Seaside. I've heard her mention the bumper cars and the turnaround at the beach and the Miss Oregon pageant. I have no idea how long she's known Janine."

"See, you never know what you can pick up if you're in the right place. I take it T.G. didn't spring for all six stores at once. Did one store do well enough to finance another five? And how long did that take?"

"I'm not sure, three or four years, I think. You two had enough?"

"I don't know about Willie, but I never get enough."

"Of water!" She gave me a reproving look and took the pitcher and glasses back into the cabin.

When she was back inside the bus, I said, "Follow the logic, Annie. Assume that T.G. was reluctant to spring for more than one store So Janine and Luci talked Sharon into kicking into the pot. That still wasn't enough, so Sharon borrowed more from Mariah."

"Why would she do that?"

"Good question. Mariah told me that Sharon had found out something about the business that was suspicious. Since it was her father's money that set up the racket in the first place, maybe she wanted to protect him from scandal."

Willie said, "Shush!"

Annie and I shushed.

Willie said, "I heard a vehicle coming up the main canyon. Then it stopped."

"A vehicle? What kind of vehicle?"

"A pickup or an S-U-V, not a car."

"Fishermen?"

He shook his head. "Unlikely. No good spots to fish down there."

"Lots of bum fishermen," I said.

"Maybe you're right," he said, and went back to work.

A few minutes later, Annie said, "Finished with the screwing. Taping is next."

Willie stood again. "Good timing. Denson and I have to jack it up and put it on stands."

Annie got her masking tape and newspapers collected, while Willie and I jacked up the rear wheels and put the axles on the stands so Willie could finish the connections underneath.

When we got on with our new chores, Annie, taping newspapers over the windows, said, "Sharon had your business card in her handbag. She was on her way to see you. She knows you do a lot of environmental work. What does that tell you?"

Willie, who had been content to let me do the talking, spoke up, "You're saying that she suspected someone at Lao Tzu's was selling bear galls to the Chinese."

"If her father had inadvertently financed the selling of bear galls, yes, that would have been motive for being discreet. How am I doing? What do you two think? The Lone Ranger and Tonto."

I was at the rear of the bus, on my back feeding Willie tools. I said, "By the way, health food stores have a reputation among the police as being used to wash drug money. Did you know that?"

Annie stood over me, legs parted, taping newspaper over the rear window. "No I didn't," she said.

I started to look up, but she gave me a glance of reprimand. "Keep your eyes on your work down there. I'm not doing my turn at Mary's."

Willie suddenly crawled out from under the bus and ran inside his cabin, returning with a pair of binoculars.

"What did you hear?" I said.

"It's what I don't hear." He started scanning the distant tree line with the binoculars.

Watching Willie, I said, "You see all the questions we need answered. Let's leave that line for a second and complete the word association drill. 'Ister' sounds pretty much like the end of sister. No mystery there."

Willie handed me the binoculars. "You take a turn, Chief. Maybe you can see something I can't. I'm certain somebody is watching us from the edge of the trees."

I adjusted the binoculars. No sooner than I got them into focus, than I wheeled and smashed Annie in the back of the knees with my forearm as hard as I could, sending her tumbling to the ground . . .

. . . as the glass shattered on the rear window of the bus.

"Shit oh dear!" Willie muttered. He ran, zigzagging, to his cabin.

On her stomach, Annie said, "My God what's going on?"

"Just stay on your stomach. Whoever's out there can't shoot what he can't see."

"Who is it?"

"I'm not sure. I saw the sunlight reflecting off the end of a telescopic sight, which is when I whacked the backs of your legs."

Willie returned with his 9mm Mauser with the Leopold and Vary scope that he used to hunt elk. Squatting at the edge of his stack of firewood, he scanned the tree line with his binoculars.

Still studying the woods through the binoculars, Willie said, "Naw. A guy like that who shoots from ambush is a total chickenshit. No way he's going to stick around and risk his own hide."

In the distance, an engine started up. The vehicle started back down the hill, the sound of its engine ever dimmer. A Toyota was it? Or something else?

28 · An early morning call

I was standing in the meadow in the wee hours of the morning taking a leak when I heard a cell phone ringing in the cabin. Not my phone. I could hear a murmuring between Annie and someone through the open window. A call at three o'clock. I walked back toward the cabin and squatted, listening.

She said, "I *like* him. Not just a little bit. A whole bunch."

I got an angle on the window so I could see her.

She looked disgusted. "Truly. Hard for you to believe maybe, you're a man. What do you know about what attracts a woman?" She scratched a boob. "Oh, come on, give me a break."

The man said something more.

Finally, annoyed, she said, "Stop! Goodbye." She hung up.

I waited a couple of seconds then coughed lightly and opened the door. Should I ignore the call or confront her? I stepped into the cabin. "Who was that?"

She rolled her eyes. "That was your pal Bill Dennis. This afternoon I left a message on his answering machine telling him he could take his job and shove it. Politely, of course. He's an okay guy. I don't have anything against him. But

Luci's been riding him, and he's pissed to the max, so he calls me, not giving a damn where I am or what I'm doing."

"I see. And you're going to do what now? Support yourself by doing exercises at Mary's?"

She laughed. "No. I think I'll pass on that. I've got some money saved up. If you two guys will have me, I'd like to hang with you until you get this figured."

"Oh?"

"I've got skills and a pretty face," she added quickly. "I can get a job when I have to. Whenever."

"You want to hang with Willie and me?" I was disbelieving.

"I had a great time working on your bus. You guys are fun. Bill had a hard time believing that. He likely thinks all females have their heart set on a Sugar Daddy driving a BMW."

"What did he say exactly?"

"Mostly four-letter words. He really went off. First time I've heard him pissed."

"You sort of did leave him in the lurch, didn't you?"

"Oh, hell, tell me. When you come down to it, the truth is that job is scut work. Anybody who can boot up a computer can do it. He'll survive. What's really got him worked up is Luci's tantrum. But it's done. I'm not going back. They might as well get used to it. You didn't answer my question."

"Your question?"

"About me hanging with you two?"

"I'll have to check with Willie."

"I figured that much. But you. How do *you* feel about it? That's what I really want to know."

I grinned wickedly. "Here, let me show you."

As we lay there, feeling grand with the first hint of dawn showing above the meadow to the east, an owl outside called, *Kee-eau! Kee-eau! Kee-eau!*

Startled, I glanced quickly at the door to make sure it was closed. But the window above the kitchen sink was open and it didn't have a screen. I hopped off the bed and closed it. Annoyed, I said, "How long has this window been open?"

"Ever since we got here. I thought we needed some fresh air. Stuffy in here."

I crawled back onto the bed, looking disconsolate. I was still haunted by my night flying experience. Here I thought the house was sealed against any intrusion by shape changing owls, if there was such a thing. Now the anxieties returned.

She said, "If you think about it, I'm very much like an owl in a way."

I sat up straight. "What?"

"Isn't an owl supposed to be able to turn its head a hundred and eighty degrees? I mean, it can sit on a branch and look directly behind it if it wants. It would take a remarkable spine to pull that off."

I didn't like talking about owls. "How are you in any way like an owl?" I snapped.

Annie studied me with curiosity. "I don't get it. You have a phobia about owls?"

"Well, yes I do. Long story. If I told you now, you'd laugh at me."

"I would?"

"Believe me."

"But I take it you will tell me sometime. A fear of owls is unusual, you have to admit."

"When I get to know you better, I'll tell you. It's a long, bizarre story. Sooner or later, you've got to know it. You have a right to know it. But not now. I don't want to have to drive you back to Portland tonight."

She smiled. "Whatever. I suppose an owl phobia is better than being a foot fetishist or you wanting me to dress up like a nurse. Here, I bet this'll take your mind off owls." She bent backwards until her spine was in a loop and her face was between her legs. Looking up at me over her stomach and breasts, she said, "I bet you've never seen a naked lady like this."

I grinned. For the moment, at least, I completely forgot about her phone call.

29 · The curious drill

I had not flown out of my skin the previous night, for which I was thankful. Even after the owl had startled me with its call and its presence was fresh in my subconscious, I had stayed put. No crazed flying. Maybe the flying was over, a thing of the past.

It was the Friday of a three-day Independence Day that lasted through Monday. The sun, having cleared the tops of the Douglas firs on the eastern end of Whorehouse Meadow, was turning to late morning yellow as I walked up to Willie's cabin and gave it a rap.

"We need to talk, Willie."

He could tell by the look on my face that this was serious. "You want to take a short hike, Chief? Better to walk while we talk."

"I think so," I said. Willie and I set off up Jump-Off Joe. As we walked with the water gurgling by our side, I told him about Annie's telephone call in the middle of the night and our short conversation at breakfast.

"You didn't hear the whole conversation while she was on the phone?"

"No. Just the tail end."

"You like her?"

"I cheerfully admit that I have to pinch myself to believe she's for real."

"You believe her?"

"I want to believe her. She's a keeper, no question. But I have to ask myself, did somebody really take a potshot at her when we were working on our bus, or was that a set-up to get us to accept to her?"

Willie frowned. He appreciated my predicament. "Chief, Chief, what's it going to hurt to let her hang with us? The worst case is that she turns out to be working for Bill Dennis. So what? To be honest, Chief, all I'm wondering at this point is how on earth does an asshole like you have all the luck?"

I grinned. "Maybe Annie Dancer is a reward for clean thinking and proper living. Did you ever think of that?"

"Clean thinking and proper living? I never thought of that in the same sentence with John Denson. The bartender at the High Country Tavern in La Grande told Jonas Knowles that Wintertime Wallace made regular visits there on Friday afternoons. That's where Jonas spotted Wintertime talking to someone in a Lao Tzu's pickup. I say we go there and wait for Wintertime ourselves. If he shows up, let's see what he does and if he's part of our story."

"Take Annie with us?"

"I don't see why not."

"Monday is the Fourth of July. Maybe there'll be fireworks," I wasn't sure whether or not we were making a mistake and I knew Willie wasn't sure either. Might have been able to see the night, but he wasn't any more certain about the motives of Annie Dancer than I was.

"What do you think?" he put in. "Postpone giving her the details until we're under way?"

I thought that made sense. "I agree. Okay to take her with us, but let's take some sensible precautions."

In view of the mystery shooter who had fired at Annie, Willie and I agreed that we needed to pack some firepower on our trip to check out the enigmatic Wintertime Wallace in La Grande—he being a mountain man and maybe dangerous. We decided to use two vehicles, Annie and I in Willie's Ford pickup, and Willie in Whitefeather Minthorn's Dodge.

The bed of Willie's pickup was covered by an aluminum canopy and contained a storage box where Willie stowed food and weapons when he went hunting. I removed the plug from my Remington automatic shotgun, giving me a full five shots, and packed that in the box. Willie had removed the rear window of his cab so Annie or I could get to the shotgun quickly in an emergency.

Willie led the way up the Columbia River. If we needed to communicate, we had cell phones. A dark gray bank of clouds lay out across the sky, and the west wind blew choppy whitecaps on the river.

With the wind at our backs, we sailed up the Columbia River gorge with Mt. Hood rising high to our right. Also on our right, we passed Multnomah Falls, at 620 feet, the second highest year-round waterfall in the United States. Then came Bonneville Dam and the wind surfers at Hood River. Then, rounding a curve to our right, we came upon The Dalles, where the evergreen forests of pine and Douglas fir gave way to the semi-arid high desert of Eastern Oregon where I had grown up. Here tan bluffs rose up from the water looking like human butts and thighs.

As we drove past the Umatilla Army Ordnance Depot, near Hermiston, Oregon, I told Annie about Willie's game warden friend and his discovery of Wintertime Wallace at the High Country Tavern in La Grande. Watching her out of the corner of my eye, I said, "So, tell me, who do you think was in the Lao Tzu's pickup at Luci's?"

"A man and a woman?"

"Right."

"My guess would be either Tommy and Luci or Bill and Vera."

"Why Bill and Vera?"

"Because Bill and Vera, uh, have a thing going on the side. Or at least that's the gossip. Might be true. Might not. Also, in the middle of being pissed, Bill wanted me to tell him what you'd found out about the case."

"He's my client. He has a right."

"But don't you think he should ask you directly, not me on the side? Either way, I suspect those are your possibilities. But I don't think you can mix and match them. Tommy and Luci or Bill and Vera. One or the other. Has to be."

"And your recommendation would be?"

"That we go to the High Country Tavern this afternoon and watch it, find out if Wintertime shows up or whoever else. What's the word you private dicks use?" She arched a playful eyebrow.

"A stakeout. Yes, we watch the place."

I thumbed the button on my cell phone, followed by the two digit code that rang Willie's number. Ahead of us, I could see Willie watching us in the rearview mirror as he answered. "I told her," I said.

"And?"

"She says either Bill and Vera, who might be having an affair, or Tommy and Luci, but not any other combination. She thinks we should watch the place this afternoon and see what happens."

"She sounds up front to me," Willie said.

Watching Annie, feeling better, I said, "I think so too. Got my fingers crossed."

"Got your fingers crossed about what?" Annie asked.

I said, "Got them crossed that we don't run into some bullshit ambush."

We found the High Country Tavern at about two o'clock in the afternoon, located in a cluttered stretch of fast food outlets including a McDonald's, an Arby's, a Taco Bell, a Burger King, and a Jack in the Box at the edge of the town. The tavern, of fairly recent vintage, had small parking lots on either side and a space in back for delivery trucks. Customers who found one lot full could circle to the rear of the tavern and check out the lot on the far side. Willie parked where he could watch the closest rear entrance with his binoculars. I parked where Annie and I could watch the second lot and the far rear entrance where the delivery trucks unloaded the beer and bags of chips, pretzels and peanuts carried by the High Country for its sports-loving patrons. Both Willie and Annie and I could also see the front entrance.

At two-thirty, a Budweiser beer truck arrived and pulled up at the loading dock. The uniformed driver went inside. Five minutes later, two men emerged from the rear of the tavern and got into the passenger's side of the truck.

At a quarter to three, Willie called. "Heads up. Wintertime Wallace just parked his Cherokee and is headed for the High Country."

"Got it," I said.

We watched the bearded Wintertime enter through the front door. Ten minutes later, we saw him emerge from the delivery entrance and get into the passenger's side of the truck. I called Willie and told him what happened.

At five minutes after three, the driver got back into the beer truck and drove away. He was the only person in the cab of the truck, which left the question of what happened to

Wintertime and the other two men who had gotten into the cab.

I called Willie with this news. "What do we do?"

Willie said, "I say we split the chore. I'll follow the beer truck. You two shoot pictures of the license plates for a couple of blocks both ways and catch up with me when you're finished."

A digital image was better than simply noting the license plate numbers because it gave us the makes and models of the vehicles that we could beam to the FBI. I drove and talked to Willie on the cell phone while Annie Dancer leaned out of the window and snapped pictures of license plates with my digital camera. We shot the plates on both sides of the street for three blocks in either direction just to make sure.

Then Willie called to say the beer truck had stopped at the Ponderosa Tavern. "This time I'll park where I can see the cab of the truck." He gave us directions to the Ponderosa.

With Annie checking the map and giving me left, right, and straight ahead directions, we headed for the Ponderosa. Just as we arrived, we saw the beer truck driving down the street.

Willie called. "Four passengers in this time. None out."

"Curious drill. We'll snap more plates. Got it."

Three blocks away we saw a dark blue Toyota pickup. Annie and I hopped out and peered inside. There was nothing on the front seat that gave any clue as to who had been driving it. She said, "It's another of the six that belong to Lao Tzu's. Impossible to say which."

The truck stopped again at Weird Bob's Tavern. Willie could not get an angle on the cab of the delivery truck. But when it pushed off and Annie and I repeated our routine with the camera, we made another charming discovery: a second Toyota pickup belonging to Lao Tzu's.

Then Willie called again. "Weird Bob's was their last stop. The truck is on its way out of town, headed down the Powder River."

I told him about the second Toyota pickup. "When we finish snapping the plates, we'll catch up."

"You think they're gathering for a Fourth of July celebration?" Willie asked.

"Fireworks coming up. Gotta be."

The beer truck, with Willie trailing at a respectful distance, stayed at a steady fifty-five miles an hour, the speed limit on the state highway that flanked the Powder River. The Powder was an east-flowing stream swollen from recent rains—with more rain on the way—that emptied into the Snake River just above Hells Canyon in Idaho.

The speed of the cautious driver gave Annie and me an opportunity to catch up. When we did, Willie passed the beer truck so the driver wouldn't think he was being followed. Annie and I stayed at least two curves behind.

When the truck pulled into the Saddleback Tavern, Willie, watching in his rearview mirror, told us to pull off the road. "You two stay put. I'll watch the truck with my binoculars. We'll see if they're loading or unloading passengers."

We waited.

Five minutes later, Willie called. "With the driver serving as a lookout, twenty-three people piled out of the truck and went into the back of the tavern, laughing and having a good time. I say again, twenty-three. They must have been packed in there what with kegs and cases of beer. From my angle, I could only count legs, not see entire bodies. There were two women among them. Do you know what's on the side of the hill above the tavern?"

"Don't have the foggiest," I said.

"The old Saddleback Gold Mine. It went out of business eighty or ninety years ago, something like that. For safety reasons, the entrance has been sealed for years. It was a deep shaft mine with lateral branches. Don't you find that interesting?"

"I suppose," I said. "So what do we do now?"

"You two can't take a chance on being seen by whoever it is who drove the Lao Tzu's pickups. Best bet is for you to drive on by and watch the beer truck from my angle. You'll find a hunting road just past the second curve where you can get off the highway and hide your pickup."

"Stay out of sight," I said.

"Right. I'll go inside and talk to the owners, Shorty and Ethel Townsend, who also own the People's gas station and convenience store next to the tavern. Or did. Judging from what we've seen so far, it's my bet that they've sold it."

Annie Dancer and I drove by the Saddleback Tavern. Just past the second curve, as Willie had said, we found the hunter's road. I drove a hundred yards up the road and killed the engine. The sun was setting over the pine-covered Blue Mountains upriver to the west and the day was cooling fast. Annie and I, taking my binoculars, digital camera, and telephoto lens, hiked back in the direction of the tavern. A wind kicked up, lowing eerily in the tops of the pines.

Fifteen minutes later we got to the top of the ridge just west of the Saddleback Tavern and People's gas station. We settled in with our binoculars and camera. A few minutes later, Willie called on his cell phone.

"I'm sitting on a stall in the john, so I have to talk fast.

There's a small kitchen back here where they microwave hot dogs and frozen hamburgers. Nobody in there. There's also small storage room and cooler where they keep supplies and the beer. Nobody in there either. Where the hell did those people go?"

I didn't know what was going on, but it couldn't be good. "Haul ass, Willie. Now!"

"I'm on my way, Chief."

I hung up and told Annie what Willie had found—or had not found.

The sun settled over the mountains and it began to turn downright cold while we waited nervously for Willie.

Leaning against me for warmth, Annie said, "People hitching rides in a beer truck from taverns scattered over half of La Grande. Twenty-three people go inside the Saddleback tavern, and Willie says they're nowhere to be found. What's going on down there?"

"Jeez, it's cold," I said.

"You don't have any idea, do you? What we need is Sherlock Holmes or Columbo. They'd know what to make of this." She snapped her fingers twice. "No problem."

I said, "Those people haven't disappeared. We just don't know where they are. There's a difference."

She rolled her eyes. "Right."

In ten minutes that seemed like ten hours later, I heard Willie scrambling lightly up the slope toward our place on the ridge.

Below us, Willie called softly, "Chief! Chief!"

"Up here, Willie!"

A minute later, he was with us, squatting, catching his breath.

"So tell us," I said.

"Before I went to the back to take a leak, I had a Coke at the bar, where I asked the bartender about Shorty and Ethel

Townsend, who used to own the place. He says they sold out
and bought themselves a retirement house in Arizona. I knew
Shorty and Ethel. After thirty years of running this tavern, it
was their life. Hard to believe they'd sell out for anything less
than a bundle. They never did a whole lot of business except
during fishing season. During the winter there's hardly any
traffic at all on that highway."

"Bringing up the question, why somebody would pay too
much for it. What now?"

"There's a fisherman's place about two miles north of here,
the Chief Joseph Motel. There's a little café next door. I say
you and Annie take a couple of rooms at the Chief Joseph,
one for yourselves and one for me in case I want to take a
catnap later on, and see if you can find something on the
internet about the Saddleback Mine. In the meantime, I'll
keep an eye on this place in case there's more activity."

"Think I should call Dunsmuir in Portland? He seemed like
an okay guy to me, and I told him I'd let him know if we
found anything he should know."

"Depending on what you find out about the Saddleback
Mine. I bet the FBI could sort through those license plates in
a few minutes. But talk to me first."

"Got it, Willie." A dark bank of clouds obscured the moon
and stars. I said, "We've got rain on its way. You're going to
get wet."

"I've been wet before. I've got my poncho."

"Plus you're nursing a warming grudge."

He grinned. "That too. Get out of here. You've got work
to do."

Annie Dancer and I picked our way down the hill, slipping
and stumbling in the dark. Before we got to the pickup we
caught a gust of piney wind and in the distance we could hear
the gathering rush of rain as it moved through the tops of

the trees. Bob Dylan's song lingered in my memory: *Well, it's a hard rain's a-gonna fall.*

By the time Annie Dancer and I got settled into our room at the Chief Joseph Motel, Bob Dylan's prediction had surely come true. While Willie hunkered on the ridge under his poncho in the rain, we got cheeseburgers and cups of coffee from the café next door and returned to our warm motel unit.

Annie plugged in her notebook and set to work seeing what she could find about the Saddleback Mine. I sat with my coffee and watched the rain lashing the surface of the Powder River that reflected the lights of the motel.

Ten minutes later, Annie said, "I've got what we want, I think, from the U.S. Office of Surface Mining, which keeps a map of all recorded mining claims and their locations."

"And?"

"In 1889, one George Coontz discovered a vein of gold in Saddleback Mountain. He registered his claim with the government in August of that year. Two years later, the Saddleback Mountain Mining Company began work on a deep shaft mine. The mine has one main shaft that goes nearly three hundred yards deep, with two lateral shafts running south, two running north, and one running east at a downhill angle toward the river."

"Toward the current Saddleback Tavern."

"It sounds that way. Hard to be sure. There are no maps of the shafts, although those are available by snail mail for a fee. The mine eventually ran out of profitable amounts of gold and closed down in 1921. The exterior buildings burned in a forest fire in 1947. In 1962, the entrances to the shafts were sealed for safety reasons. Three different mining corporations have subsequently gotten permission to check out the veins worked by the original company to see if newer technology would render them profitable."

"And the last time that happened?"

"The Big Sky Mining Corporation checked it out five years ago. Its engineers spent ten months exploring the shafts to see if any of them were potentially profitable. Big Sky then withdrew, saying it had found only 'trace amounts' of gold."

" 'Exploring' the shafts. Nice word. Which means they could have extended a shaft if they had wanted. What happened to Big Sky?"

Annie grinned. "Another database maintained by the Office of Surface Mining keeps tabs on active and inactive mining companies. Big Sky Mining declared itself inactive three months after withdrawing from Saddleback Mine."

"At just about the time somebody paid too much for the Saddleback Tavern."

Annie looked from her computer. "Seems that way."

"Can you beam those license plate images from the camera into a single file that can be downloaded?"

"No problem," she said.

While Annie moved the images onto one file, I called Willie and told him what Annie had found. "Under the circumstances, I think the smart thing to do is pass what we've found on to the FBI."

"I agree, Chief. Do it."

I hung up and gave Dunsmuir's card to Annie. "He said he'd be notified immediately of any important e-mail incoming."

"You want me to beam him the license plate images? I can do that."

"I'll write a cover note." I switched seats with Annie and wrote Dunsmuir a short note telling him about the action at the High Country and the Saddleback Tavern plus what Annie learned about the Saddleback Mine and giving him my cell phone number. When I finished, I turned the computer back to her. "We'll see if all this means anything to the FBI."

When Annie finished beaming the note and license plate images to Dunsmuir, she joined me at the window looking down on the river, which was swelling by the minute.

"What do you think?" she said.

"I think my phone will likely be beeping in a few minutes."

I had hardly got the sentence out of my mouth when it did just that.

31 · *Burdens of the potato chip man*

The morning was a leaden gloom beneath the low bank of black clouds that stretched from the Blue Mountains in the mist to the pine forest to the west of the river. The hard rain continued without respite. At nine o'clock, Dunsmuir called saying it was okay for us to join him and Willie on the top of the ridge.

Willie, who had spent the rainy night watching the tavern, didn't look a whole lot worse for his ordeal. In fact, he seemed downright passive. It was somehow reassuring to know that the Federal Bureau of Investigation had not seen fit, out of some kind of twisted pride, to establish its command at a less advantageous position just because a fifty-something Cowlitz Indian had selected the best spot. Neither had they seen fit to kick the Injun out, possibly because he had a way about him that commanded respect, and even they were not so dumb as to deprive themselves of somebody who could help them out.

Annie and I were given dark blue FBI rain slickers with hoods so we wouldn't be soaked. The slickers also served as a kind of jersey, identifying us as members of Team FBI, as opposed to our still mysterious adversary. The near freezing rain rattled against our slickers like angry BBs.

Gregory Dunsmuir had earphones under his hood and a mike around his neck so he had both hands free to blow his stuffy nose and drink coffee while he deployed his agents. When he had his first free moment, Dunsmuir offered his hand. "I've thanked your partner already. I owe you as well, Mr. Denson. The two of you have managed to do what we couldn't after years of investigation."

"Lucked out," Willie said.

Dunsmuir said, "I thought we were getting close. And I'll say it, won't kill me: I thought you two were an accident waiting to happen. We're waiting for all our quarry to get into place before we do anything. You want to take a look?" He handed me a pair of FBI binoculars that were far better than my own.

I adjusted the binoculars. I could see what had been the entrance of the mine at the base of a granite rimrock directly above the tavern and gas station. A no trespassing sign posted by the State of Oregon said entrance into the mine was prohibited. Two other signs simply said, in large, red letters, NO TRESPASSING, DANGER. Four agents in rain slickers squatted on both sides of the entrance, their backs turned against the pelting rain.

Listening to a voice in his earphones, Dunsmuir glanced at his wristwatch. "Got it." To Annie and me, he said, "A Wonder Bread truck showed up with a load of a dozen passengers shortly after nine. Now we've got a Lay's potato chip truck on its way. The driver of the Wonder Bread truck seemed to know when a vehicle was approaching from east or west, so on a hunch I had a single vehicle with a photographer make a reconnaissance run. Look at what I found." He showed me two photographs encased in plastic to protect them from the rain. I glanced at the first and gave it to Annie.

The photographs were of cameras mounted at the tops of

poles that delivered telephone, cable and power to the areas. "Security cameras!"

He said, "One camera monitors traffic from the north. The other records the traffic from the south. Earlier, I sent an agent inside to have a cup of coffee. He tells us that the bartender appears to be watching a monitor tucked under the end of the bar. If a vehicle is coming, he apparently beeps the truck driver, who halts any unloading until the vehicle is past."

As he said that, the Lay's potato chips truck turned off the road and parked at the loading entrance at the rear of the tavern. We watched through our FBI binoculars as a uniformed Lay's driver got out and strolled inside the tavern. A customer drove a Honda Civic into the People's station. A young man pumped the fuel, self-service gasoline stations being illegal in Oregon.

When the Civic was on its way, six men hopped out of the back of the Lay's truck and went into the back of the tavern. The driver went to the rear of the truck and, with the help of the young man from the People's station who had pumped gas, began carrying large heavy boxes from the rear of the truck.

"Pretty heavy boxes for potato chips," Dunsmuir said.

"Some potato chips," I said. "I'm betting steaks, hamburger and hot dogs for the grill and tubs of potato salad for a good, old-fashioned Fourth of July picnic. Maybe jars of pickles. Mustard. Ketchup. Barbecue sauce."

Dunsmuir looked grim. "That's what we're thinking. If we were going to choose our holiday gathering to bust, this would be it."

The gas station attendant jogged back to the station. Thirty seconds later a Dodge Caravan rounded the curve and pulled into the station. The attendant, chatting amiably with the driver as he squeezed a zit on his face, filled the minivan with gas. He waited until the Caravan had left the station and disappeared around the curve before he went to the back of the tavern. He and the Lay's driver resumed their duties of unloading boxes.

When they were finished, the Lay's driver got back into his truck and drove back up river toward La Grande. I could see that he was being tailed, at a discreet distance, by a helicopter.

"We'll give them until one o'clock to finish their deliveries then we'll make our move," Dunsmuir said.

" 'Them'? 'They' being?"

He said, "By such research as we could conduct this morning, we know that the same people who owned Big Sky Mining paid Shorty and Ethel Townsend four hundred thousand dollars for their tavern and gas station. We think Big Sky used its ten months of 'explorations' to extend the lower east lateral tunnel to a point directly under the back of the Saddleback Tavern. They've been using both genuine and bogus beer and grocery trucks to ferry supplies and people back and forth."

"Bear poachers did all that?"

Dunsmuir ignored my question. "Our warrant came through an hour ago. We have a choice here. We can be all polite and civilized and give a knock, knock on the trapdoor in the back of the tavern that leads to the tunnel and have a florist deliver roses along with the warrant. Or we can fire tear gas into the tunnel and down the main shaft and see if we can flush 'em out."

"I believe I'd go for the latter," I said.

"A sensible decision, but you don't work for the FBI. We're perfect, see. Never mind that the morons down there are maniacs, the drill is that if anything goes wrong, we'll be at fault. It's a lose, lose situation. If what we do works, and we arrest people without anybody getting hurt, well, we were only doing our job. Remember that woman customs agent in Washington state who caught the Al Qaeda people on their way into the

U.S. to blow up the Los Angeles Airport? She wasn't just good at her job, she was an ace. The torment she spared the country is beyond measure. But does anybody remember her name? Do you know it?"

I shook my head.

Dunsmuir glared bitterly down at the tavern. "On top of all that, I've got the lives of my people to consider. But who the hell wants his career destroyed over another Waco or Ruby Ridge?"

At the mention of Ruby Ridge, Willie said, "You still haven't told us who those people are and what they're doing."

Dunsmuir said, "Somewhere in that mountain is what those assholes call a 'Freedom Armory,' paid for by, among many ways, computer theft, selling stolen weapons on the international market, growing marijuana, and selling bear galls to the Chinese."

I glanced at Willie. "You suspect this?"

"The thought occurred to me. I didn't have any idea about the other stuff, just the trade in bear galls."

"What's the name of the militia?" I asked Dunsmuir.

"The Timothy McVeigh Brigade," he said.

I closed my eyes. "The 'patriots' lately given to blowing up American mosques and mailing anthrax to Islamic governments."

"The very same."

I said, "What do you think they have in that armory of theirs?"

"Enough C-4 plastic explosive to blow up half the mountain. Enough M16s to equip a battalion of marines. That's not to mention hand grenades, grenade launchers, machine guns, shoulder-launched anti-tank and anti-helicopter gunship rockets. You want a full list or will that about do it?"

"Where did they get all that stuff?"

"Their followers enlisted in the army and marines and stole

it from various armories, from Fort Dix, Fort Lewis, Fort Bragg, you name it. That's how we know what they have. They used to have their 'headquarters' and armory in northern Idaho until they got word we were about to bust them about five years ago. They suddenly vanished, and we've been looking for them ever since. If you thought I was being mysterious when you visited me in Portland, this is why. This is what we've been after."

32 · Response of proper patriots

The Timothy McVeigh Brigade ran the their shuttle of Wonder Bread and Lay's potato chips trucks all morning. It now fell upon Special Agent Gregory Dunsmuir, who in another incarnation might have been a marine captain at Guadalcanal or Iwo Jima, to direct the action at Saddleback Mountain. He chose to remain on our ridge where he could get a panoramic view of the action from the tavern and gas station facing the highway and the river to the west to the entrance of the mine at the base of the rimrock above it to the east.

We had delivered the McVeigh Brigade. For that Dunsmuir was grateful. But as to what would happen next, he was tight-lipped. His career was likely on the line, and he had things to think about other than being a charming host.

At ten o'clock, waiting for Dunsmuir to give us some sort of cue as to what would happen next, we heard the distant clatter of helicopter blades coming out of the Blues. Licking his lips, rain lashing against his face, Dunsmuir said, mildly, "Those would be four Apache attack helicopters sent down from Fort Lewis last night on flatbed trucks. A battalion of Rangers from Fort Lewis were flown down from McChord Air Force Base."

"Rangers?" I said.

"In the good bad old days before September 11, we had to burp domestic terrorists like this so the administration wouldn't be embarrassed on CNN. Can't forget that there are voters out there who are sympathetic to their cause. Now, at least with respect to militiamen who have stockpiled weapons and explosives, things have changed. Forget the Oregon National Guard. We can call in Rangers."

He stopped talking momentarily as the choppers put down somewhere behind us and the clatter of their blades wound down. "Bottom line is that the mass media cannot abide it when something goes right. *Borrrrrring!* Somebody has to screw up in order for them to score decent Nielsens. Without fault, there is no drama. No drama, no Nielsens. No Nielsens, no money. The media are money-making machines fueled by fault." He looked momentarily forlorn. "And yet, we keep trying. Dumb."

"So what's the drill?" I asked.

"When the delivery trucks are parked in La Grande, and the Rangers are in place, we'll deliver the search warrant and say, 'Pretty please let us into your secret underground compound where you're stashing all those illegal weapons. We would like it so very much if you would come out so we can have a nice chat. We've got hot coffee and glazed donuts, plus you can smoke 'em if you've got 'em.' That's the ritual, demanded of us by the ACLU and the fault finders. If the pricks resist or fire on us, I call in the Rangers, commanded by one Major Darryl Williams."

"Major Williams. I see. And he being where?"

"Getting his troops into place, briefing his commanders, and waiting for me to give the word for them to kick butts and take names. The Rangers are tired of training all the time and listening to NCOs tell them what it was like in Afghanistan. They want a little action."

We fell silent, watching the tavern below us. The rain continued to fall.

At length, Dunsmuir said, "We think they've most likely extended the bottom, southern shaft to the rear of the tavern. We have no idea what tunnels they might have dug in case of an emergency."

"Your hope being?"

"Our fantasy is that we will find the trapdoor in back and go through the ritual, and they'll come out like amiable chaps. They'll most likely tell us to fuck off, and we'll be forced to fire tear gas down the tunnel to flush them out. I hesitate to add that we hope nobody gets hurt."

At eleven o'clock, the state police choppers in La Grande reported that the delivery trucks were parked in their respective lots. There was no activity to be seen. The shuttle was apparently finished for the day.

At one o'clock, after a two-hour hiatus in which no more trucks left La Grande, Dunsmuir, chewing on his lower lip, gave the go-head into the microphone attached to his neck. "Let's do it. Go." He glanced at Willie and me. "Well, there it is. No turning back."

A battered pickup truck pulled into the lot from the tavern. A sloppy-looking man dressed in dirty coveralls hurried inside the tavern.

Watching him, Dunsmuir said, "He's ours." Licking his lips, he waited intently. Then he said, "Bartender quiet. Go." To the Ranger commander, he said, "Our people are on their way in, Major. Stand by."

A minute later vans rounded the bends from the north and south, six in all, and began pulling into the parking lot of the tavern both from the north and from the south. FBI agents in their blue rain slickers got out and ran into the tavern.

Watching this, Dunsmuir sighed nervously. He waited, then said, "Okay. Do it. I don't want anybody hurt. Do not, I say again, do not enter that tunnel without my explicit permission. Let me know." He went back to chewing on his lower lip. The longer he waited, the more punishment his lip took.

Listening to the progress reported by his people, he said, "They've found the trapdoor and announced the search warrant. They've asked the militiamen to assemble peacefully in the tavern."

It was hard not to laugh at that. I said, "That's like expecting a teenager to use a condom. These guys go to bed every night pulling their peepees at the thought of heroic battle."

Dunsmuir held up his hand again, listening intently. "Tell them to come out or tear gas is next."

The militiamen's July Fourth weekend had been rudely interrupted; what was a proper patriot to do?

"Oh, they did? I see. In the ear. How rude!" He tapped another button on the remote that switched signals coming into his head. "Major Williams, you're on. Go for it." To us, he said, "We've been told to fuck ourselves in the ear. We'll see."

Below us, the Saddleback Tavern went up in a shocking explosion. At the base of the rimrock above the tavern, automatic weapons began chattering.

Behind us, just over the ridge: the whacking of helicopter blades.

Dunsmuir shouted, "They've blown up the tavern, Major."

As he said that, I could see that the FBI agents at the upper entrance were down.

Four Apache attack helicopters clattered overhead, traveling abreast.

Truckloads of Ranger troops rounded the bend.

From the base of the rimrock, something white and slender shot up toward the nearest Apache.

Near the Apache, a burst of silver.

The Apache, having diverted the Stinger with a burst of aluminum chaff, opened fire with a modern Gatling that made a horrific *zooommmmmmmmmm* sound, evaporating the militiaman who had fired the missile. Near the smoking ruins of the tavern, the Rangers piled out of the trucks and started up Saddleback Mountain. Farther up, the Apaches circled, machine gunners firing at will from the open bays at fleeing militiamen.

Dunsmuir yelled into his microphone. "Give it to the sons of bitches, Major. I want them all. Every damned one of them. Do not let them escape. Do not!" He smiled grimly at the major's reply.

As more Rangers joined the action, Dunsmuir lapsed into nervous silence. The Apaches continued to strafe the militiamen with Gatling and machine guns. The militiamen, big talkers in the beginning, soon proved themselves disorganized and frantic under the assault of trained professionals. They ran about in confusion, shouting and firing their assault rifles at phantom targets. From our vantage point on the ridge, the scene below looked like the filming of a movie directly jointly by Salvador Dalí and Sam Peckinpah.

After a half hour of shouting and chattering of weapons, the firing subsided. The militiamen of the Timothy McVeigh Brigade, having heroically blown up FBI agents along with the Saddleback Tavern, dubiously proving the size of their balls if not their brains, surrendered their bodies in lieu of sacrificing their lives.

Annie, Willie and I joined Dunsmuir and his colleagues hurrying down the steep slope to find out if any of their agents had been killed or wounded and to see what was inside of Saddleback Mountain. The cold rain continued to pelt our slickers. As I slipped and slid on the mud and wet rocks, I wondered which among the militiamen, aside from Tommy Hilfinger, were from Lao Tzu's.

33 · Death of a general

We waited grimly for Gregory Dunsmuir and his people to search the remains of the Saddleback Tavern for the bodies of eight of their colleagues who had been in the tavern when the militiamen blew it up. A separate detail scoured the ruins for the entrance of the tunnel into the abandoned gold mine. The hard rain helped somewhat, quickly dampening the smoldering ruins. After a fifteen-minute wait, the tunnel detail found a trapdoor under what had been the refrigerated room that kept the beer cold.

After instructing his subordinates on the dangers of suicidal militiamen who might have stayed behind to make a heroic gesture, Dunsmuir strolled over to Annie, Willie and me. "You three are welcome to come inside, but not until we secure it and make sure it's safe. We don't want any lethal surprises. Also once you get inside, you are not to touch anything. This is a crime scene."

"Got it," I said.

"We'll be careful," Willie added.

The Rangers were still searching the nearby hills for escaping militiamen, so we got into the backs of their trucks to stay out of the rain while we waited for the underground compound to be secured. We drank coffee and waited.

At length, one of Dunsmuir's agents told us the area was clear, and we followed him to the entrance of the tunnel in the burned rubble. He led us down a ladder and into the shaft leading north into the base of Saddleback Mountain. After about fifty yards, we entered the tunnel that had been abandoned seventy years earlier. We continued another hundred yards until we came to an open door. We knew immediately this was it.

Annie went in first and made a noise in her throat.

Willie went next and made a clicking sound with his tongue.

I went last. And saw him slumped in a chair in camouflage fatigues, the bottoms of which were bloused airborne style into combat boots. He had inserted a .45 Colt pistol into his mouth and pulled the trigger. The back of his head was blown out. He had been wearing a black beret when he had shot himself, and the blood-stained beret lay nearly ten feet behind him. The Colt automatic lay on the parquet floor of the room in a pool of blood.

Dunsmuir, who was standing above him, looking down, said, "He's got three stars on his shoulders. A lieutenant general. Commander of the Timothy McVeigh Brigade."

"Lieutenant General Jerry Toogood?"

Dunsmuir gestured to the walls with his hand. "Take a look at the photographs. The walls were obviously covered with photographs before we showed up. Only General Toogood's and a few others are left." His "general" dripped with sarcasm.

"I wonder if he predicted stormy weather for today," I said.

Dunsmuir smiled weakly.

"No damn wonder he wanted to know what was being found in the investigation into the murder of his daughters." I perused the photographs that remained on the wall. In one, Toogood, wearing his jaunty beret and combat gear, reviewed the troops. In a second, Toogood fired a rocket from a shoulder tube. In a third, the general blazed away with an assault rifle.

As I studied the photographs, Dunsmuir said, "The arsenal is contained in three separate rooms adjoining this. We found everything we expected and more—enough to launch a war against a lot of Third World countries. There's also a kitchen down here. The power generator is located in a separate room higher up so it could be vented but not heard. An incredible set-up."

The photographs were stunning. If we had found photographs of Tom Brokaw or Peter Jennings in combat drag, it wouldn't have been any more shocking. I said, "Who else was in here, do you think?"

"Luci Douglas and Tommy Hilfinger without a doubt. We've had our eye on them for months. You and Ms. Dancer shot photographs of two Lao Tzu's pickups near the shuttle sites in La Grande. Assume they drove one and General Toogood here drove the other."

"Alone?"

Dunsmuir shook his head. "He could have, but we don't think so."

"With whom? Bill Dennis?"

"That seems most likely. Hard to say. We'll eventually find out. These shits might have made off with their incriminating photographs, but you can't tell me they wore gloves all the time. There have to be fingerprints all over the place. And I would hate to calculate the odds of any them escaping Major Williams and his men. They've got choppers. The state police has blocked off the roads. We're bringing in dogs. We'll get 'em."

I frowned. "I've always liked Bill Dennis. He's a good guy. Are you sure it's him?"

Dunsmuir nudged Toogood's corpse with his toe. "In this

business, I've learned never to be surprised by secrets people keep. Everybody thought the weatherman here was a good guy too. He was supposed to be the highest paid local weatherman in the country. And who does he turn out to be?"

"Jerry Toobad," I said.

To Annie, Dunsmuir said, "How can you stand hanging with this man, a good-looking young woman like you?"

Annie gave him a wry grin. "It's not always easy."

I said to Dunsmuir, "When I talked to T.G. after Mariah's alleged suicide, he seemed genuinely distraught. Do you believe he ordered the murder of his own daughters because they had found out he was a militia general? I find that hard to believe."

Dunsmuir nodded. "Doesn't figure. I agree."

"Here's something else that's hard to figure. What on earth would motivate somebody like Jerry Toogood to join the Timothy McVeigh Brigade in the first place? If I'm right, the profile of most of those guys is that they're losers or wanna-be soldiers. Tommy Hilfinger, for example. Tim McVeigh himself served in the Gulf War. They hate Jews, blacks, and almost everything foreign and all religions except Christianity. It's an 'us versus them' kind of thing. T.G. was educated, articulate, warm, an attractive television personality with a huge following. Why would he be a lieutenant general in the Timothy McVeigh Brigade?"

Dunsmuir said, "Curious, I agree. Doesn't fit the profile. If it wasn't for all the photographs of him reviewing the troops and firing his M16, I wouldn't believe it for a second. There has to be a reason."

34 • Ms. Styx has her way

In the night, I heard it. A bump. Or rather, heard it early in the morning. Woke me up.

Annie heard it too. Beside me, she said, "Did you hear that?"

Warm she was, and she smelled so damned good. I heard footsteps crunch, crunching on the gravel parking lot in front of the units, which faced the river.

Another bump. The sound was coming from the motel unit next to us in the direction of the office and café.

Reluctantly, I got out of bed and pulled on my Wranglers.

I opened the venetian blinds on the windows facing the Powder. Above the tops of the pine trees down river, a glowing sliver of orange. The rain storm and had passed, and the horizon was a grand cerulean blue.

Another bump in the unit next over, the end unit.

Annie also popped out of bed and began pulling on her jeans.

A key in the lock of the door.

Before Annie or I could do anything more, the door flew open with a horrific bang as the knob bounced against the wall.

And there stood Tommy Hilfinger in a black beret and combat fatigues soaked in mud and blood. He was pointing an M16 at us, held at hip level. Or should I say Capt. Tommy Hilfinger, for he had double-silver bars of a captain on the lapels of his shirt. He stepped aside to make room for Col. Luci Douglas, her wet fatigues soaked in mud, but not blood. They were like demented figures from an unfunny opera, all bedecked in their military gear. Lethal. Crazy. All of that and more.

"Had to have Tommy take care of the rest of the people in this place so we could have a little peace and quiet. A question of means and ends. What good were they in the long run?" When Luci talked, her thin little lips, bearing too much lipstick in an effort to make them look larger, moved like two hyperactive, evil worms.

Annie's mouth dropped. "You murdered the other people here?"

Luci shrugged. Her scarlet, malevolent slit said, "There was only the manager and his wife plus fishermen in two other units. They didn't have any brains or they'd have known it was going to rain this weekend."

"No fishing when the water is high and dirty," Hilfinger added.

"Wrong place. Wrong time," Luci said. "Which brings us back to you, Mr. Denson. I told you something about me that day when you came nosing around my store. You obviously didn't listen. What did I tell you?"

"Told me to beat it."

"I told you to lay off your investigation. I told you that I was smarter than other people. Certainly smarter than you. I do not lose. I say again, I do not lose. Ever. I win. I get my way. And when I am challenged, I make sure that person never forgets who is the smartest and who prevails. It is me. Always. People do what I tell them to do. You didn't."

"I see. So you're going to prove your point by gunning us down. A sport on top of everything else."

She smiled grimly. "Now that wouldn't be any fun, would it? Simply shoot you and the fun would be over just like that." She snapped her fingers. "You wouldn't get an opportunity to regret challenging somebody smarter than you are. If you want to die now, challenge me again, and Tommy will blow you in half. I propose to give you a chance to live. And to regret. In your regret is my victory." She stepped back. "Okay, the two of you outside."

"Okay to finish dressing?"

"You won't need shoes or shirts where you're going. Out!"

We did what we were told, followed by Tommy Hilfinger and his M16. I was in my jeans, Annie in her jeans and bra. The air was cold and damp.

"Go to the dock around back."

As I stepped outside in the bracing air, I thought I saw movement in one of Lao Tzu's blue pickups. Then nothing.

The motel was located on a promontory around which flowed a narrow, deep bend in the river, so that the current was a few feet from the docks. When we got to the dock, I saw that all but one of the boats that had been there the previous night were gone. There remained an aluminum drift boat. The river, at flood stage, was within inches of the dock.

Luci looked at me with her cold, off-gray eyes. When she talked, I saw flashes of rodent teeth. "Turn around, both of you." she said. "Hands behind your backs."

We did as we were told.

Tommy Hilfinger tied our four hands together, lashing us back to back.

"Get into the drift boat."

We did. And we waited while Hilfinger tied our feet together, then lashed them to the middle seat of the boat.

"It is important for you to acknowledge that I am smarter

than you. I know what is best for you. I am always right. I always win. Tell me who won, Mr. Denson. Perhaps I'll have mercy."

I said, "Who killed Sharon and Mariah Toogood?"

The slit that masqueraded as her mouth said, "You think you're going to solve your stupid mystery just minutes before you die?"

"What's for you to lose?"

She smiled crookedly. "You think Tommy or I killed the stupid bitches? All I have to say, Mr. Denson, is that you are some kind of pathetic detective. Maximum dumb."

"Not so dumb as to figure that if you're about to drown me, you don't have any reason not to admit murdering the sisters. That means somebody else did."

Evenly, she said, "It means no such thing. Tommy and I might have murdered them or it might have been somebody else. The victory is in letting you take that mountain water into your lungs having been beaten by Luci Douglas and with your mystery unresolved. Such frustration! Do it, Tommy!"

Hilfinger fired several rounds into the bottom of the drift boat and used both feet to push us into the current.

A cheerful Luci called after us, "The river here makes a dogleg right through rocks, then you come to the fun stuff. It must be really something after a rainstorm like we've had the past couple of days."

Taking on water from the bullet holes, we were propelled downstream by the current that increased its speed, if that was possible, after it passed by the Chief Joseph Motel.

Luci Douglas, enjoying her triumph, watched us from the dock along with the enthusiastic Tommy Hilfinger. He had joined the FBI in battle and now he was retreating to regroup. For him, all this violence had been a dream come true.

Then two quick, echoing reports from a high-powered rifle sent Luci and Tommy pitching forward into the swollen river.

Their murderer, taking no chances, had blasted them in the back.

It took a second for me to comprehend what had happened. I said, "I thought I saw someone in the pickup when we stepped outside."

"Someone ducking down," Annie said. "So did I."

We drifted in silence for a half a minute. Luci and Tommy had sought us out with intent to kill. Whoever had murdered them had taken no chances that something could go wrong or that we might escape.

I said to Annie, soft against my back, "If we survive the run down the Powder, we emerge in the Snake River just above the upper end of Hells Canyon. It's seventy miles along, a couple of miles wide, and at its deepest, from rim to river, a little more than a mile deep. Willie says his Nez Perce friends have some fascinating creation myths likening it to female anatomy."

"I bet."

"A place where one can easily imagine epic birthing. Do you know your Greek mythology?"

"A little."

I said, "Styx is the personification of the river that winds nine times around the underworld. As a vile, treacherous stream, it is a kind of moat. If ever there was a Styx, it is Luci Douglas."

"Ahh, I see. We ride the River Styx to Hells Canyon," she said.

"No reason to suspect Luci was the human Styx when I met her in the store that day. She just came off as an odious bitch."

Annie made a noise. "But now you know."

"Now I've found out. Bound, we drift toward the underworld, a nightmare of the ancient world. A classic ending. Two doughty and determined travelers are we, floating in a stream of venom."

35 · In the current

I heard shouting and the honking of a horn. I looked up, and on the highway flanking Powder River was Willie Sees the Night driving Whitefeather Minthorn's pickup with reckless abandon. "Denson, Denson! Annie, Annie!"

Never mind that Willie couldn't hear me, I shouted at him, "Willie, you wonderful son of a bitch. I love you. Do it! Do it! Do it! Do your coyote thing!" The question was what could Willie possibly do? Already the cold water was working its way up our feet. He could drive ahead and get out and try to swim out to pull us back, but we would likely slide under the water and drown before he could do that.

"There's something I have to tell you," Annie said.

I could feel the cold water moving toward my ankles. "Better make it fast."

"When Dunsmuir found out that Tommy Hilfinger was a regular at Mary's, he planted special agent Alice Harkenrider there as a dancer. She was detailed to come onto Hilfinger to see what she could learn. Talk about a sick assignment! Fat Slob took the bait like a shark."

"Say again?"

"Nobody murders an FBI agent and gets away with it. The

Portland police agreed to delay arresting Hilfinger until we figured the poaching connection to the Timothy McVeigh Brigade. First things first."

"So the FBI decided to try it again with Special Agent Annie Dancer. Sweet move." The water was well up on my ankles.

Annie said, "I asked Dunsmuir to hold off on telling you because I wanted to do it myself."

On the highway beside us, Willie, shouting something I couldn't hear, waved his hand wildly in a circle above the cab of the pickup. What did that mean?

I could feel Annie twisting to get a better look. She said, "Helicopters maybe."

"They're likely still in the area. If he called Dunsmuir, that's possible." My head snapped, as the drift boat bounced off a rock.

Annie said, "I was prohibited from taking the assignment as far as Alice did. No going home with the murderous bastard. Hear that?"

I did. Helicopter blades in the distance. "And how was it that you were the lucky female who got picked?"

"All special agents have special attributes listed in a computer database."

"Young. Slender. Good looking. Double-jointed." Our drift boat was about a third full of water.

"That was for Mary's, Hilfinger bait. I had the skills and training in accounting useful to score the job at Lao Tzu's. The bureau wrote and documented the Hong Kong legend."

We swept into a raging, deafening chute of white water.

As we whipped from side to side, the water was butt high, six inches from the gunwale of the drift boat. We bounced off another rock, then another.

The sound of the helicopter, while still distant, was getting louder.

"We're sinking," she said. I read her lips. "Chopper have a chance?"

I shook my head. The water was like ice as it enveloped my genitals.

In the pickup, pointing in the direction of the chopper, Willie lay on his horn without stopping.

The helicopter was closing fast.

"Boy meets girl. Boy likes girl," I said slowly and loudly. "Thank you."

The rump-deep cold water was turning my testicles to raisins.

"Let me try something." Annie twisted. "Try to scrunch down and pull your hands up behind your back."

I saw what she was trying to do. I did my best.

"Not far enough." She had managed to contort herself into a bizarre angle, even for someone who was double-jointed.

"That's as much as I can manage," I said.

Her voice had an edge of pain. "We can put your shoulders back in place later. Do it."

The pain was excruciating, but I did my best. I pushed my shoulders into a zone of unimaginable pain. Finally, as I literally forced my shoulders out of their sockets, I felt her teeth working on the knot that bound our hands together.

The chopper blades were making a horrific clatter. My eyes glazed with pain, I could see Willie still beside us, still honking his horn. He was not honking it to let me know the chopper had arrived. It was too late for that. We were sliding under the water.

The chopper was directly above us. The wash of the blades beat against us.

The bay was open.

A rope ladder dropped.

Too late.

I felt her suck in all the air she could.

I did the same.

Willie Sees the Night, lying on his horn, waved goodbye as Annie and I disappeared into the evil Ms. Styx's moat of the underworld. Looked like she was going to win after all.

The water was frigid. I stretched my arms for all I was worth to help keep the tangle of knots within Annie's reach. The pain in my shoulders. She gnawed at our bonds like a frantic rat. The pain! The pain! And I couldn't breathe.

The drift boat bounced on the river bottom and began tumbling in the current as the remaining years of our lives flowed as frigid seconds. In the deep. In the deep. In the deep by-and-by.

36 · *The author T*

I rise and look down at the Ranger medic working on my body. There is what appears to be an oxygen mask over my face. Willie Sees the Night and Annie Dancer are watching the medic at his labors. I have no idea how we got out of the Powder, although I assume it was because Annie managed to rip the knot apart with her teeth. At least Annie survived, for which I feel relieved. I do not know if I will ever regain consciousness.

I remember Willie saying that some, but not all travelers experienced one or more spontaneous, recurring trips. That is happening to me now. I am about to fly again; there seems to be little question about that. The first time I flew, I was skeptical. A hallucination, I later thought. A dream. Nothing more. Now, looking down on my body in the ambulance, I am again beset by doubt. The clarity of my existence, wherever I am, is once again astonishing.

A private investigator follows all possible leads. This time I am determined to be more observant. Since this is my second trip, I will surely emerge from the other side, the spirit world or whatever it is, more confident of the truth. I will *know* whether this is an interior trip in the zone of imagination and desire, or an external journey in Willie Sees the Night's spirit world.

In the chopper, Willie's face is a grim mask. Annie's face is twisted by grief and desperation. She is beautiful in both *thymos* and body. Watching her face as she urges my body to fight on and survive, I feel both humble and grateful for having met her.

I fly through the side window of the helicopter as though it did not exist. I look at the helicopter as it flies toward La Grande. Leaving it behind, I fly high above the pine trees of the Blue Mountains. I fly across the high desert where I grew up. I follow the Columbia River downstream. I see the Columbia River Gorge passing beneath me. I pass over Portland. I cross the Coast Range of mountains. I fly over the Oregon coast.

Then I am alone flying above the Pacific Ocean, heading west. Out there, somewhere in what I assume to be Southeast Asia, I know that my creator, or the man whom I imagine to be my creator, lives with a house full of jabbering women with light-brown skin.

In a heartbeat, I am there, back in the house. This time the women are in the kitchen, still babbling happily in their language. They're chopping meat and vegetables, among which I see eggplant, chayote, purple onions, green onions, garlic, stubby, thick carrots, small potatoes. The radio is on, and they sing as they work. Three little girls, about eight or nine years old, burst excitedly into the room, slip off their thongs, and run upstairs.

I don't have to be told the way to the writer's room. I go there straightaway.

The author is at his computer as before. On a small table by his computer is a basket of mangoes, papayas and small lime-green fruit slightly smaller than a golf ball, and two six-ounce cans of guava juice. He is eating half of a papaya with a spoon. Watching me, he cuts one of the lime-green fruits in half and squeezes it into the papaya. He says, "I've been expecting you." He holds up the papaya. "Want some?"

I have no idea whether or not flying spirits can eat, but I'm not hungry. I want to explore this, savor it, get past it, and get back to Annie.

He says, "This little fruit is the local citrus. The native name is *kalamansi*, but the locals also call it a lemoncito. It's got a wonderful flavor. Not as strong as a lemon, but more poop than an orange. Too many seeds, but worth it." He quickly slices another lemoncito and holds it up so I can see off-yellowish orange flesh. "So, have a nice trip, did you? Out there flying."

He is flip, but that is his way of dealing with the harshness of life. He is no comedian. He is serious. I say, "It was up, up and away and I was here in the batting of an eye. Hated to leave Annie there in that ambulance though, I admit."

"I bet. I think I'd miss her. Isn't she something?"

"She sure is."

"Don't say I've never done you a favor. Turns out she's an FBI agent. And double jointed too! Isn't she a little pistol?" He rolls his eyes.

"Okay, okay," I say, "enough already. What do I call you, by the way? I assume you have a name."

"You can call me anything you want as long as it's not late for supper."

I make a sound in my throat.

"You can call me T if you want. That's not my real name, but something for you to figure out, you being a hot damn private investigator and everything. So now that you're here, what is it you want?"

"I assumed that the evil Ms. Douglas and her fat friend murdered Sharon and Mariah Toogood. Luci and Tommy had means, motive and opportunity. But after her little fun at the

Chief Joseph Motel, I'm not so sure. I assume you know who murdered them and why."

T twists on the end of his mustache, thinking. He turns his head slightly, and leans forward. "I am you, but you are not me. Does that make sense?"

T is me, but I'm not him. If he truly is my creator, that does make sense. I say, "Give me something to work with, T. Anything all. A hint. A clue. If Luci and Tommy did kill the Toogood sisters, I want to know for certain so I can get it behind me."

He digs his spoon into the papaya and takes another bite, wiping juice from his lips with the side of his forefinger.

I said, "Mariah was a wonderful person, high-spirited and fun. Whoever murdered her was chickenshit cubed."

"Sharon and Mariah were both daughters of the weatherman. I think it should be obvious that we're dealing with the highs and lows of human emotion. We're told the circulation of fluids is the ultimate cause of all weather. A hot spot develops in the Pacific Ocean off Ecuador, and we have El Niño. Nine months later we're told El Niño is causing hurricanes in Florida, droughts in Texas and all kinds of crap. No peaches here. Bad wheat crop there. No snow pack for the ski resorts in Utah. Everybody suffers." He picks up the second half of his papaya. Then he cuts another *kalamansi* in half and squeezes it onto the papaya.

I wait.

He takes another bite of papaya, chewing contentedly.

I wait some more. Finally, I say "Is that all? Just horseshit about the weather?"

He pretends to be offended. "Horseshit, you say?"

"Since this is all about the weatherman, and you're the alleged creator, I've got brains enough to figure the weather likely fits in somewhere."

"Highs and lows. Circulation of fluid. You're a big boy. Take it from there."

"Asshole," I mutter.

Holding both sides of his mustache, he bursts out laughing.

"Sick bastard," I add.

T, sounding like a braying donkey, laughs louder still, *haw, haw, haw!* "You and Willie have solved one of the three mysteries you faced, the second remains open, the third is unknowable and unsolvable. Tell me, what are those mysteries?"

I said, "We know who poached the bears and why."

"The Timothy McVeigh Brigade. Mystery one. Right."

"We don't yet know with certainty who murdered Sharon and Mariah Toogood."

"Mystery two. Correct."

"The identity of one's creator, in the sense of the corporeal, is unknowable. One can guess. One can speculate. One can surrender to faith. But ultimately it is a mystery that cannot be solved."

"It's nice to know that I've created a private investigator who's not a complete idiot." *Haw, haw, haw!* "By the way, Denson, my readers and your clients are exactly the same. They expect us to deliver justice."

"I agree," I say.

"In the mystery of the murders of the Toogood sisters, can you think of a lead that you haven't investigated? Luci is supposed to have worked in a health food store in Seaside? If I recall, you didn't follow up on that. No telling what you might find. Also why would Jerry Toogood join the Timothy McVeigh Brigade? You never know, the answer to that is some kind of clue. My advice is to keep searching. I've heard that owls can float all night without touching down. Is that true?"

I look down. I am a bird. An owl.

37 • Baaad, baaad fathers

When I awoke from my coma in a din of chopper blades, Annie Dancer and Willie Sees the Night were both there. Above me loomed the crewcut Ranger I had seen earlier. He had THOMPSON on his nametag. He was a corporal. Corporal Thompson said, "He's coming around. We'll see if his brain went too long without oxygen."

Willie said, "He doesn't have a whole lot of brains to begin with. It's about damn time, Chief."

Annie gave me a kiss. "Willie's right. You!"

My shoulders ached. "You did it then. You got the knots untied."

She squeezed my hand. "Just before I passed out. The Rangers jumped in and pulled us out."

"My shoulders hurt."

"I had to shove them back in their sockets," Thompson said. "They'll be sore for a while." He began packing his gear. "Other than your shoulders, you seem okay, Mr. Denson. Not a whole lot you can do now except maybe have a good lunch and get some rest. Where you folks want us to set you down?"

Willie said, "My pickup is at the Chief Joseph Motel. If you drop us off there, we can take Willie back to Whitefeather's Dodge."

"I'll tell the pilot," he said, going forward toward the cockpit.

I looked up at Willie. I said, "Went flying."

Willie grinned. He knew what I meant.

To Annie, I said, "Are you willing to go with me to Seaside to check the health food store where Luci Douglas used to work?"

"Sure, I'll go to Seaside with you. If you'd like I can use my notebook to download maps to Seaside's health food stores."

"Thank you. Plus I'll need photographs of Luci, Tommy, Bill Dennis and his friend Vera." I paused. "And Janine Toogood. Good to include 'em all." I thought a moment. "And if he wasn't killed or caught in the roundup of the McVeigh warriors, I would like a mug of the Humphrey Bogart clone. I assume Dunsmuir has one on file somewhere."

"Consider it done. We should probably have ourselves a good breakfast before we go. It's a six or seven-hour drive to Seaside."

Willie, Annie, and I ordered disgusting breakfasts of fried eggs, bacon, hash browns, and toast plus a bottomless cup of mud in the Powder River Café ten miles upstream from the Chief Joseph Motel. The talk among the other customers was of the action at Saddleback Mountain and the murders of the owners of the Chief Joseph. If the gossip was accurate, the Rangers were still pursuing pockets of militiamen into the Blue Mountains.

While we waited for our food, I said, "How long was I unconscious before I woke up?"

Annie shrugged. "We'd been in the air ten minutes or so when you came around. Seemed like a week at the least."

To Willie, I said, "Saw my Creator again."

"Oh?"

"He calls himself the author T."

Annie looked puzzled. "T?"

"Most likely after Plato's term, *thymos*. For what we variously call spirit, life force, or essence. We create ourselves. T urges me not to give up on my murder investigation. He doesn't think I've followed up on all the leads. I think he's right."

Studying me, she said, "I take it you're not going to tell me more about T just now."

"Not now. Later yes, certainly."

"I told Willie who I was."

"Special Agent Annie Dancer." Willie looked amused. "See, Chief. I told you to have faith."

Annie opened the top of her notebook and began calling up images I had requested, after which she downloaded Yellow Pages maps of Seaside showing the location of Seaside's four health food stores.

After lunch, Willie set off to visit some friends on the Nez Perce reservation. I filled the tank of our pickup in the station next door. When I went back to get Annie, she was talking on her cell phone.

She said, "Read it again?" She listened, grinning. "All right! That sounds perfect. And they should look good, you think. Clear. Professional." She paused. "Just like downtown?" She laughed. "That ought to do it. Can I pick them up later today?" She waited, looking pleased. "Ah, good. What time do you close?" Her shoulders slumped. "How about if I give you my credit card number on the phone? I'm an agent of the Federal Bureau of Investigation. You can call the Portland field office to check me out."

Annie waited, listening to whomever it was she was talking to. "Extra for the rush job, I understand. I don't mind springing for a rush job as long as I get them, and they look good. Is there someplace you can leave them in case I don't make it on time?" She listened, then said, "In the drop box on the front door. Got it. If for some reason I can't pick them up tonight, I'll drop by the first thing in the morning." She hung up.

I said, "The pickup's full of gas. Oil is good. What was that all about?"

"A present for you and Willie."

"Oh?" A present. I was curious.

"In appreciation for not throwing a fit over my little deception, plus all kinds of reasons too numerous to detail here now, besides which it would take away the surprise."

"Well, that's thoughtful. Read it again, you said. Read what again? And where are you supposed to pick this up, whatever it is?"

She laughed. "At a place in Astoria, and don't be so nosy. Do you have to know everything? Let yourself be surprised once in a while."

"Mysterious," I said.

"I'm a mysterious kind of woman."

Our day had started at the first light of dawn, and three hours later, eight o'clock, we were on our way for the seven-hour run to the Oregon coast. We took turns driving, whipping east on I-84 at a solid seventy-five to eighty miles an hour. If we got pulled over, we hoped Annie's FBI boxtops, and maybe an added call to Dunsmuir, would see us through.

Seven hours later, we were on state Highway 26 approaching the summit of the Coast Range, closing in on Seaside. As I neared the crest of yet another ridge, I saw a light green Chevrolet Blazer repeatedly pop into my mirror as I rounded corners. This was a curvy road, often with two lanes. Oregon

State law required that if a driver saw four cars lined up behind him, he had to pull over to let them pass—a sensible enough law for a state full of twisting mountain roads. It was both courteous and prevented unnecessary head-on collisions caused by drivers, impatient at the slowpoke in front of them, passing when they shouldn't.

I said, "We've got somebody following us."

"A Chevy Blazer. I've been watching it in the mirror. After that ambush business, we need to be careful."

"I'll slow down and let the cars back up behind me, which will give me a chance to pull over. We'll see what happens."

As the cars started backing up behind us, I came upon a roadside turnout and overlook and pulled over to let the trailing vehicles pass. The driver could hardly pull over beside us. There was nothing for him to do but keep going.

I said, "One of us needs to put a good lens on my digital camera and snap the occupants as they go by in case we need an i.d."

"Let me do that," she said.

As she got my camera into position and adjusted the lens, she said, "There's one other thing, I guess I should tell you."

"And that would be?"

"This is my first assignment in the field. My ordinary job is tracing the bank accounts of terrorists and drug smugglers. I not only trace bank accounts, I sometimes steal bank accounts from creeps like the supporters of Al Qaeda. A professional, legal thief." She grinned wickedly.

"Hacking Annie!"

"That's precisely what they call me. It hasn't done me much good at Lao Tzu's. At the same time Luci hired me to set up a supply of medicines from Hong Kong, she yanked the computer that she used to keep records of her business with Win Ho Eng. She gave me a clean computer."

"Just in case."

"Sure, just in case. Even if she had deleted their data on the old computer, I could have recovered it. Our thinking was that if Luci Douglas was that paranoid, it had to be for a good reason."

Just then, the Blazer passed as Annie snapped away with the camera. I recognized one of the two occupants. "My buddy the bogus Shearer is driving. No idea who the other guy is. Suggestion?"

"We keep going while I beam this to the Bureau to see if we can find out who the second guy is." She then punched another number and told Dunsmuir what we had found. When she finished, she said, "The national media have descended and Dunsmuir has his hands full. He says if we have the perps photo in our data bank, someone will call us with his name."

"I bet he does have his hands full. Big story."

"He says we should keep trucking, but be careful."

"As long as we're on this main highway, we should be safe enough. But if they try to force us down one of these mountain roads, we're in for it. One of us will have to drive and the other will have to crawl into the back and get the shotgun." After the Blazer passed, I waited a few minutes then started buzzing back up the mountain. Shortly past the summit, we spotted the Blazer parked slightly off the road in a small park with a picnic area.

A couple of miles later the Blazer was back behind us again.

After we descended the Coast Range, with the disconcerting presence of the Blazer still behind us, we came to Seaside, an ocean-side resort town much loved by Portland residents, especially those with kids. The main drag of town ran east-west ending in a turnaround overlooking Seaside's nice white sand beach. This street was lined on both sides by bars, restaurants, boutiques, places selling knickknacks, seashells, taffy, plus places with video games, and my favorite as a kid, still there in an improved version, a emporium of bumper cars. The Miss Oregon contest was held annually in Seaside, and now, as a result of the fashionable use of gambling as a form of taxing the gullible, a casino.

Annie and I consulted our computer downloads for the directions to the first store on our list.

38 · A woman named Janice

As I pulled to the curb in front of the last store on our list, Settle's Health Food on Highway 101 by the northern city limits, the Blazer parked across the street a block and a half behind us. Doing our best to pretend we weren't being watched, Annie and I went inside—Annie with her notebook computer in hand. The single clerk, a small, middle-aged woman with a nice way about her, was busy with customers.

We browsed among the aisles while we waited our turn, perusing several kinds of medicine containing astragalus, which turned out to be milk vetch. The compound, obtained from the root of milk vetch, was prescribed for fatigue, diarrhea, lack of appetite, prolapsed uterus, anus or stomach, and uterine bleeding. It also allegedly promoted drainage of pus, urination, reduced postpartum fever, and reduced edema. All that. And the seed! Well, the seed was good for lower back pain, frequent urination, incontinence, and premature ejaculation.

We looked at the boxes of four kinds of medicines containing magnolia. Some contained compounds of magnolia flowers. Others featured bark. Magnolia allegedly cured intestinal gas, diarrhea, and heartburn. The flowers reputedly dissolved metals or bones lodged in the throat. The bark compounds cooled fevers, healed blisters, helped combat alcoholism and mental illness.

There were rows of this stuff, from this or that plant, all purporting to cure a wide range of maladies. Now why didn't I believe any of it? And why did people buy it? They bought it because they had faith. I had to have science. If I had a headache, I took ibuprofen or aspirin because they were anti-inflammatories that had been proven to work by clinical test. They did work. So did antibiotics. At least most of the time.

This all brought me back to questions that had haunted me ever since my fleeting moment with the fading *thymos* of Sharon Toogood and my surreal, yet real night-flying. There was clinical evidence, I knew, that showed that these crazed medicines actually did some good to people who truly believed they worked. Faith delivered.

Finally, the clerk was free. Annie stepped forward and flashed FBI boxtops. "I'm special agent Annie Dancer. This is my colleague, John Denson."

The clerk introduced herself as Etta Skaugsett, the owner of Settle's.

Annie said, "Mr. Denson and I are conducting a routine investigation. I'd like to show you some images of people to see if you know them."

"Anything I can do to help the FBI," Etta said.

Annie opened the screen of her notebook computer and tapped a key. Up popped the image of Luci Douglas.

Etta made a face. "Luci! Yee!"

"She work here?" Annie asked.

"I'm afraid so. Four or five years ago. She could turn on the charm or the fury like flipping a switch. The latter mostly. She drove customers away."

"So you had to get rid of her?"

Etta puffed her cheeks. "If we hadn't, she'd have put us out of business."

"Was she married or have any boyfriends that you knew of?"

"Luci? Married?" Etta out laughing. "Have you ever met her?

Annie looked chagrined. "Yes, I have. Stupid question, I suppose."

"Well, there *was* the fat one, but I don't think he was her boyfriend or anything."

Annie put Tommy Hilfinger on the screen.

"Him. That's the one," Etta said. "Always wearing one of those military combat uniforms. You know, the ones with a camouflage design on them."

Annie tapped another key. Bill Dennis appeared. "Him?"

Etta shook her head.

Annie replaced Dennis with Vera Hauser. "Her?"

"No."

She called up the bogus Shearer.

The clerk squinted, uncertain. "He came in once to see Janice with some kind of big news. I remember because he looked just like Humphrey Bogart. Put a fedora on him, and he could play Bogie in the movies. I suppose, you'd have to be old enough to remember Humphrey Bogart movies for him to make an impression."

Annie hit the key again. Janine Toogood made an appearance.

The clerk leaned forward, studying the screen. "That would be Luci's friend Janice. She worked for me for a while too, on the weekends."

"Janice?" I said.

Annie said, "Janice. You're sure about her name."

"Janice, yes. Luci's friend, and she worked for me part time for maybe six or eight months."

"You're sure it was Janice. Not something else."

"It was Janice. She was okay, though. A very nice, personable young woman. Friendly. Nothing at all like Luci Douglas. I have no idea why you might be interested in Luci, but I can tell you my oh my that woman was something else! Nuttier than a fruitcake!"

"I see," Annie said. "And you said the man who looked like Humphrey Bogart came here to report good news. What good news?"

Etta said, "I have no idea. Janice went outside to hear the details. She and Humphrey stood in the parking lot, and she got very excited while she listened. When she came back inside, Luci wanted to know what it was all about, but she wouldn't say. Hard to forget an incident like that. It was all so mysterious and everything. I was as curious as Luci, I have to admit."

"And what was Janice's last name?"

"Fallon."

"Janice Fallon. I see. What can you tell me about her?" Annie asked.

Etta wrinkled her face, thinking. "Nothing really. She never talked about her private life."

"And you buy your Chinese homeopathic medicines from what buyer?" Annie asked.

"Win Ho Eng out of Seattle."

39 · *Incident on Elk Creek*

When Annie Dancer and I slipped onto the seat of Willie's pickup, we were grateful to notice that the Blazer was nowhere to be seen. We headed north on Highway 101, headed back to Astoria on our way to Whorehouse Meadow. It was again my turn to drive, and I kept a watchful eye on the rearview mirrors. Nothing. The malevolent presence of Shearer and his youthful pal was no more. Nevertheless, I was grateful I was driving the pickup, not my bus. The pickup had some real poop to it. If I had to scoot, I could.

Just past the golf course north of Seaside, Annie got a call from the Portland field office. The driver of the car, the Humphrey Bogart look-alike, was George Michaels, a private investigator out of San Francisco. His passenger was Lewis Parker, the driver of the beer truck that had ferried militiamen to Saddleback Mountain. Interesting that Ms. Etta Skaugsett of Settle's Health Food Store had recalled that her employee Janice Fallon, lately Janine Toogood, had a special friend who looked like Humphrey Bogart.

I turned off the highway at the Costco outlet near the Fred Meyer's store at Warrenton, just west of Astoria, to pick up a four-liter plastic jug of olive oil. Annie, glancing at her watch, fidgeted when I pulled to a stop in the parking lot.

I checked my own watch. "I'll just be a minute."

She shrugged. "No problem. They'll leave my package in a drop box when they close."

At six-thirty, we were cruising down the main street of Astoria that ran parallel to the Columbia River.

She said, "It'll be a couple of blocks east of the Maritime Museum. Do you know where that is?"

"I do." A block after Astoria's Maritime Museum, I slowed. "What is the 'it' we're looking for?"

"Rainy Day Printing. There it is."

So it was. I pulled into the lot.

Annie hopped out of the pickup. "I'll be right back."

I did as I was told and a few minutes later, she emerged from the printing shop with a plastic bag in her hand and a huge smile on her face. As she slipped onto the seat, I said, "Looks good, does it?"

"Wow! Beautiful. Just right. They understood what I wanted and did a first rate job."

I reached for the bag. "Let me see."

Enjoying herself, in high spirits, she snatched it away from me. "You're awful. When the time is right, bub. Not before."

We still had seen no sign of the Blazer when I turned off the main highway and headed up the road flanking Elk Creek. As we drove Annie couldn't resist taking quick peeks into the bag of whatever it was she had picked up in Astoria. She was so damn pleased, I could tell it was hard for her not to show me. As we approached the spot where I had encountered the fish storm and Sharon Toogood's body, I saw something in the rearview mirror that made me forget all about the bag and what might be in it.

"Behind us," I said.

Annie glanced in the side mirror at the green Blazer. She gnawed on her lower lip. "What do we do?"

"We've got the shotgun in the back."

"The shotgun?"

"Just in case."

"Your shoulders are still a little stiff. My duty." Saying no more, she dropped her plastic bag and slithered through the window into the shelter of the aluminum camper.

"Use the buckshot," I called back.

"Got it."

I could hear her load it up.

"If you have to use it, splatter their windshield."

"Best bet. I agree."

Before I could react, Blazer was on its way around us. "Flatten out," I said. I ducked. The glass of the window beside me exploded, ripping glass pellets into the side of my neck and my head. My cuts burning, I simultaneously cramped my wheel and slammed on the brakes.

The Blazer dropped back, preparing for another run.

"Get ready back there," I shouted.

Annie could see the blood on my neck. "You okay?"

"Burns like hell. Carotid's intact."

The Blazer was faster than Willie's pickup and despite my best efforts, it gained steadily on us.

In the mirror, I could see Annie getting into place at the rear of the pickup bed. I said, "That buckshot will spread fast. They closer they are the better. Tight pattern."

"Understood."

Closer the Blazer got. Closer still.

I had the pickup nearly topped out and was barely able to control it around the curves. Below us and to our right, downhill, flanked by rocks, lay Elk Creek.

Annie opened fire *whoom, whoom, whoom, whoom, whoom!* In the mirror, I saw the Blazer's windshield explode. The rig soared off the shoulder of the road and plunged down the bank, landing upside down, on rocks at the edge of the stream, its wheels still spinning.

As I braked to a stop, Annie, soaring from the adrenaline, crawled back into the cab.

"Rambo action," I said. "Annie Rambo!"

Her eyes were wide. "I never shot anyone before."

"Had to be done. Them or us. Lady, you're a-shakin' like a dog shittin' peach pits! Do you know that?"

"You should see yourself, Mr. Cool." Her hands trembling, Annie used her cell phone to call 911, after which she called Dunsmuir and told them what had happened. Catching my eyes, she said, "He says the Saddleback raid has given him enough media drama for one day. He says to check them out. If they're still alive, stay put. If they're dead, he doesn't want an FBI agent anywhere near this place."

"Good thinking," I said.

"Rest your arms and take care of your cuts," she said and piled out of the back of the pickup. I eased the pickup to the edge of the road and left the motor running as I watched her scramble down the steep slope of the riverbank and peer into the Blazer. Then she was on her way up again, using both hands and feet.

Breathing hard, she slipped onto the seat beside me. "Both dead. Let's get out of here."

By the time we got to Whorehouse Meadow we were laughing like fools, glad to be alive. Giggling all the while, we attacked the refrigerator and made ourselves sandwiches of sharp Tillamook cheddar slathered with strong brown mustard, and we popped the caps off some cold bottles of Oddball Ale. It was no time for mild. It was time to savor the flavor. We popped homemade Sees the Night dill pickles into our mouths and chomped. It felt wonderful to be alive.

Was the private investigator George Michaels working for Janine Toogood, or had he visited her in Seaside on behalf of somebody else? He had tried to kill us. Why?

40 · Data chase

While the raid by army Rangers on the Timothy McVeigh Brigade and its amazing armory was dramatic in the extreme, the twenty-four-hour cable news channels knew the story would dim without a more lasting ratings jack. Inasmuch as the First Amendment protected the circus along with the sober, Gregory Dunsmuir was now called upon to answer the inflammatory leading questions of this or that politician, posturing for his or her constituents, or "analysts" pursuing the inevitable charges of incompetence, malice, and the violation of civil rights by the FBI.

Insulated from the media noise, Annie Dancer and I went to work in my cabin in Whorehouse Meadow. Annie had FBI software enabling her to enter the computer systems of the Portland Police Bureau, the Oregon State Police, and the county, state and federal agencies with records pertaining to immigration, naturalization, birth, adoption, marriage, divorce, and death. Following the 9-11 terrorist attack, such access was considered mandatory for the FBI, and increasingly, much to the alarm of civil rights purists, such data were routinely shared among the FBI, CIA and other investigative agencies plus the INS and the IRS. Data that were previously disparate and scattered were now routinely pooled. And FBI computer experts like Hacking Annie Dancer were necessary to follow the data trail into computers all over the world.

Annie keyed instructions into her notebook and up popped a brief FBI bio of Luci Lynn Douglas. I looked over her shoulder at the screen and learned that Luci Lynn Douglas was born in Multnomah County, Oregon. She was adopted by a Darrin and Darlene Bonner in Portland, where she attended elementary school and David Douglas High School. She graduated from Washington State University, in Pullman, Washington. She was a sociology major. When she was twenty-three, she married Leon Buster Douglas, of Coeur d'Alene, Idaho, and was divorced from him six months later. She had no listed criminal record.

"What do you see there that's interesting?" Annie asked.

"One possible link," I said.

"And that would be?"

"Coeur d'Alene is in Northern Idaho. Northern Idaho is the land of the Aryan Nation and screwball militia groups. Do we have the possibility of a continuing contact stemming from her time there?"

"Very good. Wait until you see Tommy Hilfinger."

"Oh?"

Her fingers danced over the keys until up popped the FBI's bio of Tommy Hilfinger. "Tommy Hilfinger grew up in Sandpoint, Idaho. He has a juvenile record that remains sealed. He was kicked out of high school in his junior year and did not graduate."

"Sandpoint! Just east of Coeur d'Alene."

"Hilfinger has no military service. He tried to enlist in the marines but got turned down for having flat feet."

"I find that interesting what with all his swaggering about wearing combat fatigues. Too much reading *Soldier of Fortune* magazine. Such was the base of the Timothy McVeigh Brigade."

"There are scores of Douglas and Hilfingers in the Portland telephone directory. Any one of them could be related to Lucy or Tommy. We've got people currently working on that. We're talking door-to-door stuff, ringing doorbells and asking questions."

She turned to Bill Dennis's bio. Dennis turned out to have been born in Longview, Washington, and educated at Whitman College in Walla Walla, where one of his classmates had been Jerry Toogood. Originally trained as a geologist, he had gone to law school in his late thirties.

"Who established the Win Ho Eng connection?" I asked.

"Luci, wouldn't you think? Ms. Charm worked for Settle's Health Foods in Seaside as you know. Settle's used Win Ho Eng for their supplies of Oriental medicines."

I said, "Luci dropped Win Ho Eng as Lao Tzu's supplier yet still has lunch with him. Who's next on our list?"

"Vera Hauser. Bill Dennis has an eye for her. She sucked up to Luci. She had enough juice to rate one of the Toyota pickups."

I added, "And she was maybe the female I glimpsed that night outside Luci's."

Annie keyed in the request for the FBI bio on Vera Hauser. She was born and educated in Yakima, Washington, and was a graduate of Western Washington University, in Bellingham. She was a botany major. She had no criminal record.

I said, "Note a whole lot there. Let's try Janine Toogood, a.k.a Janice Fallon. She talked both Sharon and T.G. into investing in Lao Tzu's. For some reason, she likely hired the private investigator George Michaels. She's the mother of the proud new owner, little Carrie."

Annie looked up the record of Janine's marriage in Portland to Jerry Toogood six years earlier. The new Mrs. Toogood listed her maiden name as Janine Fay Shepherd.

"You showed her Janine's picture, she identified her as Janice Fallon. No hesitation."

"She seemed like a responsible woman. She didn't have a Seeing Eye dog. How about legal name changes? Can you trace them?"

"Yes, I can. We're very interested in people who change their names. Most of the time they're women wanting to take back their maiden names. Sometimes they're criminals wanting to put a felony conviction in their past. They could be running from child support, or even be a Muslim terrorist here to kill people for the sport of it."

"Suggestive if we could find a name change for Janice Fallon."

Annie clicked the mouse. "We'll start with people from the Pacific Northwest, including Montana and Idaho." It took her several minutes to run that hole dry with no matches. "No name changes in this part of the world."

"Try California, Nevada, and Arizona," I said.

Five minutes later, Annie said, "Oops, what do we have here? Five years ago in Las Vegas, Nevada, one Jerelyn Marie Bonner had her name legally changed to Janine Faye Fallon. Ms. Bonner, an American citizen born in Acapulco, Mexico, was adopted by Darrin and Darlene Bonner, of Portland, Oregon. I don't have access to the Mexican data."

"Whoops!"

"Double whoops! Jerelyn Marie Bonner, also known as Janice and Janine Faye Fallon, also Janine Fay Shepherd, lately Janine Shepherd Toogood, is Luci Douglas's sister by adoption."

"Now there's one of your garden variety suggestive coincidences. Why change her name from Bonner to Fallon?" I asked.

Annie paused, then her fingers began hopping again. "I

can't find any legal convictions for either Jerelyn Marie Bonner or Janice Faye Fallon."

"Marriages?"

Annie searched for twenty minutes then gave up. "Nothing. Which doesn't mean that she wasn't married before, only that I can't find a record. She might have been married in the Dominican Republic or Belgium. Who's to know? She might have been married, divorced, and went back to being Fallon. Hard to know. Oh, oh. We've got a second legal name change, six months before she married Jerry Toogood, she changed her name from Janice Faye Fallon to Janine Fay Shepherd. That was in Tucson, Arizona. Give me a minute."

I waited.

She frowned. "No legal convictions or marriages for Janine Fay Shepherd, which takes us back to her original name of Jerelyn Marie Bonner."

"Are there any Bonner families in Portland?"

She checked the white pages on the computer, then sat back. "A bunch."

"You getting a little pooped?"

"A bit. Hard to concentrate after a while. Let's check Darrin Bonner and see what we can find."

What Annie found was that Darrin Bonner was dead, but his mother, Mrs. Oswald Bonner was still very much alive. Gladys Bonner, age 84, lived in a house in east Portland.

"We need to talk to Mrs. Bonner tomorrow," I said. "Now's the time for some Oddball and the other."

She grinned mischievously. "Oddball and the other. I agree. But I wouldn't want to hurt your delicate shoulders."

41 • *The nature of private investigators*

I'm on a crowded street. The street is packed with home-made vehicles that I recognize as Filipino Jeepneys, belching black smoke. They are painted wild colors, green, blue, yellow, red and orange, with horses, dolphins, mermaids and other chrome decorations. The air smells like a sewer. There is garbage in the gutter. I see the author T, wearing walking shorts, standing by a vendor's cart. His gray hair is a tangle. He needs a haircut. His mustache needs trimming. He sees me. He gestures for me to join him. He waves with the palm of his hand turned down, not up.

"And we are where?" I asked.

"Sanciangko Street, one up from Colon, the main drag. This is downtown Cebu; uptown is also more upscale. Better air. Nice restaurants. You want some Indian food? Or maybe I should say Hindu food. I know a place. Good biriyani."

The young woman running the vending cart eyes me as she stirs some round white balls, the size of large marbles, cooking in a wok full of boiling oil.

"And these would be?" I gestured at balls.

"Squid balls. They're great if you don't mind a little garlic.

Here, try one. Dip it in the sauce." He hands me a small paper container with a thin, orange-colored sauce.

I dip a ball into the sauce and taste it. "They are good, you're right."

In the blinking of an eye, T and I are in a dark room. The music is too loud. Above us, looking down at us, grinning shyly, a Filipina wiggles her butt at us. She is timid at first, then wiggles with enthusiasm, pleased at the reaction on our faces. T is an unabashed admirer.

This is not a dream. It is real. I am in Cebu in the Philippines, having flown here from Whorehouse Meadow. Watching the sensual, hypnotic butt above me, I tell T what Annie and I had learned about Janine Toogood's oft-changed identity and about her apparent relationship to the private investigator who looked like Humphrey Bogart.

T nods. "You're gaining on it."

"I want help."

Not taking his eyes off the dancer above us, grinning with appreciation at the girl, not my request, he twists the end of his mustache, saying, "Listen, Denson, I have a general idea of where I'm going with your story. I have a few thousand words to go. No telling what ideas I'll get between now and then. I've got a lot of responsibility here. The fates of all the characters are up to me. No fun without discovery and a little surprise now and then. Would you really want to know the exact ending without the mystery of the in-between?"

"Aw come on," I say.

Still watching the girl, he chews on his lower lip. "What comes next? If you think about it, that question is critical for every animal on the planet. Is there food or a predator lurking around that leaf or rock or tree or bank of coral or mountain or across that river or stream or stretch of snow or desert or jungle? Our brains are more complicated, so our questions are more complicated. Solve the puzzle yourself, Denson. Follow the evidence."

I think about that for a moment. "Okay, tell me about the process. How do you come up with the story? Maybe that will help."

He shrugs. "The stories well up out of the murk in bits and pieces."

"The murk?"

"My subconscious. I see a character, names, hints of motive, glimpses of relationship. I see revealing detail, complications, and suggestive metaphors. All of this out of order, mind you. I keep rearranging character, motive and incident until I come up with a solution that makes sense. I try to rule nothing out, no matter how unexpected."

"You're describing my job."

T looks at me like I'm an idiot. "Well, of course, but with a twist. An author assembles. A detective disassembles."

"I disassemble?"

"I put the story together. You tear it apart to see how it works." He licks his lips. "You're really something, you know that, Denson? Worrying about all this stuff with a hot little butt wiggling a foot from your face. How do you do it?"

I sense something up close and personal. It's the girl's rump, inches from my face. Only it isn't the behind of a Filipina. It's Annie Dancer. She gives me a wink. "What you think, big boy? You like the action?" She looks me straight in the eyes, flirting.

"Very much," I say.

Annie motions with her fingers, palm up, western style.

I stand and turn my head toward her lips.

She whispers into my ear. "My double joints let me bend into dreams. Girls with regular spines can't do that. I am a willow. I flow with the wind." She blows into my ear. "I like your wings."

I do have wings. I check my bird feet.

Annie stands, still moving. A tease, she is. "Very hip," she says. "You know how to tickle a girl with those feathers of yours?"

I call, "*Voo-hoo-hoo-hoo! Voo-hoo-hoo-hoo!*"

She laughs, still flirting. "My, oh my, you *are* a sweet talking man. I bet you say that to all the girls, don't you? Mr. Smooth."

The author T morphs into me, John Denson, admiring Annie dancing above him. Annie morphs into an owl. The owl cocks its head. Then it looks at me. Its large, yellow eyes blink twice. "*Kee-eau! Kee-eau! Kee-eau!*"

I woke up with Annie sleeping beside me. I had been right all along. I didn't fly outside my skin. I am no owl. Nor do I host the spirit of an owl. I flew inward. The clues to my interior journey were clear. Willie recently cooked his deep-fried venison balls for Annie and me, so it made sense that I imagined T buying squid balls from a street vendor. I met Annie at Mary's, so I dreamed that T took me to a girlie bar in the Philippines. And there, logically enough, Annie made an appearance.

But whatever its origins, the journey had been productive. I hadn't completely disassembled the mystery of who murdered the weatherman's daughters. It only appeared that I had.

When the dying Sharon Toogood looked into my eyes, her *thymos* evaporating and with salmon falling all about us, I was confronted with two mysteries: murder and the nature of *thymos*, or spirit, which is who we really are, not our bodies. T did not create me. It was the other way around. I created T, who was me, my *thymos*. That is why T morphed into me in the girlie bar. I imagined T as an author because I understood intuitively that we all write our own lives, a succession of stories, call them novels, that evolve as we get older. It was also logical that I had created myself as a private detective. Those people who think about the nature of their lives are the most private of private investigators.

In the dim light, I looked at Annie's face as she slept beside me. She was a companionable, lovable, loving young woman, a welcome addition to my changing life. I hoped she would remain a central character in the serial stories of John Denson.

42 • Mrs. Bonner's memory

Gladys Bonner was a short, stumpy lady in her early eighties wearing a flowered blouse and brown polyester trousers. She had a wrinkled face and an outsized nose. Her blue eyes peered up at Annie and me through horn-rimmed glasses that had bits of reflecting sparkle embedded in the plastic. Her thinning hair, artificially colored a light brown, had been permed by a beautician in a doomed attempt to take advantage of what hair she had left. The result was sort of a soft, short Afro. She had bad knees and hobbled when she walked.

Her eyes widened. "My! CIA. Can that be so? Spies? Arab terrorists."

"FBI, ma'am. No spies. No terrorists."

She said, "All that violence! You mind if I sit in my chair while we talk?"

"Oh, sure. Be comfortable," I said.

As she led the way into her tiny living room, I saw that the walls were covered with shelves containing ceramic cows, hundreds of ceramic cows. A cow stepping on its tit. A Holstein being milked by a ceramic man. A white cow that was a creamer. It was nothing short of bizarre, all those cows. A deliciously crazy obsession was Mrs. Bonner's collection of ceramic cows.

Mrs. Bonner caught me staring at her cows. "You like cows?" she asked.

"They can be cool," I said.

"And you? Do you like cows too?" she asked Annie. She acted like she had just asked a naughty question.

"I like milk and ice cream."

Mrs. Bonner, climbing as though she were Sir Edmund Hillary crawling up that last torturous yard on all fours, slowly ascended a recliner covered with shiny purple plastic until she reached the summit, a place to kick back and relax. She pursed her lips in concentration. Her pace was glacial, but she made it, and once in place, set about finishing her routine. She used an electric control to boost her feet up. She pulled a cotton blanket with what looked like Native American designs on it over her lap. A black and white cat hopped onto the blanket.

Thus ensconced, comfy, snuggly, cat in her lap, she was ready to talk. "They tell me that I forget things. I can go along okay and then I just forget. There's no explaining it. My arthritis is acting up. I can tell it's going to rain. Whenever it's getting ready to rain, my arthritis starts acting up."

"You must be pretty miserable living in Portland. It rains almost nine months out of the year."

"Every time it rains, my arthritis starts acting up. I've had operations on both my knees. Nothing helps. Sometimes I don't know about these doctors." She looked sour.

"I milked cows from the time I was a girl. Until a few years ago, I lived on a small farm in Eastern Oregon. I milked three cows morning and night, until my husband died. Then my son and daughter-in-law got killed in a car accident. I couldn't take care of my cows by myself. I moved here because my sister lived here, and there were better doctors here. Or so I thought. Then my sister died, so now it's me and my cat and my ceramic cows. What was it you said you were after?"

"I'm trying to find more about a young woman named Jerelyn Marie Bonner."

Mrs. Bonner made a spitting sound like she had something on the end of her tongue that she couldn't get rid of. "Jerelyn? She's been gone for years."

"Oh? What can you tell me about her?"

"She was my son Darrin's daughter. I say 'daughter.' She was adopted, you know. You never know what you're going to get, taking pot luck like that. They wouldn't listen. You know how that goes. Turned out Jerelyn was a wild one." Mrs. Bonner made her spitting sound. She did not actually spit, but there was something about the tip of her tongue that she found annoying. An imaginary something that she wanted to get rid of but couldn't. "My son and his wife moved to Idaho. Jerelyn disappeared one day when she was thirteen years old. We never knew what happened to her, whether she ran away or somebody took her or what."

Annie said, "That's too bad. We're sorry to hear that."

She made the spitting sound. "It was a blessing, if the truth be known. But Darlene, my daughter-in-lawn, couldn't have children of her own, and she wanted one. Look what she got." She bunched her mouth and shook her head, looking bitter at the memory.

"And Darrin and Darlene were killed an automobile accident," Annie said.

"Ten years ago. The doctor told my son and his wife that Jerelyn was a mistake made by the daughter of a wealthy Portland family and her boyfriend. Good family? I always found that hard to believe." Mrs. Bonner made the spitting sound, which this time sounded like an editorial full stop. "The girl supposedly went to Mexico to have the baby, which is where Darrin and Darlene went to fill out the adoption paperwork. You know the Mexicans will do anything if you pay them enough money. They're as crooked as a dog's hind leg."

"Did anybody let slip the name of the birth father?"

She concentrated. She frowned.

"You don't remember?"

Mrs. Bonner looked angry, not at the question, but because her memory was going on and off like a refrigerator motor.

"How about the doctor's name? Can you remember that?"

Mrs. Bonner shook her head. "Oh, no. It's been so long ago. He had an office next door to Providence Hospital. Or was it? I can't remember. I told my son and his wife that I didn't trust him any farther than I could throw a stick, but they wouldn't listen." Spit! Spit!

Annie said, "Do you have a picture of Jerelyn?"

"Oh sure." She turned and pointed at a wall covered with shelves of ceramic cows. "Up there behind the Guernsey with the cactus in its back."

I saw the Guernsey that was also a planter. Behind it, was a framed photograph of a skinny blonde girl. I stood and retrieved the photograph, studying it. "Say, you wouldn't mind if I borrowed this photograph, would you?"

Mrs. Bonner made the spitting sound. "If you promise to bring it back. I haven't seen her in all these years, and she was adopted and everything, but I still want to keep it. Pictures and my cat and ceramic cows are just about all I have these days." She sounded vaguely bitter. She made her spitting sound.

I started to go, then thought of one more question. "Your son and his wife didn't adopt any other children, by any chance?"

Her tongue began spitting again, rapidly and with passion. Spit! Spit! Spit! "Lucinda, a year older than Jerelyn. They were inseparable when they were little girls. Luci went to college at Washington State and married a man from Idaho. That didn't last. A man would have to be too stupid to pour pee out of a boot with the directions on the heel to marry that female. Her face was enough to stop a clock, and her temper!" Spit! Spit! "I think she runs some kind of health store here in Portland, but she never comes to see me. I never saw her after Darrin was killed. She's crazier than a cracked bedbug. Mean too. Didn't even go to my son's funeral. Maybe it comes from being adopted. No real sense of belonging." Spit! Spit!

"Did you ever see Jerelyn as an adult?"

Spit! Spit! She shook her head.

"Did anybody come round asking questions about her biological parents?" Annie asked.

She blinked. "Why yes, as a fatter of fact."

"I see," Annie said. "Can you remember the man's name?"

Mrs. Bonner accepted a black and white cat that hopped lightly onto her plump lap and stared at me with yellow eyes. "Oh heavens, I can't remember. He looked like a movie actor, I know that. I used to have dogs, but I couldn't take care of them when I got older, so I switched to cats."

"Like Humphrey Bogart?" Annie said.

"Yes, that's it. Humphrey Bogart. Now I remember. Isn't that something? Sometimes I can't remember what I did five minutes earlier, and other times I can recall something that happened ten or twenty years ago like it was yesterday. People probably think I'm nuttier than a fruitcake. Addled old lady."

43 • *The turmoil of fluids*

The next morning as Annie Dancer and I sat down for a breakfast of Raisin Bran and coffee, watching a tube news report on the militia bust, the phone began beeping. The new weatherman at the station, or rather a weather young woman, was telling us there would be rain in the morning with patches of clearing in the afternoon. I started munching on Raisin Bran, wondering about Rosie's mysterious friend, when the phone beeped. It was for Annie, from Gregory Dunsmuir.

After listening to Dunsmuir's report, saying little herself, Annie hung up. "Dunsmuir says Janine is still part of the federal investigation of domestic terrorism. He agrees it's curious that Janine Toogood changed her identity with every full moon. He says the fact that Luci is her sister by adoption and worked with her in the Seaside health food store is circumstantial. But . . ." She turned up the palms of her hands.

I said, "But all those circumstances lie in the murky territory of reasonable doubt, a zone of shifting definitions. Maybe she's an heir of Family X, seeking to combine her take with Jerry Toogood's bank account and Sharon and Mariah's inheritance from their mother."

"They're checking the histories of seven wealthy Portland

families represented by Bill Dennis to see if Janine might be an embarrassment of an errant son or daughter. Dunsmuir says Janine was at Saddleback Mountain the day of the raid on the Timothy McVeigh Brigade and may well have murdered Luci and Tommy after they sent us down the river. He says the Portland Police Bureau and the Oregon State Police are holding off talking to her until his people finish sifting through the militia records, plus they've scored search warrants for all six Lao Tzu's stores and the Toogood residence."

"Where is Mrs. Toogood during all this?"

"Dunsmuir's people are watching her around the clock."

"Anything more on the murders of Sharon and Mariah Toogood?"

Annie shook her head. "He believes Luci most likely ordered Tommy Hilfinger to kill Sharon after she found out what was going on at Lao Tzu's. She ordered Tommy to murder Mariah in case her sister told her anything. He says if you can reconstruct the murders better than that, by all means be his guest. He's open to alternate explanations."

"You think your forensics lab is finished aging the face in that photograph Mrs. Bonner loaned to us?"

"Let me check." Annie opened the lid of her notebook computer. The FBI forensics laboratory had indeed completed its rush job. I stood over Annie's shoulder as she printed the reconstructed image. It was little doubting that the little girl, Jerelyn Marie Bonner, was now Janine Faye Toogood.

The phone beeped again. This time it was from Rosie Garza, inviting Annie and me to join her for pizza and beer to celebrate the Nature Conservancy's bonus for our role in busting the bear poachers. She said Willie had already agreed to come and she wanted me to meet a friend.

I could hear her sigh heavily. "It's time, I think."

"For me to meet your friend?" I said.

"You'll understand. If you can come around about noon,

you can follow me to a place in Scappoose that I've found. Good pizza."

"Well, sure," I said. "Annie and I'll join Willie. We'll be there."

Willie and Annie and I piled three abreast in his pickup for our celebratory lunch with Rosie Garza, with Willie at the wheel and Annie in the middle. I tried to be cheerful, although my mind was gnawing on the murders of Sharon and Mariah.

As we rolled down the highway flanking Elk Creek, Annie took a small box out of her handbag. Opening it, she said, "Here is my present for you guys. You don't have to answer now if you don't want." She handed me a business card.

I read it and blinked.

Willie glanced at me. "Chief?"

I studied the card.

"I can't read and drive. Read it to me, Chief."

"It says Denson, Dancer and Sees the Night. Private investigations. It has an e-mail address at the bottom, 'We solve mysteries at whorehousemeadow dot com.' "

Willie gave me a lopsided grin. "Say what?"

I read it again, aware that Annie was studying me.

I cleared my throat and said nothing. We drove in silence.

Finally, Annie said, "Well?"

Willie waited, making her suffer. At last he said, "What do you think, Chief?"

Determined to keep a straight face, I said, "Hey, I don't know, Tonto."

We continued in silence.

Annie looked annoyed. "Say something, one of you."

Hesitantly, Willie said, "Would this mean we have to build you your own cabin? You're looking at plumbing and wiring and the rest of it. We'll have to dig another septic tank. That's hard work. That's not to mention applying for all the permits and the rest of it."

She groaned.

"Or are you thinking of moving in with me?" I asked. "Using me for sex. A sex object."

She closed her eyes, looking disgusted.

"Because if you are, I'll go for it. If it's okay with Willie, I say Denson, Dancer and Sees the Night it is."

"You!" She leaned against me, smelling grand.

"Ah, ah! Don't count your chickens. Willie has the veto."

Willie said, "But there would be conditions. You need to understand."

"Conditions?"

"You don't have to make coffee, but you're the whiz with a computer, so you'll have to keep tabs of our expense records. Denson and I are terrible at that."

She smiled broadly. "Consider it done. I'll keep the books and do your hacking.

Willie said, "What do you say, Denson, thirdsies with the profits?"

"You want to give her a third?" I asked. "Pushy broad," I muttered.

"Chief Dumsht," she said.

Willie laughed. "Sensible woman. You're going to fit just fine."

We arrived at Rosie's houseboat in high spirits, and there was the inevitable Lance, hanging out on the boat the next moor over. He looked startled and not a little concerned at our arrival, suddenly shouting, "Rosie! Rosie! Denson and Willie are here!"

Why was he shouting? I gave him a look as we hopped aboard Rosie's houseboat.

Behind me, sounding annoyed, Lance said, "Don't you people ever call before you show up at someone's place? Jesus!"

Rosie appeared at the door with a young woman. "It's okay, Lance. I invited them."

Lance said, "Really?" He grinned broadly. "Good for you, Rosie!"

I understood immediately the reason for his concern. The young woman with Rosie, leaning against her, was clearly expressing more than platonic friendship. She was Rosie's girlfriend. That's why Rosie lived in a houseboat in a community of gays. Contrary to being in any way put off, I was relieved. Since I met Annie, I had moved on emotionally.

Rosie said, "John, Willie, I would like you to meet my friend Lynn."

Lynn, so small she'd have to run through the shower to get wet, looked up at me with shy brown eyes. I shook her hand. "Pleased to meet you, Lynn. I would like you two to meet Annie Dancer, formerly of the FBI, now a member of Denson, Dancer and Sees the Night."

"Ah, a new partner! Well, congratulations," Rosie said.

I summoned my best imitation of a male short-eared owl. *Voo-hoo-hoo-hoo! Voo-hoo-hoo-hoo!*

Rosie looked confused. She had no idea whatever that I was mimicking an owl.

"All right!" I said, relieved that she had no idea.

Dryly, Annie said, "Dumsht has this owl thing. Won't say what it's all about, but I'll get it out of him eventually."

Rosie laughed. "When you do, will you let me know what it is?"

I said, "Let's go for the pizza. We've got a lot to celebrate. Friends, lovers, and Denson, Dancer and Sees the Night." Yet my mind kept twisting in the wind. Two murders.

We followed Rosie and Lynn to Shive's Tavern in Scappoose, which made its own pizza as well as its own lager, ale and stout, brewed on the premises. These tavern breweries, a recent, civilizing appearance in Oregon, served a variety of great-tasting brews. Having come out of the closet with no embarrassing consequences, Rosie was in a buoyant mood, and Lynn too seemed more relaxed as we settled in and ordered a pitcher of a strong amber ale called Panther Piss.

While we waited for our Shive's Crazed Special pizza, we drank Panther Piss and talked about Annie and Lynn. But we were soon distracted by the television set above the bar, which was tuned to Jerry Toogood's station. The station had put together a biography of the much-loved weatherman who had turned out, to the shock and dismay of his many fans, to be a self-styled general of the Timothy McVeigh Brigade. Lieutenant General Toogood? It didn't compute.

The question, understandably enough, was how had T.G. been able to hide his right-wing political sympathies and his abiding antipathy if not outright hatred of the United States government? His colleagues at the television station all said the same thing. T.G. kept his politics to himself except for an occasional complaint that the courts did not defend the right of privacy with vigor. Turned out, T.G. had hated Ronald Reagan's nomination of Robert Bork to the Supreme Court because Bork argued that a right of privacy could neither be found in the Constitution nor deduced from it.

Three years earlier T.G. had been interviewed on the occasion of his twenty-fifth year at as the station's weatherman. A good-looking young woman, in obvious awe of the storied weatherman, went through the drill of mandatory clichéd questions. At the end, she asked if through the years T.G. had gained any kind of insight that he would like to share with the viewers.

Jerry Toogood started to answer with that natural charm

that had buoyed his television ratings, but then he stopped, as though he had suddenly remembered something. He ran his hand across his face as if to wipe away his amiable T.G. persona. He seemed caught in the grip of an odd compulsion over which he had no control. The weatherman had been asked a question for which the interviewer hadn't expected an answer that anybody gave a damn about, and he had decided, for whatever reason, to answer it truly, from the heart.

His voice low and grave, rattling as the lungs of the dying, he looked straight at the red light. "Every weeknight for twenty-five years, I have appeared before you talking about highs and lows and fronts and moisture blowing in from the Pacific. Rain squalls followed by periods of sun. Snow in the West Hills. Freezing rain in the gorge. What, my interviewer asks, have I learned that is memorable? An important question! How truly, beyond the data collected by the National Weather Service, does one forecast the weather? Take it from the weatherman when I tell you that the abdication of personal honor is a form of malevolent heat that saturates our lives, dissipating so slowly it cannot be measured save for the inadequate speculations of moral philosophers. It lingers for decades. Both the storms in the fields and the torments in our homes are caused by the turmoil of fluids."

Having said his piece, T.G. looked like he was about to weep. His eyes watered up. His chin began to bob. He struggled to maintain his composure.

The floor director switched the shot to the interviewer. The young woman blinked her blue eyes. She flipped her long mane of blonde hair as though nothing untoward had happened. "Would you tell us about your roses? I understand you've won several international prizes."

My jaw dropped. Jerry Toogood had almost certainly revealed why he had been drawn to the Timothy McVeigh Brigade.

"What is it?" Annie asked.

I said, "Dunsmuir told you he has Janine Toogood under twenty-four-hour surveillance. Do you suppose you can sweet talk him into giving me fifteen minutes to sit down with her? If he does, tell him I might be able to crack this thing. If he wants, I'll wear a wire."

44 · *The weatherman's forecast*

Janine Toogood, dressed in a trim white suit and with her short hair fashionably cut, sat at a window table in the lodge at Multnomah Falls with a BLT and a glass of red wine. When she saw me coming, she brightened and said graciously, "Mr. Denson! Won't you join me?"

I said, "I'd like that, thank you. We need to talk, Mrs. Toogood."

"Janine, please."

"Janine, it is." I sat. A waitress arrived immediately. I said, "I'd like a Full Sail Ale please." Full Sail was brewed locally in Hood River.

Janine took a sip of wine, watching me. "And to what do I owe this visit? And how did you find me?

"I'm here about two unsolved murders. Annie Dancer is an FBI agent. We planted an electronic tailing device on the bottom of your vehicle."

She scowled. "An FBI agent? The little bitch. I should have known. The morons lost one female agent, so they risked the life of another. Determined." She glanced out at the parking lot.

"Annie's waiting for me. We're alone. No wire. Getting to

the truth of these murders is personal thing with me. I'll let them collect their own evidence."

In fact, I was wired. In the parking lot, Willie, Annie and Dunsmuir were listening to our conversation from a Ford Explorer. Oregon State Police officers in civilian clothing were scattered about the lot in unmarked cars.

Janine may have believed me, but more likely she felt compelled to tell someone her story, and I was it, to hell with the consequences. It wasn't enough to have prevailed. Someone else had to know what she had done.

I said, "Annie and I talked to Etta Skaugsett in Seaside and to Gladys Bonner in Portland. Gladys is an oldie, but still alert."

"You've been very busy. And you learned what?"

"That Darrin and Darlene Bonner adopted you through a doctor at Providence Hospital. You were born in Acapulco, Mexico, but the doctor told the Bonners your biological father and mother were from wealthy Portland families. Mrs. Bonner loaned us her photograph of little Jerelyn, to which the FBI added twenty years." I showed her the original plus the reconstructed image that Annie had downloaded. "Pretty good work, don't you think? They did it overnight. Rush job."

She picked up the image. "Very good. It looks like me!"

"You went by Janice Fallon when you and Luci Douglas worked for the health store in Seaside. You apparently hired George Michaels three years before you married Jerry Toogood. Why would you hire a private detective?"

"You figured the answer to that one, did you?"

"Earlier today, I saw a television biography of T.G. The mystery isn't so much that he committed suicide, which I don't think he did, but that he was a member of the Timothy McVeigh Brigade. He was educated, warm, charming, very popular with television viewers. He was apparently not political, although he was concerned about the erosion of the right of privacy. You were married to him for five years. How was it that he had become a lieutenant general in a right wing militia?"

"Luci introduced him. You're right, the loss of privacy is one of the militiamen's main complaints. They hate it that the Social Security card is everything short of a national identity number. Jerry wasn't just concerned about the issue, he was obsessed. He couldn't express his rage in public, but the militiamen understood his complaint. He fit right in."

"And he got his rank how?"

"Luci essentially sold it to him. She was the real commandant of the brigade. She loved being in charge. She imagined it as her private army. She set up the sales of bear galls to help raise money. She pushed the militiamen to increase the acres of pot they had planted in the mountains. She got them involved in selling stolen arms."

"I take it T.G. had some kind of secret to keep."

"He was tormented, poor baby," she said mildly.

"Tormented by guilt, I take it."

Watching me, Janine's face was a spooky mask. She leaned across the table, her face inches from mine, her eyes bonfires of fury. Such rage! "Guilt? You *bet* he felt guilty. You *bet* he was afraid his past would catch up with him. You *bet* he was obsessed with privacy."

Looking at me evenly, she took a sip of wine. "When I was fourteen, I ran away from my home in Portland vowing to have my revenge on my biological parents who abandoned me in Mexico. No matter what happened, I would prevail. I kept switching identities so nobody would know who I was. For years, I found no hint, not a clue, but I never quit, never. Eventually, I caught up with Luci again. She was then divorced and working in the Seaside health food store." She signaled to the waitress. "I would like another bottle of Merlot please. And another Full Sail Ale for the gentleman." To me she said,

"The triumph is not fun if nobody knows what I did. Besides, it's my word against yours, right."

"Correct," I lied.

"Luci had found a private investigator who would do anything if the price was right, as you found out."

"You got that right."

"George had found the identity of Luci's biological parents, so I hired him to do the same for me. The doctor who arranged Luci's adoption kept a list of babies he had helped place with new parents. A baby girl with my birth date was born in Acapulco, not in Portland as my birth certificate said. George went to Acapulco, and after spending fistfuls of American dollars for bribes, he concluded that my biological parents were most likely Jerry Toogood, the son of the Toogood family who owned the newspaper in Oregon City, and Samantha Moultine, the only child of Donald and Ruby Moultine. Ring a bell?"

"I know the family."

"What happened was that the Toogoods and the Moultines sent Jerry and Samantha to have a nice holiday in Acapulco before Samantha's pregnancy began to show. The protected ones got married two weeks after they returned to Portland, then proceeded to have two more baby girls over the next three years." Janine waited while the waitress delivered her fresh bottle of wine. "The baby girl they gave up for adoption was me. Had to be. I felt it in my bones. I had been casually dumped, like so much trash, so as not to embarrass the Moultines and the Toogoods. Well, ta, ta, ta." Janine tilted her head, pushing up the end of her nose to indicate snobbery. "Lacking any other way of learning the truth, I seduced Jerry Toogood. I married him and fucked him blind until I was pregnant."

"The man you thought was your father."

"Call it fury. Call it rage. Call it whatever you want. But let me tell you, John Denson, if you do to somebody what those bullshit families did to me, you have to expect it will come back on you." Her face twisted by rage and raw hatred, she said, "Jerry hired you to look into his daughters' deaths because he was concerned about his image, a Toogood through and through. Image is everything in the television business. He loved the admiration and adulation of being the famous T.G. with his face on billboards all around town. He was not tormented because he cared what he had done. He feared loss of respect.

"I delivered Carrie and bided my time. Finally, DNA testing became available to the larger public. I raked his back with my fingernails during a wild screw and sent some of his skin and some of my own to a laboratory in Phoenix. He was my father all right, there was no denying the DNA evidence. A few days before his anniversary interview, I sent him an anonymous note saying I was his Acapulco daughter and asking for money to keep silent."

"Which led to his revealing outburst. And then what happened?"

"The note just about totaled him. He couldn't keep it to himself any longer. He had to tell someone, so he told me the story of the daughter he gave up for adoption. He was looking to his sweet wife for emotional support. Called the writer of the note a malicious bitch! Can you imagine?"

"He had no idea she was you."

Janine looked amused. "Are you joking? The young woman who sat across the breakfast table from him every morning and periodically fucked his eyes out? His daughter? The woman who had delivered his granddaughter?" Janine looked bitter. "Fun to watch him suffer after I sent him that letter. Then I began sending him anonymous notes several times a week, tormenting him. He couldn't go to the police without revealing his secret. What could he do without revealing his past? Nothing. I never let him forget that I was out there, and

I knew. At the same time, mind you, I played the sympathetic, understanding wife.

"Remember Robert Duvall's line in the movie *Apocalypse Now*, 'I love the smell of napalm in the morning. It smells like victory'? For me the smell of victory was plain old hot coffee in the morning. I loved the odor at the breakfast table, watching Jerry brace himself for another day and possibly another note from his lost daughter, wondering when his image as the amiable weatherman was going to come to an end." She smiled at the memory.

I took a sip of Full Sail. "Who else knew this?"

"Nobody. I arranged for the DNA test myself. Jerry was trapped. No way to escape that evidence. It was so, so very sweet. There is nothing finer in this life than absolute, total revenge." She laughed triumphantly. "I encouraged T.G.'s involvement in the McVeigh Brigade as a favor to Luci. Other than to encourage Sharon and Mariah to invest in Lao Tzu's, I avoided any connection to those nitwits."

"When did you decide to murder Sharon and Mariah?"

She said, "One day Sharon asked me if there was any chance I had been born in Mexico, not Portland. I had no idea on earth what she had learned or how. When Bill Dennis let it slip that she was asking about a private investigator, I told Tommy Hilfinger she'd likely figured out Lao Tzu's connection to the bear poaching and was going to rat us out. He stole a pistol from Mariah's apartment, and when Sharon was driving toward your place, he ran her off the road and threatened her. No problem. She told him what he wanted to know. Turned out she'd found an envelope tucked behind the lining of her mother's antique hope chest. The envelope had the seal of a Mexican hospital on the flap and contained a lock of hair and a note in Spanish, saying the baby girl was six pounds ten ounces. The date on the note was the same as my birthday.

Tommy gave me the envelope like a big old, faithful, dumb dog. Had no idea what it was all about."

I said, "Maybe your mother wasn't all bad. She hung on to physical evidence that you existed. If she hid the envelope in an antique hope chest, maybe she suspected it would be found one day, or even wanted it to be found."

She frowned. "My mother is dead. We'll never know, will we?"

"Still, a hint of guilt there, don't you think?"

Janine was on a roll. There was no way she was going to be dissuaded from the object of her rage. Ignoring me, she said, "Now we're getting to the good part. You're gonna like this. Before I shot Jerry in the McVeigh headquarters, I told him who I really was. He couldn't do much but listen, what with the muzzle of my pistol a few inches from his face. I told him it was me, his long-lost daughter, who had been writing those notes. I had delivered his granddaughter. I asked him if he had enjoyed the sex. I even asked him if he thought it was possible that I gave as good a Clinton as Monica Lewinsky." Janine burst out laughing. "You should have seen the look on his face! He didn't seem in the mood for jokes, though. His mind was on the muzzle of my pistol."

Janine took another bite of her BLT, chewing thoughtfully and with no apparent regret. Plato and Hegel were both right about *thymos*. It was prideful. It thrived on recognition, demanded it. She studied me, her eyes heavy-lidded and lethal. "You know what he called me just before I shot him?"

"I have no idea."

"Ice woman." In saying that, she betrayed no emotion.

She was cold, I'll give her that. A low pressure area blown in from Jerry Toogood's past.

She retrieved a padded manila envelope and two vials from her handbag. The envelope, which contained a note, was addressed to the *Portland Oregonian*. One vial was filled with blood. She unscrewed the lid from the second. She retrieved a small penknife from her handbag and nicked the tip her finger. As she dripped blood into the vial, she said, "T.G. told his interviewer that the storms in the fields and the torments in our homes are caused by the turmoil of fluids. He was referring to oceans and water and rain, yes. But he was also thinking of semen and blood, through which family secrets can now be definitively traced. He predicted his own downfall. Good work."

She screwed the lid on the second vial, and put both containers into the envelope and sealed it. "My job isn't done until the public knows the whole truth about their wonderful T.G. We'll let the *Oregonian* see to the DNA tests this time. More convincing that way." She motioned for the waitress. To me, witness to her triumph, she said, "So much blood! Don't you just love it, Mr. Denson?" When the young woman arrived, Janine gave her the envelope and a hundred-dollar bill. "Could you please mail this for me? The money is yours."

The waitress looked astonished. "A hundred dollars?"

"Enjoy."

"Are you sure?" the waitress said.

"Mail it please."

Glancing at me, waitress left.

The rain began to hit the windows. "Always raining in this part of the country," she said. "But this is a rainbow kind of day, patches of blue between the clouds. Rain now. Sun in twenty minutes. Then back to rain again."

She finished her wine. She stood and strode out of the door facing Multnomah Falls. Before I could do anything to stop her, she started sprinting for the base of the trail that zigzagged up the mountain.

45 · The flight of Takenah'ah

Gregory Dunsmuir, Willie, Annie and I gathered in the swirling mist in the huge hollow at the base of Multnomah Falls, wondering if the Oregon state cops were going to catch her before she got to the top. We looked up at the white sheets of water cascading at high speed from the top of the precipice 620 feet above us. Above the top of the falls the dark bank of rain clouds moved on, revealing a warming sun and a pale blue sky.

Above us seagulls floated, squealing. Multnomah Falls, being a tourist attraction, was a good source of discarded food scraps much loved by the scavenging gulls. Waiting, it occurred to me that without a doubt that semen, seed of our treasured sons and daughters, could be the sweetest of all the biological fluids. It could also be the most bitter, surpassing even the bile produced by the gall. Janine Toogood had been so caught up in her need for revenge that she hardly mentioned her own little girl. Just mentioned Carrie in passing.

I almost missed Janine's tiny figure standing at the top of the falls, silhouetted against the blue. Without a word, she leaped into the void, floating silently down from the top of the falls. She was as a ghost, fleeting, falling as the salmon fell that afternoon and as I fell when I flew that first night. I had at least some idea of what she was experiencing. For her as for me, her remaining years were compressed into heartbeats. Was her revenge worth the premature plunge? The falling salmon were an omen, Willie had said. Maybe he did see the night, after all.

She landed silently in the roar of the water crashing into the pool at the base of the falls. The squealing gulls, curious, wondering if there was food to be had, circled over the corpse that floated minus the complicated *thymos* that had so craved recognition of birthright. *Acknowledge me*, the abandoned Jerelyn Bonner had demanded. *Give me what is rightfully mine.*

As the uniformed policemen set about retrieving the body, I mopped mist from my face with the back of my arm. "The Zen Buddhists believe we rise up from the great river of humanity and sink back down."

Willie said, "If that is what the Buddhists believe, they're likely right. This one was Takenah'ah, the jealous one, daughter of the seahawk Tookla'ah, the keeper of fluids."

Annie said, "Oh?"

Willie always had a myth appropriate to the occasion. I was never certain if they were genuine myths or whether he made them up to fit the circumstances. I didn't care. They were fun and many of them were remarkably similar to the Greek myths I had learned as a student at the University of Oregon.

Willie said, "In seducing her father, who had abandoned her as a baby, the vengeful, ambitious Takenah'ah rode the winds of envy so high that the air was too thin to fly. She dropped toward the earth, furiously flapping her wings. But she was going so fast she couldn't slow down even when the air was thicker. She plunged into the river and drowned. The hungry seagulls, flying rats who will eat anything rotten, waited for her body. But her bitter remains tasted so foul that they spit out her vile flesh, screaming in loathing and disgust.

We can hear their plaintive cries blowing in the wind, *eeeeee, eeeeee, eeeeee!*

Annie was impressed. "Nice!"

Willie glanced at me, looking amused. "What do you think, Chief?"

"Very clever," I said dryly.

"You think I just made that up?" He pretended to be offended.

Annie, Willie and I left Dunsmuir and his subordinates to their grisly chore of retrieving the corpse from the pool beneath the falls. The patch of blue closed, another bank of dark clouds moved in, and a light mist returned. We walked thoughtfully through the rain down the trail to our pickup. As we climbed onto the front seat, the seagulls floating high above us said goodbye with screeching cries, *eeeeee, eeeeee, eeeeee!*

The flesh of Janine Toogood contained such bitterness. Such resentment. She would not be denied. See her. She existed.

Eeeeee, eeeeee, eeeeee!

As Denson, Dancer and Sees the Night, we headed west on I-84 to Portland, the first leg of our trip back to Whorehouse Meadow. We still had work to do on my Volkswagen bus.

I said, "For what it's worth, Willie, on my first time flying out of my skin, I had wings. I never saw myself in a mirror, but I clearly had wings."

"Oh? You were a bird then. What kind of bird?"

Having no real idea what we were talking about, Annie said, mildly, "He thinks he was a short-eared owl."

I twisted my shoulders that were still a little bit sore. "Annie's right. Just like the bird that hangs out in Whorehouse Meadow. What goes in, comes out. It's a logical world, Willie."

Willie sighed. "What did I tell you, Dumsht? You're unchanged. Still the rational warrior. It's why we animal spirits recruited you. By the way, it was your computer skills that caught their attention, Annie. They've had their eyes on you for some time."

Annie blinked.

Willie Sees the Night rolled his eyes in abject disgust. "Annie! Annie! You think your winding up with us was some kind of fortuitous accident? The intersection of Mars with the last phase of Venus or other such claptrap? Please. Spare me!" Willie burst out laughing at Annie Dancer's naïveté. But of course, *post hoc, ergo propter hoc* turned on its head. By Willie's reckoning both Annie and I had been recruited by the animal spirits to help preserve the natural world. Maybe he was right. No proof that he wasn't.

Willie said, "You want to give us a little owl talk, Chief?"

I decided to humor him. Why not? "*Voo-hoo-hoo-hoo! Voo-hoo-hoo-hoo!*"

Willie looked pleased. "What do you think, Annie? Not bad. He's getting the hang of it. In time, he'll be able to give his various calls with proper inflection and real feeling."

I called, "*Voo-hoo-hoo-hoo! Voo-hoo-hoo-hoo!*" I was reluctant to admit it, but I was getting better, a disconcerting skill.